Advance Praise

"*The Gym* is darkly funny, written with wry spark and a keen eye for killer details. There are also humane and wistful notes, a tribute to the way Kevin Cowherd has coped with a lifetime in bruising, big-city journalism. Not every writer can pull that off."

— Carl Hiaasen, bestselling author of *Hoot*

"Kevin Cowherd's latest left me convulsing in laughter and tears. The brilliance of *The Gym* is in its fresh take on the pain and complexity of divorce, from the perspective of husband and father. A good and decent guy can move on, with a little help from his friends. The novel is brimming with truths and insights but with lightest of touch and a big, beating heart. Anyone whoever grunted through a workout (at a modest fitness center) will adore this Baltimore tale."

— Michael Davis, author of *The New York Times* bestseller *Street Gang: The Complete History of Sesame Street*

THE GYM

Kevin Cowherd

Apprentice
House Press
Loyola University Maryland

First Edition

Library of Congress Control Number: requested

Hardcover ISBN: 978-1-62720-496-5
Paperback ISBN: 978-1-62720-497-2
Ebook ISBN: 978-1-62720-498-9

Design by Claire Marino
Cover photo by New Africa, Adobe Stock

Published by Apprentice House Press

Apprentice
House Press
Loyola University Maryland

Loyola University Maryland
4501 N. Charles Street, Baltimore, MD 21210
410.617.5265
www.ApprenticeHouse.com
info@ApprenticeHouse.com

For Madeline and Jack, and Llewyn and Lily.
They give us hope for the future.

"The battleline between good and evil
runs through the heart of every man."
—Aleksandr Solzhenitsyn

1.

At a little after 8:30 on a warm evening in September 1980, Alejandro Ramon Maldonado returned home from another long day running the thriving carpet store he owned in Baltimore.

He walked into the kitchen and said hi to Carmen Elena Maldonado, his wife of 16 years. Carmen stood at a counter preparing Alejandro's dinner; initially, her back was to her husband.

Turning to greet him, she was undoubtedly surprised to see Alejandro wearing a pair of bright red oven mitts. Even more startling was the fact he now brandished a 12-inch cast-iron skillet, which contained the roast, red potatoes and honey-glazed carrots that had been simmering on the stove.

In the next instant, Alejandro raised the skillet high in the air and brought it crashing down on her skull.

Many of us have wondered what flashed through Carmen Maldonado's mind in the milliseconds she had to absorb that surreal scene.

Bad enough to die in a hail of stringy cooked meat and gravy-flecked vegetables, of course. But to have as your final earthly vision a greasy black saucepan hurtling toward your cranium like a runaway asteroid seemed especially cruel and capricious.

According to the police report, the two Maldonado children, a 16-year-old boy named Joey and a 13-year-old girl named Olivia, were upstairs in their respective bedrooms doing homework at the time of the murder.

Both would later claim to have been wearing headphones and listening to music, and therefore were unaware of any disturbance below. Both would also say they eventually went to sleep without saying good-night to their mother and father – not an unusual occurrence in the Maldonado household.

After a brief period of time – again, this is per the police report – Anthony dragged his wife's body down to the garage.

He stepped outside and unhurriedly smoked at least one cigarette. (The crushed butt of a Winston, burned all the way down to the filter, was found in the small garden where Carmen Maldonado raised her prize tomatoes.)

Alejandro then retrieved an 8x10-foot remnant of Karastan carpet, one of the early Persian stain-resistant varieties that he'd brought home that evening. Carefully, he rolled his wife's corpse in it. He secured the roll with duct tape at both ends. At some point, he transferred it to the trunk of his late-model Oldsmobile 98.

The body would not be found for almost a week. It was finally discovered in a heavily-wooded state park 25 miles north of the city by a pair of teenage hikers who had ducked off the trail for the express purpose of having sex.

Grinding into each other with primal urgency and moaning with desire, the two had quickly shed their backpacks in a grassy clearing and stripped off their clothes. Flopping onto the ground, their heads grazed against something lumpy in the underbrush. This turned out to be the rolled-up carpet, now covered with mud, leaves and twigs.

The sight of one of Carmen's pale, desiccated arms jutting from the thick, woven fabric quickly tamped down the carnal desires of the young woman, who screamed "JESUS FUCKING CHRIST!" and leapt to her feet.

Frantically gathering up her clothes, she bolted from the clearing over the protestations of her boyfriend, who failed to understand why he couldn't at least get a quick hand-job before they set off to report the remains to the authorities.

The murder weapon itself also turned up quickly. The skillet, now cleansed of any stubborn skull fragments or clumps of hair, was spotted for sale at a neighborhood flea market by a sharp-eyed detective, acting on a tip by a member of Carmen's extended family. The price tag on the handle read: "A steal at $3.75!"

Alejandro Maldonado, who had reported Carmen as missing, was soon arrested and charged with second-degree murder. According to testimony at the trial, he and Carmen had quarreled loudly and frequently in the months leading up to the murder.

Alejandro, five years older than his voluptuous 35-year-old wife, had repeatedly accused her of having an affair with her boss, a supervisor at the textile company where Carmen worked as an office manager.

On the witness stand, Joey Maldonado told a rapt courtroom that his father had frequently berated his mother with taunts of: "Think I don't know about that fat, sweaty dago you're banging?"

Joey also testified that Alejandro had threatened Carmen on multiple occasions with numerous kitchen utensils, including a rolling pin, a stainless-steel meat tenderizer and a four-speed Proctor Silex hand-mixer.

"So of *course* he would decide to end this poor woman's life with yet *another* implement from the marital cupboard," the prosecutor thundered in closing arguments. Pointing an accusing finger at Alejandro, sitting meekly at the defense table, he went on: "Colanders, strainers, peelers, spatulas...all were potential instruments of death in the hands of the monster who sits there before you."

The lurid trial played out daily in the pages of the *Baltimore Herald,* the city's newspaper of record. It even made national headlines. One of the supermarket tabloids went so far as to dub Maldonado "The Oven Mitts Killer."

To many, this seemed to confer on him a weird mantle of both evil and domesticity, as if when he wasn't busy making plans to snuff out his life partner and the mother of his children, he could be found happily baking assorted cookies, pies and muffins for the family.

Maldonado was quickly found guilty of second-degree murder and sentenced to 25 years in prison. At the maximum-security Maryland Correctional Institution in Hagerstown, he was said to be a model inmate who devoted many hours to obtaining an advanced degree in Eastern philosophy while also developing cutting- edge physical fitness routines for himself and his fellow convicts.

Yet gradually, the memory of him and his horrific crime faded from the minds of most Baltimoreans.

I myself knew nothing about his story until last year when I joined a local gym and one day found myself grunting and straining on a bench-press machine, trying for even a semblance of muscle definition in the flabby mass that was my chest.

That's when someone pointed out the fit-looking elderly man on the exercise mats. He wore a tight black sleeveless T-shirt, black sweatpants and black Nikes. He wasn't very tall, maybe 5-foot-9, but seemed to command the room with his very presence. Even at rest, the muscles in his chest, shoulders and arms rippled like whipcords.

What happened next remains, to this day, one of the most

astonishing things I have ever seen.

It began with the old guy bending slightly at the knees and executing five perfect backflips in a row, a feat that would result in a frantic ambulance ride to the emergency room for someone decades younger.

From there it got even crazier.

Man, I thought, *whoever this dude is, he's serious.*

Of course, back then I had no idea how serious.

2.

The gym saved my life.

Maybe you rolled your eyes at that statement. Maybe you think it's hyperbole. Maybe you think I'm a diva or a drama queen or whatever. But it's true. The gym saved me in more ways than I could ever explain.

Before I joined and began working out to stave off the massive coronary that surely loomed in my future – before ever laying eyes on the wondrous geezer described earlier – I never much cared for exercise. Any old photo of me would confirm that. What you saw was a pale, doughy man who appeared in desperate need of a place to sit, preferably one where you could also order a burrito.

The gym was called Ripped! It sat in a forlorn strip mall on a hill near the confluence of the Beltway, Route 40 and I-95, which, if nothing else, allowed management to advertise "Convenient From Anywhere!" and not technically be lying.

On the commute to and from work every day, I used to gaze up at the big Ripped! billboard. It pictured a handsome, buff-looking guy lifting dumbbells and a smiling, attractive woman – maybe the buff-looking guy's wife or girlfriend? – running on a treadmill.

They looked so happy and healthy and care-free, to the point where I knew if I ever met them in person, I would hate their guts.

Yet as the weeks went by, that sign gave me the first stirrings of hope, maybe in the same way a church steeple appearing out of the gloom can inspire the downtrodden.

One day, almost as if the car had a life of its own, I found myself veering off the highway and into the gym parking lot, arriving in a squeal of brakes and a spray of gravel that signaled the urgency of my mission.

I walked in and a young woman in a black T-shirt and black sweatpants popped out from behind the counter. She pumped my hand with alarming intensity and smiled broadly.

"Welcome to Ripped!" she chirped. "Looking to get healthy? Oh boy, have you come to the right place!"

The whole time we talked, I couldn't stop staring at her teeth.

Later I would discover that her name tag said Tami. But who could look at her chest? No, I was transfixed by those magnificent choppers, all perfectly aligned like two rows of gleaming white Chiclets encircled by a layer of perfectly-applied cherry-red lipstick.

"Let's get you started," she said. She picked up her iPad and jabbed it with a manicured forefinger. "What are your goals?"

Um, my goals?

I stared blankly at her. It wasn't a great time to be talking about goals.

For starters, my marriage of 15 years had just broken up. Maybe shattered is the better word. All because of what Beth claimed was "one silly little incident," the silly incident being that I walked in on her, during a drunken New Year's Eve party, going down on Dan Henson.

How do you stumble upon your wife performing fellatio on the next-door neighbor and go on with life as before? How do you just shrug it off, as if it were no more consequential than a parking ticket?

The answer: you can't. Not that we shared any of the sordid details with the kids the next day when they bothered to look up from their tablets and iPhones long enough to ask: "Where's Daddy going with the suitcases?"

There was also this: my job at the *Herald* was on life support. Another round of layoffs was rumored on the way. At age 45, as a columnist with a salary slightly higher than the galley-slave wages paid my reporter colleagues, I was definitely in management's cross-hairs as a cost-cutting target.

Of course, there were days when I practically *prayed* to be fired, too. The staff was ridiculously over-worked, for one thing. No one had gotten a raise in years. Plus the place was run by a cadre of clueless, back-slapping shitheads who cared not a whit about good journalism or employee morale, who worshipped solely at the altar of on-line page views, blog hits, Facebook posts and all the other niggling, soul-sucking tasks that —

"I mean your *fitness* goals," Tami added helpfully.

Oh. Well.

I wasn't sure I had any of those, either.

LOOK AT ME! I wanted to scream. *YOU CAN'T GUESS WHY I'M HERE?!*

For starters, I weighed in at a nifty 220 pounds. This was fine for a chiseled 6-foot-4 NFL wide receiver, but not so good for a lumpy newspaperman a shade over 6-feet with zero energy, aching knees and hypertension.

I ate too much, drank too much, worried too much.

My fitness goals?

How about this? *Hoping not to keel over in the next five minutes.*

But I doubted that would be detailed enough to satisfy Tami, who continued to fix me with a penetrating gaze. Head tilted sympathetically to one side, she wanted desperately to understand how the good people of Ripped! – and she herself as the proud front-door ambassador, the keeper of the sweat-soaked velvet rope, so to speak – could help the battered and broken wretch who stood before her.

So I made up some bullshit story about seeking a total lifestyle change.

I talked about how slouching toward the Big Five-Oh had me determined to shed the pounds piled on over the years by the unhealthy eating habits, ritual after-work beer-swilling and generalized sloth in which I'd wallowed for so long.

I even threw in something about eventually wanting to train for a marathon, and if that went well, maybe even an *ultra*-marathon.

"And this ultra-marathon?" I continued. "I'm thinking of one of those grueling torture-fests where you run hundreds of miles across a burning desert. Only the race is run at night, because it's like 160 degrees in the daytime, and the whole time you're scared shitless about being bitten by scorpions and rattlesnakes. Or you're worried you'll snap an ankle in some goddamned gopher hole.

"If they even *have* gophers out there," I said with a shrug. "I don't pretend to be a zoologist."

Oh, yeah, I was laying it on thick. So thick it almost made *me* gag.

But not Tami, bless her heart.

Dutifully, she entered all this in her tablet without comment, without even the tiniest smirk or eye-roll. *What a woman!* I wondered if I were falling back in love already.

Was this the infamous "rebound" effect everyone talked

about? Where a mope like me, confused, angry and vulnerable after a marital crash-and-burn, dives into another relationship right away with zero caution and even less self-awareness?

Sure, Tami was probably 20 years younger than me. But you can get past the age barrier if both partners truly enjoy each other's company, if they make each other laugh, if they're committed to making the relationship work and —

"Ready for a tour?" Tami chirped.

Um…a *tour?*

I took another glance around.

It wasn't as if I'd never been in a gym before. This one looked to have the usual set-up: industrial-gray carpeting, rows of treadmills, stationary bikes and elliptical machines up front under banks of large high-def TV's.

The free-weight area was off to one side, where the customary gaggle of wanna-be muscle-heads could be seen grunting and clanging barbells and taking long, unselfconscious looks at themselves in the floor-to-ceiling mirrors.

A spinning class was taking place in a glass-enclosed room to my right. A dozen gaunt-looking women and one cadaverous man in the back row sat hunched over their bikes, sweating small rivers and pedaling like it was the closing kick of the Tour de France, all while the blonde pony-tailed instructor shrieked commands over pulsing techno-music.

Signs for the men's and women's locker rooms loomed on the far wall. And there was another sign for the child-care area, where harried young moms and dads, desperate for a quick workout so they wouldn't snap the next time a sippy cup was whipped at their face, could leave the little monsters in the care of an 18-year-old staffer with an ever-present smile, boundless energy and the patience of Mother Theresa.

Finally, all the way in the back were the tanning booths, standing ready to dispense the pulsating, skin-damaging UV rays that devotees laughably claimed lent them a "healthy glow."

Hell, I had the lay of the place already.

What else was there to see?

But I sensed from Tami's eager expression that she'd be crushed if I didn't let her show me around.

"A tour would be great," I said.

Tami smiled ecstatically. You'd have thought I promised to donate a kidney to her dying mom.

For the next 15 minutes, we wound our way through the facility, Tami pointing out the vast array of high-tech machines (PRECOR! Cybex! LifeFitness! Live Strong!, Stairmaster!) and low-tech exercise options (barbells! dumbbells! kettle balls! jump ropes!) that would be at my disposal.

"Would you want a personal trainer?" she asked. "We have three on staff."

Three!

And all three, Tami assured me, were the best personal trainers in the area, personal trainers that even *other* personal trainers consulted for personal training advice.

These were personal trainers so committed to serving the needs of their clients, Tami added, that they gave out their cell phone number and urged clients to call anytime – day or night – with their fitness-related questions.

"No, seriously, *anytime,*" she said. "Joe Ameliore? He's been on the staff the longest. He had a member call him at 1 in the morning. From a bar, natch. This guy had been trying to lose weight for weeks. And now he was absolutely shit-faced, OK?

"And because he'd just pounded, like, two dozen wings, he was desperate to schedule a workout first thing in the morning.

To, y'know, redeem himself. And Joe accommodated him. Met him here at 7 a.m., handed him a Dunkin' macchiato, and the two of them went to work. *Hard! That's* the kind of dedication our trainers have."

She shot me a sideways glance. "Are you a bar person?"

Well, yeah. But I couldn't picture myself with half a load on reaching for my cell phone with greasy, Buffalo-sauce-stained fingers to ask someone to punish me in the gym the next morning. No matter *how* guilty I felt.

(On the other hand, in the interest of full disclosure, I *did* call Beth a few times at 2 a.m. right after we split up. Yes, I was hammered. I'm sure that shocks you. And, no, that didn't go over well. I'm sure that shocks you, too.)

As my tour with Tami wound on, I saw that, up close, the gym was a lot smaller than it appeared from the outside. It was far more worn-looking and scruffy than I'd initially noticed, too.

The carpet was discolored in several places from where the roof had obviously leaked during rain-storms. Quite a few machines were affixed with "Out of Order" signs. The men's locker room was cramped, with only a few showers, and the outdated lockers were so tiny they seemed designed for the Keebler Elves.

As we passed the water fountain, I saw a man bend over to take a drink. Suddenly, he straightened, scowled and smacked the push bar.

"Fucking thing hasn't worked in weeks," he grumbled.

Over-hearing this, Tami held up her hand, like a sheriff signaling a halt to a posse. The expression on her face said it all: an important matter of customer relations needed her immediate attention.

"Sir," she said evenly, "the replacement part has been ordered.

I'm sure it'll be here in a day or two."

"Yeah, right," the man said. He glanced at me, shook his head in disgust and muttered: "This place just *sucks . . .*"

But to tell the truth, I was fine with all of it. God knows I was more than a little worn and scruffy-looking myself. Besides, fancy, pretentious gyms always gave me the creeps.

I didn't need all their shiny bells and whistles and snotty airs. I didn't need a gym that offered aromatherapy, eucalyptus-infused towels and a snack bar serving 15 different organic smoothies and 10 different healthful salads.

I just needed a place to sweat and get in some semblance of shape. A place that didn't cost an arm and a leg, either.

That was the other thing: Ripped! was 30 bucks a month cheaper than any other gym around. That could be key, I knew, for the day when I got the inevitable tap on the shoulder from some management flunky at the *Herald*, along with a whispered: "Big man wants to see you in his office."

This was how they killed you now in the newspaper business. They didn't send a hulking, ink-stained Luca Brasi. (If they even *had* a hulking, ink-stained Luca Brasi, he would have been laid off by now. And filing for unemployment benefits while looking for job openings at Target.)

Instead they sent someone like the former restaurant reviewer, who was now helping out on the obituaries desk because management gutted the entire features section, including the "10 Best Places to Eat!" guide that made the reviewer a minor celebrity among the foodie set.

They sent some poor, timid soul who was terrified of being down-sized himself and was only too willing to be the messenger boy for another hit that might save his own sorry-ass job for a few more months.

At least that's how my editor, the ever-gutless Thomas P. Halloran, would do it. Then when you got the flunky's message and took the long, dead-man-walking slog to Halloran's office and slumped in the chair across from his desk, heart pounding, forehead slick with flop sweat, he'd fix you with those sad, basset-hound eyes, spread his arms in a gesture of helplessness and say: "You know this isn't anything I wanna do, Jackie. Right?"

Oh, sure, Tommy. It's not you. We know your hands are tied. It's those cold-hearted dickheads at corporate making you do this, right?

Back at the front desk, Tami and I quickly closed the deal on my new membership. I slid a credit card her way, signed a couple of papers and had my photo taken.

And that was it.

For better or worse, I was now banking on the redemptive powers of Ripped!, a gym so seemingly insecure it needed an exclamation point tacked to its name to convey a sense of excitement and the promise of wellness within its walls.

Tami beamed, giving me one last flash of her glorious molars.

"I can promise you one thing, Mr. Jack Doherty!" she said, handing me my receipt. "You won't regret this!"

Sure. That's what Tischler the Lawyer said when he first urged me to sign off on the divorce terms Beth was demanding.

And look how that turned out.

3.

I settled into a standard Monday-Wednesday-Friday workout schedule, vowing to also come on the odd Saturday or Sunday to further accelerate the stunning physical transformation that surely awaited me.

Weekend attendance, however, would depend on the severity of that day's hangover. And whether it was my turn to have the kids. God, I missed them so much!

The plan was to hit the gym first thing in the morning before work. This, I hoped, would help blunt the overwhelming urge, triggered the moment I walked into the *Herald* newsroom, to strangle any editor who pushed another shitty column idea on me, or pored over my expense vouchers like an SEC auditor.

We were a diverse group, the M-W-F early risers. With an almost equal mix of whites and African-Americans and a decent number of Asians, we were probably the most heterogeneous gathering in Baltimore, a city with a checkered (to say the least) history of race relations.

There was a diversity of body types, too.

There were, to be sure, plenty of fatsos like me, jiggly guys with big guts groaning through sit-ups and bench presses for the first time in ages. There were plus-sized women in billowing T-shirts and yoga pants huffing and puffing through floor exercises, or pumping out another grueling series of "waves" on the battle ropes that made their flabby, middle-aged arms burn.

But there was also your usual core of incredibly fit members, bursting with an otherworldly energy and enthusiasm that could be terrifying. These were the 30- and 40-ish guys with washboard bellies and hulking shoulders, grunting and throwing around massive amounts of iron in the free weights area.

These were the sylph-like women with gym-toned biceps and determined expressions pounding away on the Sole Stepper and the elliptical machines while talking to their brokers the minute the markets opened in the morning.

Naturally, we in the hefty contingent couldn't stand these people. Their very presence depressed us. They caused us, the serially un-fit, to look inward too much. They drove us to ruminate over what had gone wrong with our lives, to obsess over the demons that, for years, made us blow off, say, a four-mile run in favor of binge-watching "The Office" and devouring a plate of nachos the size of a hubcap.

Some of us were socially awkward, too, and favored early-morning workouts as a way to avoid interaction with others.

A small, bird-like woman who flitted silently around the gym's perimeter to warm up for her workout was a case in point. No matter how many times someone called out "Good morning!" as she traversed her tight, 50-yard loop, she seemed startled by the greeting and incapable of answering with anything but a stammered "Uh,…yeah. You too."

There were also the obvious obsessive-compulsives in our ranks. These were the folks who tended to work out on the exact same machines, in the exact same order, at the exact same time each and every day.

When they were done with each piece of equipment, they didn't just wipe the perspiration from it, as per standard gym etiquette. No, these people would practically polish it to a high gleam with their ubiquitous little hand towels, as if it were the hood of a shiny new Lincoln Navigator.

Harvey Volker was the first of the morning regulars to befriend me. He was about my age and worked as a real estate scout for a chain of frozen yogurt outlets. Pale, painfully skinny, with long, unkempt hair, he exuded the same healthy aura as a hostage chained to a basement radiator for months.

Our initial introduction was awkward. Two weeks after I joined, Harvey marched up to me as I did triceps pushdowns.

"Quick," he barked, "what's the world's most popular site for suicides!?"

I stared at him uncomprehendingly. *What in the blue hell was this?*

"Uh, no idea," I said finally.

His eyes narrowed. "What kind of fucking answer is that?!" Now he was practically shouting. "AT LEAST TAKE A GUESS, FOR GOD'S SAKE!"

"Fine. Golden Gate Bridge?"

He made a loud buzzer sound – "AARRGGHH!" – like when a game-show contestant blows an answer.

But he didn't go away. I tried again to appease this lunatic.

"Niagara Falls?"

"AARRGGHH!"

He shook his head mournfully. "Jesus, I thought everybody knew this! Give up? It's the Nanjing Yangtze River Bridge! In China!"

"Sure," I said. "That was my next guess."

But this bit of deadpan elicited no reaction from Harvey. Not even the *hint* of a smile.

Instead he stuck out his hand and said: "The name's Harvey. If it makes you feel better, the Golden Gate's no. 2."

It didn't make me feel better. Yet after that little theater of the absurd, Harvey and I hit it off. In the days that followed, he sought me out often to shoot the shit. At first, I was flattered by his attention. *Hey, look at that! This guy likes me! He wants us to hang out!*

But before long, a fuller understanding of the social dynamic between us emerged.

Harvey, it turned out, was a non-stop talker. It was like the old saying: ask him the time, he'll tell you who made the watch. And I was simply fresh meat, someone who was – at least initially – polite enough to feign interest in whatever he was blabbing about.

So desperate was Harvey to bloviate that he would often forego his own workout and follow his latest victim around the gym as he or she lifted, or did ab crunches or Kettle bell exercises or some kind of cardio. Then, after flapping his gums for 45 minutes or so, Harvey would get back in his car and go off to work without ever breaking a sweat.

A Japanese friend once told me about the phrase *kuuki yom-enai.* Translated literally, it means "can't read the air." In our culture, it would refer to someone who can't read the room. Someone oblivious to facial expressions, verbal cues, the body language that signals impatience and a desire to, for instance, exercise without some emaciated-looking windbag yakking in your ear the whole time.

This was Harvey Volker to a T. No wonder he was nick-named "the Workout Killer." Harvey was where your endorphins went to die.

Despite this, everyone seemed to like him. And he knew everyone in the gym. Pretty soon he was introducing me around like a cruise director working a deck party.

Invariably, with his arm slung around me, he'd also volunteer: "Check this out: Jack here walked in on his wife giving head to the guy next door. You believe it!?"

After the third or fourth time this happened, I took him aside and whispered: "Um, maybe we could leave out that part of the bio . . ."

But Harvey had no filter, either on his thoughts or what came out of his mouth. There would be an awkward silence after he disclosed the blowjob back-story to yet another member he wanted me to meet. Then I'd get these looks that ranged from sympathetic to horrified to *seriously? Tell me more, dude!*

Not until I threatened to strangle him with a resistance band did Harvey stop with the hummer story intros. And by then he'd already told half the membership. I might as well have worn a T-shirt that said: "Ask me about being cuckolded."

In any event, that's how I managed to fall in with him and his motley band of gym rats, most of whom had been Ripped! members for years.

One was R. Jamison Winthrop, the lead investigative reporter for local TV station WBGB ("Your Most Trusted 24-Hour News Source.") Tall and handsome, he also had the perfect name for his chosen profession. It was a name that signaled gravitas and sense of purpose, along with a lofty, Presbyterian disdain for the hypocrisy, fraud and malfeasance he regularly ferreted out in Charm City.

(*"For a special I-Team report, we go live now to West Baltimore, where R. Jamison Winthrop is standing by with the owner of the brothel where the mayor and six members of the City Council were discovered in a pre-dawn raid by police . . ."*)

Jamison also had the perfect head of expensively-coiffed salt-and-pepper hair considered *de rigueur* for a 40-something big-city on-air talent.

"Oh, yeah," Harvey cracked, "no one ever looks at Jaymo and thinks: 'Another satisfied client of Big Andre's Discount Cutz.'"

Mikey Conroy was another member of our group, a grizzled community college phys ed teacher and Vietnam War vet in his late 60's. From the beginning, it was apparent that the others had nothing but respect and admiration for Mikey's two tours of duty with the Marines and the fierce, unrelenting combat he'd seen in the steamy jungles of 'Nam.

"Baby-killer!" Harvey hissed the first time we all worked out together.

"Tell the truth, Mikey," Jamison added. "How many 'villes did you torch back in the day?"

To me, Jamison whispered: "We're all waiting for Mikey to snap from some horrible flashback and open up with an AR-15. I keep telling him: 'Just give me a heads up. I can have a videographer here in 10 minutes.'"

Invariably, Mikey met this torrent of abuse with a roll of his eyes and a weary shake of his head.

"Nice to see you slap-dicks don't deal in any old, discredited stereotypes," he said that first day. "But if you *must* know, I was only involved in two or three civilian massacres. OK, *four*, tops."

Courtney Mancini was the most intriguing member of the bunch – at least to me. A pretty, dark-haired single mom in her late 30's, she was an ER nurse at the University of Maryland Shock Trauma Center, probably the busiest such facility in the entire country.

"You're probably wondering why I work out with these pigs," she said, gesturing at Harvey and the others when I met her. "Tell you a story. A couple weeks ago, the ambulance brought in this kid. He was, I don't know, 17, 18, something like that. He'd been in a horrible car accident. And now he was screaming in pain, lower torso bathed in blood…just *awful* to see.

"When I bent over the stretcher to look at him, I accidentally brushed against his leg. *And it literally fell off! From the knee down!* It landed on my shoes, bounced up and fell to the floor. And the other nurse picked it up like it was *nothing!* Like you'd pick up a log to toss on a fire. We laughed about it later. But crazy shit like that happens on every shift."

She gazed affectionately at Harvey and the others. "Pretty sure nothing *these* clowns do is gonna get to me."

I was still picturing the gory runaway limb caroming off her Nikes when she grabbed my elbow, suddenly serious.

"Just do me a favor," she said. "If you're gonna stare at my boobs, don't let me catch you, OK? It makes me *really* self-conscious."

I promised I'd do my best to honor her request. And for the longest time, I did.

Within weeks, for reasons known only to him, Harvey took to calling us The Big Five. He also suggested that we start wearing matching T-shirts in the gym. Mercifully, this was soundly hooted down.

"Maybe we could all hold hands while we work out, too," Mikey growled.

"Yeah," Jamison sneered, "and get in a circle for a team cheer when we're finished."

"Or maybe," said Harvey, turning a deep shade of red, "you two could go fuck yourselves." He grabbed his towel and bag and stomped out the door to his car.

Oh, this was going to be fun.

From what I'd seen so far, these people were raw, edgy, volatile. They were ready to give the needle to each other at a moment's notice, to jab it in hard and deep, too, simply for the sport of it.

A lame joke, the slightest verbal stumble during the telling of a story, the voicing of an idea deemed hopelessly dumb or impractical – any of these would invariably trigger a torrent of ridicule from the other group members.

An apology by the chastened offender, or the hasty back-tracking from an ill-advised remark, only made things worse. These were taken as signs of weakness or vulnerability; the attacks would only double in intensity after that.

But I was ready for all of it.

To me, it felt like just another day with Beth.

4.

On the day we first set eyes on the chiseled old guy, a nasty dispute broke out between the CNN and FOX-News partisans over territorial rights to the TV's.

A bit of background: on most mornings, the banks of televisions spread around the gym offered just four programming choices: the "Today Show," ESPN, a movie channel and a cable news channel.

Occasionally, HGTV was on for those lost souls who wanted to watch Chip and Joanna Gaines of "Fixer Upper" gleefully attack a wall with sledgehammers, argue over shiplap and distressed woods, and somehow transform another Texas hovel into a glittering showpiece in 45 minutes.

But that was basically the sum total of entertainment options at Ripped!

Apparently, management's feeling was this: if you couldn't slap in your earbuds and be content watching Savannah Guthrie and Hoda Kotb wax orgasmic over a roasted squash and burrata salad; if you were too good to take in another exhaustive update on LeBron James' strained hamstring from the Worldwide Leader in Sports; if you were going to whine about having to endure "Jurassic World III" for the umpteenth time or yet another cable discussion on whether Stormy Daniels was a great patriot or an opportunistic (and possibly disturbed) harlot, then you, dear member, were a royal pain in the ass.

And Ripped! had no need for your presence.

Don't like the programming here? Too low-brow for you? There's the door, Your Royal Highness. Find another place to sweat, Mr. Albert Fucking Einstein. That seemed to be the unspoken message.

Understand, this business philosophy was never articulated out loud. But we members weren't dopes. The stunning lack of viewing options and management's indifference to improving the situation was obvious to anyone with half a brain.

On this particular day, "Fox & Friends" was the featured cable news show when someone on one of the elliptical machines – OK, fine, it was me – had a simple request.

"Could we get rid of this crap," I asked Bryan, the gym manager, "and put on CNN?"

Watching the Donald Trump sycophants on FOX's signature morning show, with their fake, toothy smiles, forced bonhomie and eagerness to disseminate the president's lying bullshit, was giving me a headache. Harvey, chattering away on the machine next to mine, didn't seem to care one way or the other.

Yet for me, it was always better to start off the day with CNN, where the undisguised loathing of the despicable Imposter-in-Chief was so much more uplifting.

Bryan clicked the remote and suddenly the earnest faces of "New Day" anchors Alisyn Camerota and John Berman filled the fourth screen. They were grilling some poor, sputtering GOP operative who seemed clearly unnerved at the prospect of having to defend the most clueless Oval Office occupant in history to a vast audience of seething libs, all of whom dropped to their knees every night praying for Trump to choke on a Big Mac.

As soon as Bryan changed the channel, though, a howl went up. It came from two men on the last row of treadmills across the aisle.

"*H-e-y-y-y!*" came a plaintive wail. "Put FOX back on!"

Bryan grabbed the remote and quickly complied. Then he rushed over to us and apologized profusely.

"Forgot they were still here," he said, nodding toward the MAGA whiners. "They asked for FOX first. Soon as they leave, we'll switch to CNN."

This seemed like a perfectly fine compromise to me.

To prove it, I waved to the two Trump cultists, whom I now noted looked very large, very pumped and possibly in the throes of a steroidal rage, too.

The wave was meant to signify: *Heh-heh, no problem! New guy still learning the ropes here! A thousand apologies if we interrupted your daily briefing on Wingnut TV.*

Harvey, however, seemed intent on imparting a different message.

"Right-wing asshats!" he hissed, glaring at the two men.

"Liberal jerk-offs!" one hissed back.

Judging by this snappy exchange, it was clear the level of discourse would not be rising significantly anytime soon. Therefore, I felt it was imperative to convey to Harvey my earnest wish for him to, well…shut the fuck up.

For one thing, I was reluctant to make waves and get tossed out, seeing as how even my modest attempts at weight-lifting and cardio work were beginning to pay off. (Down six pounds! Hot damn! The beefy journalist was on a roll!)

More importantly, I had no desire to get my ass kicked by the two right-wing neanderthals glowering at us now.

"Fuck 'em!" Harvey replied sweetly. "Let 'em *try* to start something."

You had to admire the man's *cojones,* of course. But this sounded more like a death wish than anything else.

Harvey stood all of 5-feet-8-inches and weighed *maybe* 145 pounds – and this only after one of his world-class pig-outs at the Akbar Palace lunch buffet down the street. Having him on your side in a brawl was like having Bambi watch your back.

There was also this: I was not exactly Mike Tyson myself.

The only fistfight I'd ever been in – if you could even call it that – was back in my junior year of high school, when the evil Teddy Mozak jumped me one day. This was 15 minutes after the final bell, as my girlfriend Kaitlyn and I walked home.

Teddy had been angry at me for a number of perceived slights, the latest being that I had accidentally set his shirtsleeve on fire in chemistry lab that morning and laughed about it. Actually, it had been more of a high-pitched, terrified giggle, because even as he cursed loudly and frantically tried to tamp out the flames on his ratty flannel shirt, all I could think was: *I'm a dead man.*

Oh, there was no doubt about it. Teddy Mozak was going to bust me up good at the first available opportunity.

So when he and two of his thuggish sidekicks materialized that afternoon from behind a stand of trees as Kaitlyn and I cut through the park, it was clear that Judgment Day had finally arrived.

Grunting like a wild boar, Teddy rushed me. I took a feeble swing at him, which he swatted away effortlessly. Then he threw me to the ground and jumped on my chest, his knees pinning my shoulders.

Grinning maniacally, he drew back his arm and cocked his fist, prepared to deliver the avenging haymaker that would knock me senseless. (If I close my eyes, I can still see his hairy, scarred knuckles poised in mid-air, like some kind of hideous, otherworldly creature sent to our solar system specifically to re-arrange my face.)

I cringed and whimpered inwardly, determined not to let Kaitlyn see me cry no matter how savage the beat-down. Which was when she crept up behind Teddy and – in possibly the most heroic move I'd ever witnessed – bit his shoulder.

Chomped down on it hard, too.

Hard enough to cause an impressive spurt of blood to shoot from under the dirty mohair sweater he'd exchanged for the singed flannel ensemble.

Yelping with pain and swearing ferociously, Teddy jumped off me and chased after Kaitlyn. But that was a futile exercise. Kaitlyn was a track star. She was the anchor on the girls' 4 x 100-meter relay team and had already opened up a big lead.

The chances of the hulking Teddy – already a wheezy, pack-a-day smoker with the unmistakable beginnings of a beer gut – catching her were non-existent.

Kaitlyn and I rendezvoused at my house a half-hour later. We had the place to ourselves. My little sister and brother were still in school and my mom had gone off to her job as a nurse at the psychiatric hospital on the outskirts of town.

Deftly steering Kaitlyn to the couch, I attempted to express my gratitude for her bravery by mashing my lips into hers and fumbling with the buttons on her blouse.

Initially, she seemed interested to see where all this would lead. But after a moment or two, she abruptly stood, pulled herself together and announced she was leaving, apparently having decided that geometry homework was more exciting than the pitiful face-sucking and juvenile groping she'd just endured.

In any event, that long-ago run-in with Teddy made for a pretty skimpy fight resume if Harvey and I got into it with the two scowling MAGATS. Which now seemed inevitable, as both had just climbed off their treadmills and were headed our way.

"Uh-oh," I murmured to Harvey. "Say a prayer."

"Sure," he said, glaring at the advancing meatheads. "How about this one? 'DEAR GOD, PLEASE DON'T MAKE ME HAVE TO POUND ONE OF THESE TRUMPIE DOUCHE-BAGS!'"

"Maybe something more spiritual," I whispered.

Harvey grinned. "What? That's not in the Bible?"

Great, I thought. *Now he's tossing out wisecracks like it's a Jack Reacher movie . . .*

At the last minute, though, Bryan leaped from behind the front desk and intercepted the two troglodytes. He threw an arm around each and spoke soothingly for a few moments, no doubt trying to convince them it would be a waste of time to mop the floor with the pitiful snowflakes that had inadvertently antagonized them.

Finally, the two mouth-breathers stomped off to the locker room, although not before shooting us dirty looks and muttering dark threats about: "Next time, lib-tards!"

One thing was clear: I had to get away from Harvey. He was going to get me killed. My adrenaline levels were still red-lining as I retreated to the free weights area to do bench presses and calm down.

Moments later, Mikey slid onto the bench next to me to do bicep curls.

Suddenly, I saw him stiffen and drop the dumbbells.

"Holy shit!" he said. "I think that's Oven Mitts Maldonado!"

I sat up and followed his gaze. He was staring at an old guy jacked enough to be the cover-boy for *Senior Fitness Today*.

Transfixed, we watched him warm up with a series of perfect backflips, the kind you might see a perky 85-pound college cheerleader pull off. After that, he strode confidently over to the chin-up bar, head held high, shoulders back, the way a great concert pianist would move across a stage to his Steinway. Three fit-looking women, all of whom appeared to be in their late 30's or early 40's, stood nearby, following his every move.

He gave them a sideways glance, as if to ensure that all eyes were locked on him. Then, springing lightly from his toes, he grasped the steel bar.

Slowly and methodically, he began doing one-armed chin-ups – the most flawless ones I'd ever seen. He knocked out 20 in a row with each arm without breaking a sweat, smiling beatifically the whole time.

"If it's the same guy," Mikey said, keeping his voice low, "his name is Alejandro Maldonado. Killed his wife years ago. Some kind of love triangle thing. He was all over the news for weeks. Did some hard time, if memory serves."

I couldn't take my eyes off the man.

Judging by his well-lined face, he was maybe 70 years old. After he finished this incredible exhibition, he dropped lightly to the floor. Then he grasped the shortest woman around the waist with both hands and lifted her high so she could reach the bar.

Using both arms, she churned out seven superb chin-ups of her own, earning whoops of delight from her friends and a spirited high-five from the old guy.

In fact, so excited was he by the woman's performance that he suddenly bounded across the floor and did six flawless handsprings, bouncing high in the air on each before sticking the landing like an Olympic gymnast.

The women erupted in more cheers.

Mikey and I gaped in astonishment.

"*Are you fucking kidding me*?!" Mikey murmured. "If I tried *one* of those, I'd be in a full body cast, popping Percocets like they were Skittles."

"Are you sure it's the same guy?" I whispered. "What did you call him? Oven Mitts?"

Mikey studied the old-timer intently. Finally he shook his head.

"Nah, I can't be positive," he said. "All that stuff, the murder and the trial, happened back in the 80's. I was still pretty messed up from 'Nam."

He turned to me and smiled. "But you're the hotshot reporter, right? You should be able to find out."

5.

Moi?

A hotshot reporter?

Once upon a time, maybe. But not anymore.

I worked in a dying industry and everybody knew it. A priest should administer last rites to anyone dumb enough to work for a newspaper these days.

Newsrooms used to hum with activity: phones ringing, police scanners squawking, harried editors barking orders and yelling about deadlines, hard-bitten reporters banging out copy or grousing about the newest lame story they'd been assigned.

Back when you could smoke, it wasn't terribly unusual for a staffer, deeply absorbed in filing a story, to absent-mindedly flick cigarette ashes into a waste basket filled with copy paper. Within seconds, a good-sized blaze would erupt, sending a shower of sparks toward the ceiling until the reporter, with a phone attached to his ear, nonchalantly doused it with the cup of three-day old coffee languishing on his desk.

The best copy editor I ever knew kept a bottle of Wild Turkey in a satchel near his feet. By the time his shift ended at 11 every night, you had to practically point him to the elevators so he could begin the four-block lurch back to his apartment.

God, it was *heaven!*

Now, with layoffs, buyouts and all the other ways chicken-shit publishers cull their workforce following dire warnings of falling profits from corporate bean-counters, newspaper staffs were skeletal.

And newsrooms? Joyless.

Imagine the sound of crickets, pretty much 24/7.

Walk into the *Herald* at 10 in the morning and it had the same charged atmosphere as a shoe store. If you were lucky, maybe you'd see the obituary writer on the phone with a local funeral home director. Maybe you'd see the assistant metro editor heating a cup of tea in the microwave in the break room, or a yawning sportswriter heading out to Ravens training camp to start his day. So much for excitement.

God forbid the governor dropped dead of a heart attack at a morning ribbon-cutting ceremony, or a jetliner crashed in the Inner Harbor, torching the pavilions, obliterating the USS Constitution at dockside and causing a miles-long swath of death and destruction through the city.

Who would cover it?

The prevailing sentiment at the paper in regards to a big story breaking in the a.m. seemed to be: *oh, let the TV stations take that one.* At least until the rest of the paper's staff – exhausted from being stretched so thin and working so many hours – stumbled in later for the 1 p.m. budget meeting.

Under the dreary, feckless reign of Thomas Halloran, everything was about cost-cutting now.

When you pitched a story idea to an editor, it was almost as if one of those cartoon thought bubbles popped up over his or her head: *Wait a minute…you want us to spring for lunch for one of your sources? A DEA confidential informant? And you want to take him to a Panera Bread? Uh-uh. What do we look like, Fort Knox?*

Once, as I prepared to fly to the West Coast to report on a big Hollywood blockbuster set to be shot in Baltimore, a project which would have the whole city buzzing with excitement and provide hundreds of much-needed jobs for the economy, Halloran took me aside.

"The airfare for your little junket's gonna kill us," he moaned. "So you need to skimp on the hotel." He lowered his voice and look around the newsroom. "We need you staying in the kind of place where junkies shoot up in the stairwells. And hookers roam the parking lots. If you catch my drift. . ."

Oh, I caught his drift, all right.

The next day, he circled back to my desk to tell me he was just kidding, that he'd had a couple of beers at lunch that made him mouthy. The assistant managing editor, the unctuous and gelatinous Mark Minske, also assured me Halloran was kidding.

But I knew he wasn't kidding. Therefore, after touching down in L.A., I checked into the Four Seasons Beverly Hills for three days.

Not long after my return – with (he said modestly) a crackerjack story about the emotional and financial turbo-charge the new film would provide our fair city – Minske marched up to my desk. He waved a sheet of paper in my face. This turned out to be a print-out of my latest expense report.

His face contorted with anger, he hissed: "The Four Seasons? *The Four Fucking Seasons?*"

Patiently, I explained that all the places with junkies shooting up in the stairwells and hookers prowling the parking lots had been filled up.

"Marko, you didn't want me flopping on a park bench, did you?" I asked. "With all the sickos and perverts out there in La-La Land?"

Minske stared at me for a good 10 seconds, furiously chewing his gum. Finally he turned and stomped back to his office,

35

muttering a string of epithets under his breath. I was definitely on management's shit list after that.

How could anyone work in that kind of dreary, soul-sucking environment and still think of himself as a hotshot reporter?

On the other hand, I used to be pretty damn good at this job. Four years at an OK journalism school, 23 in the newspaper biz including 15 at the *Herald*, a bunch of awards, most of them gathering dust in a cardboard box in the basement...hell, I was certainly capable of finding out if a wife-killer worked out among us.

Knew just where to start, too. What I did was call on all my education and training, on the countless hours I'd spent honing my craft and the finely-tuned gut instincts that had never let me down.

Then I walked up to the gym's front desk.

And I asked Bryan: "Hey, who's the old guy back there? The one who's totally jacked? With the harem fawning all over him?"

Bryan nodded. "His name's Anthony Maldon. Goes by Tony. Been a member since the place opened. Until recently, he worked out with those gals in the evenings. Probably why you've never seen him before."

Alejandro Maldonado...Anthony Maldon...c'mon! It couldn't be that easy, could it? But maybe it could. Maybe all the clean living I'd been doing since Beth curb-stomped my heart was paying off with a suddenly enhanced aura of kismet.

"By the way," Bryan said, chuckling, "guess how old he is."

"I'll go with 70," I said. "But I'm way off, right?"

"Try 80."

"SHUT UP! Are you serious?!"

"Totally," Bryan said. "Just had a birthday last week. The women baked him a cake."

"Made of what, broccoli? The guy has zero body fat."

"I know," Bryan said. "Never seen anything like it. And I've been in this business for a long time."

From the gym, I went straight to the *Herald*. What I needed now was for someone to comb through the archives to see what we had on one Oven Mitts Maldonado. I also wanted to examine any old photos of him, to make sure he and the ageless Tony Maldon were one and the same.

A funny thing had been happening to me at work lately. Instead of wanting to smother every editor I saw, now it was only every third or fourth one that sent me into a homicidal rage.

Maybe it was the gym that was leveling my moods. Forty-five minutes of lifting weights and a half-hour slog on the treadmill every other day – hell, that *had* to get the dopamine flowing, didn't it?

Or maybe it was the camaraderie with my new workout buddies that was causing my improved sense of well-bring.

"*I hate this shit!*" was my usual sunny greeting to them every morning when I walked in the gym. And I *did* hate it. I still hadn't warmed to exercise of any kind, rigorous or otherwise. But Harvey, Jamison and Mikey were pushing me in a good way. And Courtney and I had been trading war stories about our respective divorces – which I found comforting – and about which of us had married the bigger asshole. (The consensus: it was a virtual tie.)

All I knew was that there were days now when I walked through the *Herald's* heavy glass doors and past the gigantic framed photograph of the sainted H.L. Mencken, plopped myself down at my computer and felt almost…I don't know… *mellow*.

Apparently the change in my demeanor had not gone

unnoticed by my colleagues, either. A few minutes after I arrived, Debbie Nesbo, Halloran's administrative assistant and the resident office busybody, marched up to me.

"Please don't take this the wrong way . . ." she began.

I leaned back in my chair and frowned. "Too late. I'm already highly offended. No, make that outraged. Highly-outraged is probably the better term."

She stared at me, trying to decide if I was putting her on.

Smiling hesitantly, she continued. "It's just that…well, some of us have noticed there's something a little, I don't know, *off* with you."

"*Off*," I repeated.

"Yes," she said. "You've almost been…you know…*pleasant* to deal with lately."

"*Pleasant*," I said.

She nodded. "You haven't cursed out a copy editor in weeks. You didn't throw a coffee mug at the IT guy when he accidentally erased your files the other day."

"Everyone makes mistakes," I said benevolently. "Hard to believe, but I myself have erred on an occasion or two."

"And when that memo came down about management raising our parking rates, you didn't march into Tom's office and tell him to go fuck himself. Like last time."

I shrugged amiably. "What's 15 bucks more a month? Especially for the peace of mind that comes with knowing your car is being watched over by a crack team of security professionals. Even if they *do* seem to be smoking weed in that booth half the time."

Debbie nodded uncertainly.

"So I guess my question is . . ." She looked around the newsroom and lowered her voice. ". . . Are you *on* something?

Like, you know, some kind of meds? A mood leveler, maybe? Or Zoloft? Like my sister's on?"

I didn't reply right away. Instead, I stood and motioned for her to follow me. We went out into the hallway. As usual, there was zero foot traffic.

This, in a nutshell, was the modern-day newspaper office. The few cubicle rats still in the newsroom seemed perpetually chained to their desks, terrified to gossip and schmooze with co-workers in a more private setting lest some management stooge decide they weren't working hard enough and were replaceable. The Joint Chiefs of Staff could meet in the halls of the *Herald* to mull a nuclear strike on the Chinese mainland and no one would ever know.

Leaning close to Debbie, I whispered: "OK, you got me. I *am* on something. I'm on the Toad."

Debbie's eyes widened. "On the . . .*what?*"

"Colorado River Toad. I'm serious. Google it, Deb. The extract from its glands has psychoactive properties. But it also induces feelings of calmness and well-being – at least before the intense hallucinations come on."

The smile slowly seeped from her face.

"Trouble is, the stuff's expensive," I continued. "The toads go for about two thou each. And it's illegal to transport them across state lines. So you need someone on-site, preferably a qualified herpetologist, to collect the exudate – that's the cells and fluid – and ship it to you."

I shook my head sadly. "As you can imagine, it's costing me a small fortune. And I've done some horrible things to get my hands on it – really sick, depraved stuff. Bordering on the *criminal,* really."

An awkward silence descended on us.

Appearing to brighten, I said: "But, hey, if you want to go in with me on the next batch, that'll cut expenses. What do you say? You look fairly well-adjusted. You probably don't need as many doses as I do. Which means they won't have to slice up as many of the slimy little critters. Could save us both *beaucoup* bucks."

Deb turned pale. I thought she might pass out.

She took two steps backward, eyeing me warily, as if I might pull one of the mucilaginous creatures from my pocket and fling it at her. Then she turned and wordlessly clomped back to the newsroom.

Yeah, ever the workplace charmer – that's me.

6.

My next stop was the newspaper's library – we used to call it the morgue, back in the Paleozoic Era before hedge funds hijacked journalism – to see if I could pick up the trail of the infamous Anthony Maldonado. A quick Internet search had turned up nothing. Maybe Benny could work his magic and do a deep dive into the archives for me.

At one point not too long ago, the *Herald* employed six full-time research librarians, all kept mind-numbingly busy by the information needs of a large and energetic staff of reporters and editors.

Now we were down to exactly one researcher. Luckily, though, the one who remained, Benjamin Parisi, was a rock star.

A 35-year veteran of the newspaper, he was dedicated, hard-working and tenacious, blessed with an uncanny ability to ferret out even the most arcane material from the most obscure sources. So naturally management couldn't wait to get rid of him.

They had tried to push him out the door the last two times buyouts were offered, correctly assuming they could find someone to take his place at a fraction of his salary.

But Benny wasn't going anywhere. He had no wife or family. No real life outside work. Rumor had it he was sitting on a priceless collection of World War II memorabilia, with an emphasis on the weapons, field gear and uniforms of the Wehrmacht of Nazi Germany. But that had never been confirmed.

Whether he was secretly wealthy or not, most of us had always assumed that on his final day at the *Herald*, after he was "banged out" in the customary sign of respect and affection for a departing colleague, he'd walk out into the bright sunshine, take a deep breath of fresh air – and promptly throw himself in front of a bus.

Rich or not, what would he *possibly* do with all the free time retirement offered? No, to Benny, a life without the *Herald*, would be a death sentence.

As always, I found him hunched in front of his computer on the second floor, simultaneously squinting and glowering at the blue-white screen through thick eyeglasses.

"There he is, the great Benny Parisi!" I bellowed, shifting smoothly into the fawning and obsequious mode that had always worked best with testy co-workers on whom I was suddenly dependent for help. "A shoo-in for the Librarian Hall of Fame! I'm serious, dude! You're a first-ballot selection! Goes without saying, but you got my vote!"

Only then did I recall that Benny had always seemed impervious to the world-class sucking up that I and many of his other colleagues tended to do in his presence.

Without taking his eyes from the monitor, he pointed wordlessly to a pen and pad of paper on the desk in front of him. Next to them was a small hand-written sign: "Leave your research request. Don't be wordy. Two sentences or less."

"OK, sure!" I chirped. "I can do that. Wow, we're really going old school, huh? A Bic and paper? But no problem! Hey, can I get you a coffee or anything? A bagel from the cafeteria?"

Benny's face remained expressionless. He was concentrating so hard on whatever he was reading I thought blood might start seeping from his forehead. Had he even heard a word I'd said?

Sighing, I grabbed a slip of paper and scribbled in my pathetic cursive: "Need info on one Alejandro Maldonado, aka Anthony "Tony" Malden, aka Oven Mitts. Whacked his wife back in the 80's – maybe cuz she wouldn't look up when he spoke to her."

Yes, that was a little shot at Benny. But it was fully compliant with the dumb two-sentence rule. Besides, what did Shakespeare say? "Brevity is the soul of wit?" Maybe I had a future in stand-up.

Except now Benny's rudeness was starting to tick me off. Who did he think he *was,* anyway? The head of the goddamn National Archives? He couldn't give me the common courtesy of at least making eye contact? And saying hi?

Turning to leave, I said: "OK, nice talking to you, Benny. We really should do this again soon. But maybe next time let me get in a word or two, all right? It can't always just be you yakking away non-stop."

Only then did Benny Parisi finally deign to acknowledge my existence.

With his eyes still glued to the screen and his meaty right hand curled around his mouse, he slowly unfurled his middle finger.

Oh, it was a beautiful moment! This is why I'll miss the big lug if he ever leaves.

A few hours later, while banging out the next day's column, a snappy 750 words full of righteous indignation about how the meter readers doing mass ticketing downtown were the worst human beings ever – yes, I'd been rung up, too – a message flashed on my screen: "Come see me. Benny."

I found him in the exact same position as before.

Silently he pointed to a thick file on his desk. Peeking out from the top was a yellowed clipping of an old *Herald* article, with a headline that screamed: "JUDGE TAKES GLOVES OFF,

OVEN MITTS KILLER GETS 25 YEARS."

Bless his misanthropic little heart, Benny had come through again! It was all I could do not to kiss the guy on his fat, bald, glistening head.

"You're the best, you silver-tongued devil!" I sang out. "Sure, sometimes you're just too goddamned chatty for your own good. But when the rubber hits the road, when it's a three-and-two count with two outs in the ninth and the game's on the line, when we're trailing by a touchdown and it's 4th-and-1 and we're inside the red zone with 10 seconds on the clock – am I mixing too many metaphors here? – you *always* deliver, my friend. *Always.*"

You could tell he was touched.

This time he let go of the mouse for an instant, with the faintest hint of a smile forming on his features.

Then he proceeded to give me the finger with both hands.

7.

I called a meeting of the Big Five for 6:30 the next morning.

We sat at a battered table near the snack counter, in an alcove partially hidden from the rest of the gym. This was where Tami, when she wasn't manning the front desk and flashing her blinding, All-Galactic molars, spent her day making the worst smoothies known to man. These were dense, viscous, tasteless concoctions of an iridescent green or yellow hue that left her customers fishing bits of berry stems, chia seeds and pineapple peel from their mouths for hours.

I figured the loud whine of the ancient blender would prevent any busy-bodies from overhearing our conversation. Instead, a sign was posted: "Attention members: the snack bar is closed, due to a problem with the electrical system. We apologize for any inconvenience."

"What are we doing here?" Harvey grumbled, pulling up a chair. "What's with all the hush-hush stuff?"

Courtney glared at him. "Sit your pale, skinny ass *down*! Jack has something important to tell us. It's about one of the members. And he'd rather not have everyone in the place know about it – if that's OK with you."

Looking back at me, she smiled sweetly. "Go ahead, Jackie."
Jackie!

God, it sounded lovely coming from her! Like a heavenly chorus of angels. Way better than how Halloran said it, with his smoker's pre-cancerous rasp and the perennial pissed-off edge to his voice.

"Read this first," I told the group. "Then we'll discuss."

Quickly I passed out printouts of one of the articles Benny had retrieved. It was from the August 15, 1981 issue of the *Herald*. The headline read: "Well-Known Merchant Sentenced in Wife's Death."

Alejandro R. Maldonado, the self-professed "Carpet King of Cross Street" whose tacky TV commercials with the catch-phrase "We never pull the rug from under you!" both fascinated and appalled Baltimoreans for decades, will have a new home for the foreseeable future: the state penitentiary in Hagerstown.

Maldonado, 40, was sentenced yesterday to 25 years for the 1980 murder of his wife, Carmen E. Maldonado, 35. The sensational case, rife with accusations of domestic abuse and infidelity, drew national attention. It also earned Maldonado the tabloid sobriquet of "The Oven Mitts Killer" after authorities determined he wore a pair of the protective thermal gloves while bludgeoning his wife with a hot frying pan in the kitchen of his family's home.

Before Judge Cleotis Boyer imposed the sentence, Maldonado asked to address the packed courtroom. Wiping tears from his eyes, he read a brief statement in which he expressed remorse for the killing while also urging shoppers to take advantage of his store's "tremendous upcoming Labor Day sale, with discounts up to 70 per cent off plus a two-year limited installation warranty. Ask for Lou. He'll be running things for a while."

Maldonado's elderly parents, Luis and Candida Maldonado, spoke to the media afterward. Both said they grieved for Carmen Maldonado's family. Both also said they would always love their son, although Candida Maldonado admonished him for injecting a plug for his carpet business into the solemn proceedings.

"He knows better than that," she added, "no matter how good the sale is. And I'm sure it's a very good one. They always are."

Accompanying the story was a grainy black-and-white photograph of the killer being led from the courtroom in handcuffs and leg shackles, a dazed look on his face.

"Wow," Courtney said, studying the image. "And you're sure it's the same guy you and Mikey saw the other day? The geriatric wonder doing all those sick exercises?"

"Definitely," I said as Mikey nodded. "The full head of hair's gone, of course. He's got a Friar Tuck fringe up top now. And a lot more wrinkles. And he's changed his name – calls himself Tony Maldon. But he's the Oven Mitts Killer, all right."

She shivered and looked up. "And he's going to be working out here in the mornings now? Lovely."

"Don't worry, Court," Mikey said. "I'll be happy to introduce you. In fact, gimme your cell number. I'll have him call you."

Courtney glared at him. "You are *such* a douchebag . . ."

Mikey cackled for a moment, then said: "You know what? I bet he's here now." He stood and peered over the counter. "Yeah, there he is. Way back at the Queenax. The same three babes are with him, too. Oh, and its showtime again! You gotta see this!"

The rest of us scrambled for a look.

The Queenax was a massive piece of equipment that looked like a jungle gym on steroids. Belts and pulleys could be attached to its many rungs and ladders to perform all manner of hellish exercises: squatting, pulling, pushing, bending, etc. And there, hanging by his feet in the middle of the contraption, like some kind of slumbering albino god in a white Nike T-shirt and white shorts, was Oven Mitts Maldon.

Yet instead of sleeping, he commenced doing a series of upside-down sit-ups, the kind of slow, tortuous movements that would make a Navy SEAL hurl. We watched him knock out 20 in a row with his arms crossed over his chest, back ramrod straight, each one as perfect in form as the one that preceded it.

Jamison whistled softly. "That dude's unreal! He could probably crush a beer can with those abs."

After his final sit-up, the old guy rocked forward slightly to build momentum, launched into a tight back flip and landed gracefully on the balls of his feet before bowing theatrically.

The five of us gawked as if we'd just witnessed the transfiguration.

The old guy smiled and the women smothered him with hugs. After they all moved on to the free weights, we sat back down. Courtney shook her head.

"OK, that was...*unbelievable*," she said softly. "But the whole idea of him working out here is so creepy. It's like a bad Netflix documentary: 'When the Killer Did Queenax.'"

"Or 'Evil Lurked on the Elliptical.'" Jamison offered.

"'The Butcher Did Biceps Curls,'" Mikey added, warming to the exercise.

"Uh, maybe we could move on," I said. "Think anyone else here knows he's *the* Oven Mitts Maldonado?"

"Doubtful," Mikey said. "That case is 34 years old. And he's a grandpa now. Hell, maybe a *great*-grandpa. Even if he's doing stuff no other grandpa on the planet could do. Who would recognize him after all these years?"

"What about his three disciples?" Jamison asked. "The Oven-ettes? Wonder if they know who he really is?"

Courtney snorted. "No way! What self-respecting broad

works out with a guy who offed his old lady? I'll tell you what else is creepy. How touchy he is with those three. Those hugs went on *way-y-y* too long. And his hands are sliding all over the place. You *know* he's copping a feel every chance he gets."

We sat in silence for a moment. Harvey gazed up at the ceiling, lost in thought, until Courtney kicked his chair.

"What do *you* have to say about all this, Mr. Motor Mouth?" she asked. "Usually we can't get you to shut up. Now you're, what, gazing up at the heavens in awe and wonder? Contemplating the vastness of the universe?"

She reached over and patted his shoulder. "Oh, and sorry for being a little bitchy earlier. It's that time of the month. Cramps, bloating, uterus bleeding out . . you know how it is."

Harvey made a face. "*Jesus*, Courtney! We get it!"

With that he jumped up and began pacing back and forth, hands clasped behind his back.

"OK, here's what I think," he said, finally. "I think we need to find out way more about this Oven Mitts character. I mean, c'mon! The guy freaking whacked his wife! And did a serious bit in te Big House!"

"I *love* when you do prison lingo," Courtney said. "It's *such* a turn-on . . ."

"And now here he is, working out right next to us!" Harvey went on, ignoring her. "And we're the only ones who know about his horrible past! But don't you want to know even *more* about the guy? Like what was his life like in the slammer? What's he been doing since he got out? Is he still dangerous?

"At his age you wouldn't think so," he added with a shrug. "But, hell, you never know."

He whirled around suddenly and pointed at us. "We need answers, people! We gotta investigate this guy!"

Mikey nudged Jamison in the ribs. "Oh, you mean we should form, like, some kind of a detective squad? Would we get to wear matching trench coats?"

"And matching fedoras?" Jamison asked.

As the two of them cracked up, Harvey glared and unleashed a torrent of profanities before lapsing into silence again. The detective squad, it seemed to me, was off to a rocky start. Morale was already cratering. And there appeared to be dissension in the ranks, at least at the moment, causing no small amount of consternation in Lt. Harvey.

Yet Harvey had awakened something in us, too. You could sense it as the meeting continued. He had punctured our boredom, given us a renewed sense of purpose. No longer were we just a listless bunch of everyday Joes and Janes showing up at the gym and going through the desultory motions of trying to keep the pounds off and slow the ravages of age.

Now we were also conducting a confidential inquiry into the life of a bonafide murderer – a *wife-killer, no less!* – who worked out among us and happened to be the most extraordinarily fit codger we'd ever seen.

Maybe we *were* like a detective squad, albeit a kind of half-assed one. In fact, wouldn't that look good on our business cards? *The Half-Assed Detective Agency. We'll Try to Help. But Don't Get Your Hopes Up.*

And Harvey was right: we *did* want to know more about Oven Mitts. We wanted to know his secrets. *All* his secrets. Was he still a powder-keg who could blow at any moment and hurt someone – or worse? Were the Oven-ettes, despite their relentless sycophancy and adoration, in any danger?

We were on a mission to find out. Hell, for all intents and purposes, we were working a real live *case!* Our heretofore hum-drum lives had been given new meaning. We ourselves had been given new relevance. And we were determined not to blow this opportunity.

As the meeting broke up, Courtney took one last glance at the photo of Oven Mitts.

"What do you think he's looking for?" she asked.

"Looking for?" I said. "Who said he's looking for anything?"

She gave me a knowing look. "A man who did what he did? And has lived with it all these years? Lived with the guilt and the pain, if he's any kind of human being? No, trust me. All these years later, he's looking for *something* ... "

8.

"Are these supposed to be chicken tenders?"

Emily gazed down at her plate as if it held the entrails of a ground hog. I took a deep breath and silently counted to 10. Going thermonuclear would only make things worse.

"No, sweetie," I said at last. "They're not *supposed* to be chicken tenders. They *are* chicken tenders."

"They don't *look* like chicken tenders," Liam said.

He pushed four of the suspect chunks of white meat to the far side of his plate, thus signaling they were now permanently banished from associating with the more-or-less decent food – the corn and apple sauce fit for human consumption – he'd deign to eat.

I tossed my napkin on the table and sat back.

"OK," I said, looking at both children. "What's wrong with the tenders?"

They looked at each other and shrugged.

"They're kind of...*chewy*," Emmie said finally.

"Chewy," I said.

"Yeah, like kind of, I don't' know...*leathery*."

"Leathery," I repeated.

Liam, 6, nodded solemnly, but said nothing. His 10-year-old sister was on a roll. She was representing their cause magnificently – even if he wasn't completely certain of the strange jargon being tossed about.

Emmie popped a tender in her mouth and made a face. "How long did you leave them in the oven?"

This time I counted to 15. It felt as if the top of my head would explode. I feared I'd break out in facial tics.

"I left them in the oven," I said evenly, "for as long as the instructions on the package *said* to leave them in the oven. Then I took them *out* of the oven. At precisely the time they were *supposed to* be taken out of the oven."

Emmie absorbed this new information with a worried frown.

"Mommy says that with all the demands people have on them nowadays, it's easy to lose track of time. That's probably what happened in this case."

She leaned across the table and patted my hand reassuringly. Liam nodded and patted my other hand.

"Poor Daddy," he said. "It's OK."

"You'll probably get it right next time," Emmie added sweetly.

Discreetly, she brought her napkin to her mouth and gently spat out the offending piece of chicken, wadding the whole mess into a ball which she placed on her plate. Liam mimicked her every move. Only his spitting wasn't as decorous. More like a longshoreman hacking up a loogie.

He grinned and said: "What's for dessert?"

It was one of my first full weekends with the kids since the divorce. To say things did not start off well would be an understatement. Both had seemed quiet and unsettled since Beth dropped them off at my apartment earlier that afternoon.

After handing me their overnight backpacks, my former wife felt compelled, as always, to summarize what she presumed to be the emotional and physical state of our children.

"Emily is not in a great mood because she's missing her friend Sarah's birthday party," she began. "It was going to be a big deal.

They were going to ride ponies at Sarah's mom's ex's place off Falls Road in the Valley.

"On the way over here, Emmie asked if *you* would ever buy her a pony." Beth snorted derisively. "Of course, I had to tell her no. We all remember you wouldn't even let the kids have a puppy. Or a hamster, for that matter."

I know, I thought silently. *I suck. I'm the worst human being ever . . .*

"Liam might have the beginnings of a cold," Beth continued. "His nose is runny. He feels a little warm, too. Don't get him all riled up. You know that stupid game you play with the kids? Where you're the psycho killer and you turn off all the lights and pretend it's midnight in a deserted graveyard? And you chase them around snarling and growling until one of them bangs into a chair or table and starts crying? I'd hold off on that one."

"Got it," I said. "We'll spend the weekend doing origami. And mindfulness exercises."

She sighed and shook her head softly.

"God," she murmured, "you're still *such* a tool .. ."

"Forty-five years and counting," I said proudly.

As the kids made a bee-line for the TV remote, Beth stuck a bony index finger in my chest.

"Have them back Sunday afternoon by 4," she hissed. "Do *not* fuck this up."

"Me?" I said. "Fuck something up?"

She turned on her heel and walked briskly down the walkway to her Volvo, but not before shooting me a final withering look. It was nice to see that my long streak of being a tremendous disappointment to her was still intact.

The amazing thing about the seemingly boundless reservoir of irritation Beth drew on in her dealings with me was how twisted it was. After all, wasn't *she* the one who had torched the marriage? With an astounding display of infidelity that literally took my breath away? And broke my heart in a way I never thought it could be broken?

"You're never gonna let that go, are you?" she once said to me. This was in Tischler the Lawyer's office, right before the divorce was finalized.

"You giving our neighbor a holiday hummer?" I said cheerfully. "Oh, no, I'm totally *over* that, Bethie. I only think about it 20 or 30 times a day now."

Tischler diplomatically pretended not to hear that one, developing a sudden fascination for whatever was happening outside his window. But his assistant nearly spit out her coffee. Watching her smother a laugh with a Kleenex, I almost managed a smile.

Then I remembered how much this whole sad business was going to cost me, both emotionally and financially.

Besides, how exactly do you just "let go" of something that's left you so traumatized?

This seems as good a time as any for a brief recap of the "silly little incident," as Beth called it, that ruptured our marriage.

It was New Year's Eve, 2019. We had a big party at our house. It was around 20 minutes after midnight, which means everyone had finished watching the ball drop on TV and exchanging the requisite corny toasts and sloppy hugs and kisses. A few people had left, but a lively group of guests remained, mostly from the neighborhood, many in various stages of inebriation.

I was checking on the beer supply when I heard a noise on the back deck.

At first I thought it was the raccoon again. At the time, we had a raccoon the size of Toyota Prius that regularly toppled the garbage cans under the deck and feasted on the contents.

He wasn't picky about what he ate, either. Nor did he seem particularly afraid of humans. If you snapped on the lights and ran out to scare him off, he'd stare you down until you were maybe 10 feet away.

Only then would he turn and saunter off into the woods, but not before shooting you one last icy look as if to say: *Fine, you win this one, Fat Man. But this isn't over. We both know I'll be back.*

This time, though, I decided on a new tactic.

I grabbed a flashlight and slipped noiselessly out the side door. The plan was to creep up on the voracious critter, zap him with the light and scare the crap out of him with a loud noise. Hopefully the shock would make him stay away for good.

A quick word here about the Pelican 7620 tactical flashlight I carried.

Oh, it was a beauty. The same model is used by police and military outfits all over the world. Unlike a regular flashlight, this baby threw off a wide, powerful LED beam, like the spotlight on a prison guard tower.

Tip-toeing to the deck, I was startled to hear a low moaning. I am no wildlife expert, but this did not sound like the noise your average raccoon would make as he tore through a savory buffet of rotted orange peels, old Keurig pods and smelly tuna cans.

I pointed the Pelican in the direction of the moaning and clicked the "On" button.

The deck exploded in light.

And there, leaning against the railing, with his pants around his ankles, was my good buddy Dan Henson, gazing up at the stars with a dreamy (and drunken) look on his face. And there on her knees in front of him, head bobbing up and down rhythmically, was my wife.

Well.

Parts of what happened next are still a blur.

In my mind, I grabbed my face with both hands and screamed, like the famous Edvard Munch painting. But it was probably more like an anguished yelp. My heart was hammering in my chest. I thought I was going to pass out.

Beth whirled, saw me and leaped to her feet. Dan was so hammered it took him a few seconds to realize two critical things: a) he was no longer being fellated and b) the husband of the woman who'd been fellating him was now standing somewhere off in the darkness, shooting a white-hot beam of light into his face like an angry, vengeful god on Judgment Day.

This next part I remember clearly: no one said a word.

Eyes filling with tears, Beth pushed silently past me and went back inside. She would hole up in the bathroom for the next 20 minutes, crying and splashing water on her face and hyper-ventilating until finally emerging, damp and ashen-faced, to ask if anyone wanted coffee and dessert.

Dan fumbled with the zipper on his jeans for what seemed like the longest time. He finally opened the sliding glass door and lurched inside, shooting me a scared and embarrassed look. (Although not *that* embarrassed, now that I think about it.)

A minute or two later, I watched him go over to his wife, Melanie, and whisper something in her ear. The two left hurriedly soon after. So hurriedly, in fact, that they forgot their crystal dessert tray, which I later sailed into the woods, grunting with satisfaction as it hit a tree and shattered into pieces.

Somehow, Beth and I held it together until the last of the guests left. Then it all went to hell. We were up until dawn, sobbing, shouting, throwing things against walls and angrily pointing fingers at each other.

Beth blamed her "indiscretion" – ha, another nice term for

it! - on too much booze, on the stress of her real estate job, on the guilt she felt as a working mom spending so much time away from the kids, on me not meeting her emotional needs.

That last one was a beauty.

"How does that work exactly?" I asked. "You wake up one day and think: 'Know what? I'm not getting the empathy and support I need from my husband. Think I'll go blow Dan?'"

I moved out the next day.

It soon came to light that Beth and Dan had been fooling around for some time, something I had just been too dumb (or naïve) to see. This was no drunken one-off.

Dan worked as an accountant from home while his wife Sally commuted 45 minutes back and forth to her job with an insurance agency. Beth did most of her work from home, too, while I was either at the *Herald* or hitting the streets for columns. And our kids were conveniently in school from 8 a.m. until 3 in the afternoon five days a week.

Which meant the circumstances were perfect for the two dissolute lovebirds to whet their considerable carnal appetites pretty much whenever they wanted. A skulking 20-foot tip-toe across either home's back yard and a furtive duck-in through an open sliding glass door was all it took to remain below the radar of any nosy neighbors before the eager groping, rutting and mashing of tongues into mouths could begin.

Nevertheless, Beth spent the ensuing months insisting to everyone who'd listen that I was the bad guy and she was the one who'd been wronged by a cold-fish husband – one with a host of sexual inhibitions rooted in a stilted upbringing by his controlling and domineering parents, whom she never got along with in the first place.

I was the one, she contended, who had over-reacted wildly

to a single unfortunate instance of reckless behavior on her part, brought on by an extra glass or two of wine that clouded her judgement, as it would anyone's. (Yeah, right.)

You talk about gaslighting someone. She practically had a doctorate in the subject.

During the divorce proceedings, we agreed on joint custody of the kids. Beth was a sneaky, lying little shit, a full-on adulteress and a lousy life-partner. But she was also somehow a decent mom, so we agreed the kids would be better off with her.

Between their busy schedules and mine, this meant I would mostly see Emmie and Liam on weekends, relegating me to that most pitiable of categories: wronged husband and part-time dad.

Nevertheless, I was determined to be the best dad I could be, and to wring as much joy and closeness as I could from every visit.

On the day of the chicken tenders fiasco, we went to Camden Yards and, on a gloriously sunny afternoon, watched the Orioles get their asses kicked 12-1 by the Cleveland Indians. We binged on hotdogs and sodas and cotton candy. Emmie had her picture taken with the Oriole Bird. But the furry mascot – since when do birds have fur? – freaked out Liam, who wailed as if someone was sawing off his leg.

The next day, we went to the National Aquarium and then out for dinner, my cowardly way of avoiding another harsh critique of my cooking.

We played Psycho Graveyard Killer a few times, too. Inevitably, Liam began giggling so hard he failed to watch where he was going and slammed into the coffee table, just as Beth had predicted. He ended up with a nasty bruise on his shin. But he only cried for a moment or two before wiping his tears and demanding: "Do the chain-saw noise again!"

Which I happily did. WHONNK! WHONNK! WHONNNKKKK!

I made both kids promise not to tell their mother. But I also knew they'd crack in a heart-beat if Beth pressed them, as she surely would. Her Gestapo-like post-visit interrogations – unofficially titled *What stupid shit did your father do this time?* – began the moment she collected the kids and threw the car in reverse. And these sessions were always thorough and revealing.

As the end of my weekend with the kids neared, I felt the familiar hollow pit in my stomach that came with knowing I wouldn't see them for days.

For some reason, I thought of Oven Mitts Maldon. I wondered what his relationship was with his children now. Had he had any contact with them at all? I couldn't imagine him opening any cheerful Father's Day cards from Joey and Olivia during all those years he spent in a dank prison cell in Hagerstown.

With the passage of time, was there even a scintilla of forgiveness in the children's hearts for the horrific deed done by their dad? Probably not. And that wasn't just me playing Dr. Phil and trying to get inside their heads.

I based it on another old article Benny had dug up. This one was from the mid-90's, a front-page story in the Baltimore *Bugle*, the feisty, irreverent broadsheet that had gone toe-to-toe with the *Herald* for years until succumbing to the inevitable economic pressures of a two-newspaper town.

The *Bugle* headline said it all: "'Pay up, Pops!' Furious kids sue monster dad who offed their mom!"

No, no love lost there, apparently.

According to the story, Joseph Maldonado and Olivia Maldonado and their representatives were asking for $12 million in compensatory damages and another $12 million in punitive damages. This hardly seemed like an exorbitant sum to me, given that he had changed their lives forever in a fit of rage, with a single deadly blow from a fry pan.

The article went on to say that Oven Mitts's offspring were also asking for ownership of the family home. This, too, seemed like small compensation for the harrowing lifetime of loss and pain that now stretched out before them.

As Beth's car pulled away from the curb at a little after 4 and the kids waved from the back seat, I wondered what it would be like to know your own off-spring loathed you and never wanted to see you again.

Pretty goddamn sad, was my uneducated guess.

But maybe I'd get up the nerve to ask Oven Mitts himself one day. Hell, I could still *pretend* to be a hotshot reporter, couldn't I?

Sure I could.

9.

Mikey reached for an Equal with his stubby fingers, tore it open and dumped it in his coffee.

He grabbed another packet and did the same. Slowly and methodically, he repeated the ritual five more times.

As the rest of us watched in astonishment, he added a dollop of cream and slowly stirred the concoction.

"Do you *always* do that?" Courtney asked finally.

Mikey looked up. "Stir my coffee? Yeah, pretty much."

"No, you idiot!" she said. "PUT SEVEN FREAKING EQUALS IN IT! That can't be healthy."

"Mikey, she's right," Harvey said. "There are mice in research labs dropping dead in their cages after ingesting that stuff."

Mikey rolled his eyes.

"Another tired and discredited trope," he said. "Perpetuated, no doubt, by Big Sugar."

"Maybe," Jamison said, "but those artificial sweeteners are super-addictive. Didn't you read that piece in the *Herald* the other day? Harvard Med School did a study with lab rats that were fed cocaine, OK?

"But when the rats were given a choice between the blow and artificial sweeteners, guess what? Most of 'em chose the sweeteners. What's that tell you?"

For a moment, Mikey appeared lost in thought.

"It tells me," he said finally, "that those rats have exceedingly good judgment. At my age, I'll take a nice Equals buzz over a coke high any day."

He took a loud, slurping sip of coffee and smiled contentedly.

"Jesus God!" Harvey said. "He's hopeless! *That's* what'll make him wig out one day and start shooting people! He'll be on an aspartame rager! It'll have nothing to do with 'Nam!"

Mikey said: "Think we could stop fixating on me? And get back to the matter at hand?"

Ah, yes. The matter at hand . . .

At the moment, the matter at hand was a debate about whether the late Carmen Maldonado – Oven Mitts' wife, gone from this earth for so many years – bore even the slightest responsibility for her untimely demise.

The discussion had started in the gym that morning. But it had quickly gotten heated when Harvey, during a set on the leg-press machine, loudly blurted: "I'M NOT SAYING SHE WAS A WHORE! I'M SAYING SHE HAD WHORE-LIKE TENDENCIES! THERE'S A DIFFERENCE, YOU KNOW!"

The fact that Oven Mitts and his adoring retinue were just 20 feet away – him doing 60-pound dumbbell rows seemingly effortlessly, the Oven-ettes swooning on cue as they watched him – was also problematic.

So when necks started craning in our direction to find out which whore or whore-like person we were talking about, Courtney had quietly suggested delaying the debate and moving it to another venue.

Thus it was that the Big Five reconvened an hour later just up the road at the Golden Saucer, a local greasy spoon. There we commandeered a table away from any other customers who might have had a problem hearing "SHE WAS A SLUT!" while enjoying their morning orange juice and scrambled eggs.

"OK, people," Courtney began. "Let's refocus. The testimony at Oven Mitts' trial indicated Carmen Maldonado was having an affair. We know this from the old newspaper clips, right?"

"Right," Harvey said. "Apparently she was banging her boss at Ageant Textiles."

"No *apparently* about it," Jamison said. "A private detective hired by Oven Mitts testified he followed the two to a hotel. Saw them check in at the front desk. Watched them sucking face and hanging all over each other as they got on the elevator. They sure as hell weren't there to watch 'Seinfeld' re-runs."

"And remember what else Oven Mitts told the court," Mikey added. "He said he looked out his storefront window one day after that and saw his wife and her boss drive by in the boss's car. And she was practically giving him a lap dance behind the wheel."

Harvey shook his head sadly. "How come that stuff never happens to me?"

Courtney shot him a contemptuous look.

"Yet I'm sure we all agree," she said, voice rising, "that *despite* her infidelities – which, yes, were reportedly numerous and flagrant – she certainly didn't deserve to be killed. I mean, my God! This isn't Afghanistan under the Taliban! We don't stone women to death for having trysts!"

She looked at each of us. "Right?"

The four of us stared back at her.

"RIGHT?!" she repeated.

No one said anything. I looked over at Harvey and Mikey, who were gazing down at the floor. Jamison seemed fixated with a loose button on his sport coat.

"WILL ONE OF YOU BONEHEADS PLEASE SAY

SOMETHING?!" Courtney shouted.

Harvey finally cleared his throat. "I don't know, Court. Maybe we need to re-think the laws in this country. Sure, maybe stoning's a little over-the-top. But a wife fools around on her husband…isn't ending the little tramp's life with a greasy skillet pretty much justified?"

Courtney picked up a fork and lunged at him.

"OK, OK!" he said, laughing and throwing up his hands. "KIDDING! GEEZ!"

As the rest of us cracked up, Courtney hissed: "You bony little shit! I'll stab that midget dick of yours if you keep it up."

Harvey grinned and looked at the rest of us. "How does *she* know what I have down there?" Then to Courtney: "So you've been hanging out in the men's locker room? I'm gonna have to report that to management, Court. That's a rules violation for sure."

Courtney lunged at him again. It took several more minutes for order to be restored, at which point she proceeded to mount a spirited defense for the dalliances – alleged or otherwise – of the long-departed Carmen M.

By all accounts, Courtney argued, the marriage had been a profoundly unhappy one for years.

Hadn't Carmen's parents, Martin and Eva Santos, testified that they'd begun to see red flags just months after the young couple's wedding at St. Theresa's Church in Highlandtown and their glitzy reception at Martin's West?

Hadn't the parents begun fielding more and more late-night phone calls from their daughter, during which she'd tearfully declare that she'd made a terrible mistake in marrying a man so cruel, boorish and domineering?

Hadn't both of Carmen's children told the court about their

parents' frequent and loud arguments, when Anthony would call his wife the most hurtful and disgusting names, causing her to flee to the bathroom, collapse on the cold tile floor and sob for hours behind the locked door?

Finally, didn't court transcripts show that Carmen's insanely jealous and paranoid husband threatened to kill her at various times with a rusty potato peeler, a heavy-duty garlic press or a stainless-steel herb chopper if she ever dared to stray in the marriage?

Courtney shook her head sadly. "Was it any wonder that after years of being abused and dominated by this brute, she eventually sought comfort in the arms of another man?"

"Now you sound like the jacket copy for a romance novel," Jamison said. He looked around sheepishly. "Not that, y'know, I've ever *read* one . . ."

Courtney shrugged. "Go ahead and snicker. No one's saying Carmen was the perfect wife. None of us knows how we'd react trapped in a stifling marriage like that. But only the most unhinged psychopath comes home from work one evening, strolls into the kitchen where the mother of his children is cooking dinner and decides" – here she mimed holding the murder weapon over her head – '*Bitch, your time is up.*' Like he's some kind of Lord High Executioner anointed by God."

Harvey seemed incredulous.

"So no crime of passion here?" he said. "That's your take? Oven Mitts didn't just flip out and kill her in a jealous rage? He didn't just explode one night after having her affair thrown in his face for so long? It was totally premeditated?"

Courtney nodded vigorously. "Ha! I bet he planned it for weeks. No, *months*." She turned to me. "Let's put you on the analyst's couch for a moment, big guy."

"Uh, no, that's OK . . ." I said.

"When you caught your wife with your neighbor that night," she went on," and she was, um, you know . . ."

"Polishing his knob?" Harvey offered helpfully.

"Sampling his sausage?" Mikey said.

"Laying a Lewinsky on him?" Jamison added.

Courtney rolled her eyes and sighed. "Boys, boys, boys... aren't we done with sixth grade yet?"

We weren't. Guys are never done with sixth grade. This is a fact. It's just that no one ever wants to admit it.

She looked at me again. "Simple question, Jackie. Didn't you want to kill her? After what she did to you?"

The question rocked me for an instant.

"Are you kidding?" I said finally. "Of *course* I wanted to kill her. In the most painful ways possible. Ritual dismemberment. Crucifixion. Rusty pitchfork through the neck. I would have been good with any of those. Had about 20 other ways in mind, too."

"But you *didn't* do it," Courtney said. "You never raised a hand to her. Oh, sure, you *thought* about murder. You *fantasized* about what it would be like. Every time you pictured the two of them on that darkened deck, her rocking back and forth on her knees, him slack-jawed and dreamy-eyed with pleasure, arms spread wide and reaching toward the stars as the first shudders of —"

"*Okay, okay!*" I said. "Can we do without the play-by-play?"

"Sorry. My point is, each time you thought about that horrible betrayal, the pain would overwhelm you all over again," Courtney continued. "It was so agonizing, so unbearable, you thought you'd scream. Or lose your mind. And the only way to make it hurt less was to picture her suffering some awful lingering retribution. Preferably delivered by your righteous hand."

She stared at me. "Am I right?"

When I looked down and didn't answer, she nodded knowingly.

"Been there, felt that," she said. "When I found out what Teddy was doing behind my back, I kicked him out. And all I could think about for months was grabbing my boning knife, driving over to the shitty little apartment where he was staying with his slutty girlfriend and...*gutting him like a fish!*"

She spit the words out with such ferocity that the rest of us flinched.

I made a mental note: whatever you do, do *not* piss off this woman.

For *any* reason.

"But of course," she continued, "I never acted on my sick little reverie, either." Her features had softened again. "I'm like you, Jackie. We're not psychopathic killers. We're not like Oven Mitts. We're damaged in a lot of ways, yes. We're scarred from the terrible wrong that was done to us by our partner. But we're not so deranged, so irretrievably broken inside, so hollowed out emotionally, that we'd murder someone."

It took a moment or two for this to sink in.

"So what are you saying?" I asked. "That we're too well-adjusted to kill? Not narcissistic enough? Not vicious enough? Too empathetic?"

She nodded wearily. "I'm afraid that's *exactly* what I'm saying. We're more about pleasing others, not harming them."

She reached over and patted my arm. Her long, slender fingers felt warm and inviting. Although as usual, I was probably reading too much into it.

Our little discussion broke up a few minutes later. The final consensus: Carmen Maldonado deserved some sort of retribution for her sleazy behavior, and for flaunting it in her husband's face, too. But the mother of two certainly didn't deserve to be brained with a saucepan in her own kitchen, her body left for woodland critters and vultures to gnaw on.

Did this prove the male members of the Big Five were an enlightened bunch? Progressive in our reasoning? Hardly. But maybe it *did* show that we could empathize with a woman who had fallen out of love with a cold and cruel husband and desperately wanted out of a stifling marriage.

Or maybe we were just terrified of pissing off Courtney any further.

When the check came, we all reached for it. But Courtney grabbed it first – until Jamison snatched it from her hand. She flashed a look of annoyance.

Uh-oh, I thought. Jaymo'll get gutted like a fish if she goes Chernobyl. But all Courtney did was smile sweetly and murmur: "Thanks, J."

As we said our good-byes and left, I tried to picture her furious and wild-eyed, creeping up on her sleeping ex and sinking a boning knife – her own personal, customized shiv! – into his soft, white belly.

Thankfully, the image wouldn't come. Otherwise, I'd be looking around for at least one new workout partner.

10.

As hard as the Big Five were on each other, we were even harder on our fellow gym members.

We made snap judgments about them based on superficial aspects of their persona, like hairstyles, workout clothes – *Are those yoga pants age-appropriate?* – gaudiness of jewelry, choice of footwear, even the amount of perspiration they produced relative to how hard we thought they were exercising.

We noted the level of cheerfulness or gloom they projected when they first walked in the doors, the amount of sleep crust (a mixture of mucus, exfoliated skins cells and oils) they rubbed from their eyes, their body odor levels, whether we caught a whiff of a morning onion bagel or stale booze as they passed us in the locker rooms.

From all these observations, we determined whether they were decent human beings or irredeemable losers, and therefore not worthy of our attention.

There were certain gym members we liked, many we disliked, and some we absolutely loathed.

We hated the Water Bottle People, especially the ones ostentatiously lugging around their gallon jugs to show off their superior hydration levels.

Who needed that much fluid to get through a workout? This wasn't a rainforest in Panama. The air-conditioning worked fine. Why couldn't they just drink from the goddamn water fountains like a normal person?

Even those with conventional water bottles irritated us, hogging the fountains with their endless refills. Worst of all was a particularly annoying subset of the Water Bottle People: the Supplement Nuts.

These were the individuals who stood at the water fountains adding spoonfuls of powdered mix to their bottles, then stirring the concoction endlessly, then sampling it and making that annoying little *tsup-tsup-tsup* lip-smacking sound before deciding it needed even *more* water or powder, then engaging in *another* round of serial stirring and tasting before *finally* – just when you thought you'd lose your mind and strangle them with a jump rope – getting the hell out of the way so someone else could get a drink.

We hated the Free Weight Narcissists who felt compelled to let everyone know how hard they worked with their grunting and groaning on every rep, not to mention their theatrical dropping of the weights with a loud *CLANG!* after every set.

Look at me! they fairly screamed. *Am I getting after it or what? Oh, yeah, bro! You're killing it!*

God, it all made us want to puke.

Most of all we hated the Smart Phone Dipshits, who plopped on the various machines and weight benches and proceeded to stare at their phones, rudely tying up the equipment as they scrolled through their emails, texted their friends and co-workers, hunted for new apps and engaged in scintillating conversations about what they planned to have for lunch. *("Girl, Elios has the best veggie wraps ever"!)*

"See that guy on the leg press?" Harvey said one day when we were on the elliptical machines. "Curly hair, moon face. With the big gut? Yeah, that jag-off. He's been sitting there looking at his phone for 10 minutes. I've been timing him."

"You're *timing* him?" Jamison said. "So you're ruining *your* workout by watching *him* ruin *his* workout?"

Harvey chuckled mirthlessly. "Know how we keep saying Mikey might go postal in here one day? Bring an AK and start spraying? If he ever does, I want him to take out that fat bastard first."

Now we were starting to hate Oven Mitts, too.

The man and his retinue were becoming a major pain. Whenever he worked out, half the people in the gym seemed to stop what they were doing to gawk at this geriatric superstar performing his latest otherworldly feat of strength or endurance or flexibility.

This, of course, caused a further logjam on the equipment, which served to royally piss off those of us on a tight schedule, hustling to get in a sweat before going off to our jobs. Maybe what irritated us the most, though, was how Oven Mitts pretended not to notice that his antics brought the place to a standstill.

"Oh, he knows *exactly* what he's doing!" Courtney hissed. "He's such a fucking egotist. I bet he gets off on the whole thing."

She was right. Oven Mitts basked in all the attention. You could tell. His exercise routines were getting showier and more elaborate, for one thing.

One day, as a sudden stillness descended on the place, indicating another of his "Must-See Moments" in progress, we watched him do 30 pushups with the three Oven-ettes astride his back.

Each pushup was done with flawless form: back ramrod straight, arms locked and shoulder-width apart, wrists vertical to shoulders. As always, he didn't cheat once, raising himself all the way up and lowering himself all the way down until his chest lightly grazed the mat.

Even if he'd wanted to low-key the whole thing, it would have been impossible. Not with the three women whooping and throwing their hands in the air with each rise and dip, like they were on a roller-coaster.

On another occasion, we watched him grab a jump-rope and do an absolutely insane five-minute routine full of single- and double-jumps, fancy twirls, criss-cross and double-under moves, high knee kicks and squats – all without stumbling once.

It reminded me of a mesmerizing jump-rope exhibition I'd seen flyweight boxing champion Diego Voloria put on years ago while training for a fight in New York City.

Did I mention Voloria was 28 at the time?

I should probably mention that.

How in God's name was Oven Mitts able to do this stuff at an age when many of his peers were either dead or staring blankly out a window of a nursing home, having the drool wiped off their chins by a bored nurse's aide?

This is how impressive the jump-roping was: when he finished with a dazzling 30-second flurry of sprinting in place, the rope a blur as it whistled through the air, half the gym burst into applause.

"What the fuck?" Mikey grumbled. "We're supposed to holler and cheer everything this guy does now?"

"Jesus, no!" Courtney said. Arms folded across her chest, she glared at the folks clapping and hissed: "Have some dignity, you brainless ass-kissers!"

But the incident illustrated something we'd all sensed for weeks now: Oven Mitts was becoming a celebrity.

From the moment he breezed past the check-in desk each morning, a big smile plastered on his leathery puss, porcelain veneers gleaming in the harsh fluorescent lighting, he was the center of attention.

"It's like he's running for office," Jamison said, watching Oven Mitts weave through the gym, waving and shouting out greetings before plopping his enormous gear bag on whatever piece of equipment he intended to claim first.

Once the Oven-ettes arrived, he'd give each a long, lingering hug. Then he'd announce – in a voice that could be heard in Wyoming – what core group of muscles they'd be working on that day.

"It's Back Day, ladies!" he might say, and invariably the Oven-ettes greeted this with squeals of delight, hopping up and down like caffeinated chipmunks, as if this had suddenly turned into the best fucking day of their lives.

Oven Mitts was spending more and more time at Ripped!, too. That was partly because – aside from the usual slobber-fest he attracted – so many people were interrupting his workouts now to ask for tips on diet and nutrition and lifting techniques, and especially on how to rev up their own stale fitness routines.

Invariably he played the role of the wise and seasoned health consigliere, patiently fielding their questions, nodding somberly and offering advice and encouragement in a low, soothing voice.

The man was becoming a rock star. Everyone in the place could sense it. It left my friends and me in a perpetual simmering rage.

"Ha! They wouldn't fawn all over him if they knew he'd whacked his wife," Courtney said.

"And that he's jacked from pumping iron in a prison exercise yard for 20 years," Jamison added.

"And from fending off the nightly procession of hulking cons trying to pound him in the ass in the shower," Harvey volunteered.

Courtney sighed. "Somehow I knew one of you enlightened and open-minded individuals would bring that up. Tell me something. Is that the worst fear of every goddamned heterosexual man in this country?"

"It's at the top of *my* list," Jamison said.

"Thought yours was running out of hair spray before a live shot?" Mikey said.

"Or using the wrong pancake makeup at a sit-down interview with the governor," Harvey added.

Jamison grinned and nodded.

"Fine, you got me," he said. "Both would freak me out. But going to the slammer and getting drilled every day by Big Luther the boss hog – that's definitely no. 3."

Courtney rolled her eyes and climbed down from her elliptical.

"Well, I'll leave you boys to sort out all your terrifying nightmares of penitentiary rape," she said. "I'm sure it'll be a fascinating discussion. But I'm off to work."

She shot one last baleful glance at Oven Mitts, who was doing ab crunches with the Oven-ettes as a throng of admirers looked on.

"That guy might be a big deal in here right now," she murmured. "But you watch. One day he'll get his."

"Pretty sure he already has," I said. "Two decades in the Big House – that's not exactly a stay at the Park Hyatt."

She considered this for a moment and shook her head.

"Uh-uh," she said. "He still hasn't paid nearly enough for what he did. Wherever Carmen is, heaven or hell, I'm sure she agrees."

11.

Lieutenant Oliver Barnwell peered nervously up and down the hall before ushering me into his office.

He locked the door behind us, fished a thick binder from a file cabinet and tossed it on his desk. Printed in neat block letters in the upper right-hand corner was this:

Baltimore County Police Department – Homicide Unit

Carmen Elena Maldonado.

Case no. 37303.

Pointing a meaty index finger at me, he said: "No one can ever know I showed you this."

"Understood," I said.

"If anyone *does* find out," he went on, patting the holstered revolver at his side, "something very bad could happen to you. And your entire family. Possibly your dog, too."

"Even the *dog*?" I said. "Wow. A little extreme, aren't we?"

Barnwell ran a hand through his thinning hair and glared. "I'm not fucking around here. I could lose my job, pension, everything."

"Relax, Barney," I said. "I'm a highly-trained journalist. No one's gonna find out."

Barnwell's distrust of me radiated from every pore of his being. And who could blame him? He was taking a big risk, violating protocol by sharing confidential material of a long-ago murder without authorization.

And he was doing it for only one reason: as a personal favor to Mikey.

The two had known each other since they were kids. They'd gone to Baltimore Polytechnic Institute together, played football and baseball on the same teams, even enlisted in the Marines under the buddy system right after graduation.

For this selfless act of patriotism, each was rewarded with 13 hellish weeks of boot camp at Parris Island and promptly shipped off to Vietnam. It was 1968 and the war in Southeast Asia was raging. Both soon found themselves assigned to a combat base in western Quang Tri Province, where their unit was ferried by helicopter into the steaming jungles and river valleys to engage the enemy.

One evening, ambushed by a sizeable contingent of North Vietnamese Army soldiers in a field of tall elephant grass, the men of Bravo Company were shocked to see Mikey suddenly lunge at Barney and knock him to the ground just as a round of deadly machine gun fire whistled overhead.

Dazed, his face bleeding from the razor-sharp vegetation, Barney rolled over, stared up at his buddy and gasped: "You... you saved my life!"

Hours after the battle was over, Mikey would admit to others in the squad that, far from being a hero, he had actually panicked at the sight of a small snake slithering at his feet. Squealing like a 10-year-old girl, he had accidentally bowled over PFC Barnwell in his haste to escape the harmless serpent just as the attack commenced.

But when the real story of Mikey's "bravery" was told to Barney by others in his unit, Barney would have none of it.

"BULLSHIT!" he cried. "You telling me that big ol' Marine was scared of a little bitty snake? No way. The man's a *gen-u-ine* hero! Hell, I'm recommending him for the Bronze Star."

After a while, Mikey gave up trying to set the record straight. Especially when they returned home after their tour of duty and Barney began telling the story in neighborhood bars, resulting in a shitload of free drinks for his buddy as well as the sexual favors of some of the hottest women in East Baltimore.

All these years later, Barney *still* felt he owed Mikey, big-time. But he definitely wasn't thrilled to be lending a helping hand to some pasty-faced columnist for the *Herald*, which he regarded as a liberal fishwrap that delighted in portraying the police as evil, jack-booted oppressors of a cowed and down-trodden minority populace.

As I turned my attention to the binder, Barney said: "Your boy Oven Mitts is a real piece of work. Least he was back then. Know what that sick son of a bitch did? After killing his old lady?"

"No," I said. "But I'm sure you'll tell me."

"For starters, he wedged a tomato in her mouth."

"He did *what!?*"

"Also stuffed a stalk of celery in each ear. And a pearl onion in each nostril."

"Jesus!" I stared at him. "Please tell me he left her other orifices alone …"

"No such luck," Barney said grimly. He pointed to the report. "All the pervy details are in there. With a nice little summary on page 9. Try not to get a hard-on reading it, Mr. Big Shot Newspaperman."

I looked down at the binder again. "How come this wasn't in court testimony?"

Barney shrugged. "It was. Guess the newspapers were too squeamish to report it back then. The TV stations, too. How would that have gone over on the 6 o'clock news, with families sitting down to dinner?"

Here he lapsed into a news anchor's stentorian delivery:

"A shocking new discovery tonight: The corpse of a missing 35-year-old Highlandtown woman, with a carrot jutting from her rectum and assorted vegetables wedged in other body cavities, was found in a remote stretch of northern Baltimore County . . ."

"OK, OK," I said, holding up a hand. "I'm getting queasy myself."

"These won't make you feel any better." He turned to a half-dozen black-and-white photos in the rear of the binder. They were shots of Carmen Maldonado's bloated body taken less than an hour after the two teens stumbled upon it in the woods.

There is something singularly disturbing about police photos of homicide victims. I had seen quite a few of them in my long, Pulitzer-less career. The snapshots can seem at once lurid and prosaic, capturing the doomed individual in all sorts of settings: splayed on a dirty city sidewalk after a drive-by shooting, slumped on a bed in a ratty motel room after a poisoning, sprawled under a blood-spattered tarp in a building's boiler room with a dozen gaping stab wounds.

What always fascinated me were the expressions on the faces of these poor condemned souls.

Even after a week in the wild, Carmen's body had remained remarkably well-preserved. This was mainly due to the carpet in which she'd been tightly cocooned, which prevented both forest creatures and insects from feasting on her.

But whether by happenstance or because the crime lab tech had manipulated the body in a certain way, her eyes were open in the photos. Wide open. And there was something in those eyes. It was a look of surprise mixed with curiosity. I'd seen it before on the faces of countless other stiffs in police snapshots.

It was almost as if, in the fraction of a second before the bullet tore into their gut, or the knife plunged into their chest, or the frying pan bashed in their skull, they were thinking: *Hmmm, wonder what's going on here? Could I possibly be in some sort of danger?*

"Know what the shame of it is?" Barney said, peering over my shoulder at the pics. "That was a perfectly good Karastan the guy ruined. Look at that thing! Even after a week in the elements, it holds its vibrant color."

He shook his head sadly. "Tell me you wouldn't lay that baby down in your family room in a heartbeat."

I stared at him in horror.

"Wow," I said. "You might want to think about a vacation, Barney. Hell, I thought *I* was jaded."

Barney's eyes narrowed. "Relax, Mr. Holier-than-Thou. Just a little cop humor. Trust me, you don't laugh in this business, you'll throw yourself off a bridge."

In the back of the file were notes written by a Detective Noel Romano regarding the initial interrogation of Alejandro Maldonado on the evening of Sept. 10, 1980, shortly after the body of his wife was discovered.

The first page read:

Det. Paul Zelinski and myself interviewed subject at his place of business, Alejandro's Magnificent World O' Carpets, 660 Cross Street, Baltimore. After we identified ourselves, subject immediately smiled and exclaimed: "Boys, I know exactly why you're here! Got your eyes on that sweet deal in the window, right? The Safavieh California shag? $117.98? That price, it's like I'm giving the son of a bitch away . . ."

Det. Zelinski asked the subject to be seated. Subject was then informed that the body of his missing wife had been found, and that the cause of death was being ruled a homicide. Subject expressed shock and wept softly for several minutes before agreeing to accompany us to county police headquarters for further questioning.

Before turning off the lights and locking the door, subject reiterated that the sale on the California shag mentioned earlier would extend through the following weekend, and that "There's not another goddamn carpet dealer in the area could match that price. And you can take that to the bank, buddy-boy."

I skimmed through the rest of the notes.

The final four pages detailed the lengthier interrogation at the police station during which Oven Mitts alternately wailed inconsolably over his wife's death and denied having anything to do with her murder. He also gave, apropos of nothing, an impromptu seminar on the benefits of synthetic versus natural fibers when choosing a carpet for one's home or office:

"I'm a big believer in acrylic, boys," the subject said. "Looks like wool, feels like wool, right? Only it's way, way cheaper. What do the big distributors charge for wool these days? That's highway robbery. They might as well be wearing a ski mask and holding a gun to your head."

When I was through reading, I gave a low whistle and looked up at Barney. "Wow. Incredible stuff. Can I make a copy of this?"

"No," he said.

"OK, can I take it with me? I'll bring it back first thing in the morning. Promise."

"FUCK NO! You got 20 minutes to go through it and take notes. Then I'm tossing your ass out of here."

"Fine," I said. "Just one question. How is it you haven't made Chief of Detectives yet? Y'know, with that sparkling personality of yours? And that constant, unrelenting desire to please others?"

Barney shot me a murderous look. The vein on the side of his neck pulsated wildly. I thought he'd come across the desk and pistol-whip me.

Instead, in a chillingly calm voice, he said: "Now you're down to 10 minutes, fuckwit. Got anything else to say?"

No, sir. Instead, Mr. Fuckwit pulled out a pen and began furiously taking notes.

Ten minutes later, Barney stood and wordlessly snatched up the file. He walked over to the door and flung it open. With a jerk of his head, he indicated our little meeting was over.

Out in the hallway, I turned and said: "That's it? "No 'Nice talking to you?' No 'Have a wonderful day?'"

The door slammed in my face.

"Any chance of getting my parking validated?" I said.

From the other side of the glass there was only silence.

12.

Tom Halloran leaned back in his office chair, a genuine leather behemoth befitting the bold, crusading editor he imagined himself to be.

He flashed his most pained expression, the one that made him look like he'd just swallowed broken glass. The one that said: *Why are you wasting my time with this shit?*

I groaned inwardly.

This was going to be a disaster.

After leaving Lt. Barnwell's office, I had driven straight to the *Herald* to pitch Halloran on a story about Oven Mitts. The ever-helpful Debbie Nesbo had informed me that her boss, as always, was super-busy, fearlessly and tirelessly leading the paper to ever-greater heights of journalistic excellence, all of which would undoubtedly punch up our sagging circulation figures, bring national attention to a scrappy, if pared-down, newsroom and garner a truck-load of Pulitzers.

But, she added munificently, he *might* be able to grant me a brief audience before lunch.

Lunch was Halloran's favorite time of the day. This was because it allowed him to sneak onto the freight elevator in the back of the building, ride it down to the loading dock on the ground floor and hustle across the street – hopefully unnoticed – to McGuirk's Tavern.

Now, as we eyed each other uneasily across the vast expanse

of his polished cherry-wood desk, we both knew I was keeping him from an important assignation with that first creamy pint of Guinness.

"So there's this incredible guy at my gym..."I began. "Definitely worth a story."

Halloran held up both hands.

"Whoa! Whoa!" Halloran said. "*You?* At a *gym*? Jackie, this is a newspaper. We don't publish fiction."

He threw back his head and laughed uproariously.

As he lapsed into a wheezy coughing fit, it occurred to me once more that people who laugh hysterically at their own jokes and see themselves as a paragon of wit and comedic timing are almost always – not to put too fine a point on it – complete dorks.

Halloran, bless his heart, confirmed this nearly every day.

Before he could get off another knee-slapper about my exercise habits, I quickly gave him the Cliffs Notes version of the Oven Mitts saga as it was known to us so far. Aware of Halloran's congenital prissiness, I left out any mention of orifices and vegetables in connection with Carmen's demise.

When I finished, he shrugged and said nothing.

"What? You don't think that's a story?" I asked finally.

"Eh," he said.

"*Eh*?! Guy strolls into the kitchen and offs his wife while she cooks his favorite meal? With the kids upstairs doing homework? Dumps her body near these busy hiking trails where a couple of horny kids find it? That doesn't grab you from the get-go? That's an *eh*?"

Halloran yawned. "Lots of men kill their wives. Hell, I wanted to kill Mary Jo yesterday. Right after she backed the goddamned Range Rover over my new Calloway driver."

Sweet Jesus, I thought. *Please don't let him launch into another long-winded soliloquy about golf. Especially if it's the one about playing Pebble Beach and running into a drunken Bill Murray pulling out his johnson and taking a leak near the 18th hole . . .*

"What about the *rest* of the story?" I said. "What about Oven Mitts doing hard time in one of the toughest prisons in the country? And hitting the exercise yard like a demon from the time they lock him up? Hitting it so hard that all these years later, as he continues to integrate into society, he's the fittest 80-year-old anyone's ever seen? The Adonis of the adult diaper set!"

Halloran's face remained blank. I plowed on.

"I'm telling you, Tommy, people literally gawk at this guy when he works out! The guy's entire life story, from the beginning to now, hell, that's pure narrative *gold*!"

Halloran glanced down at his watch. He shuffled some papers on his desk.

I was losing this one.

Panic was setting in.

"OK, what if I can get this guy to open up?" I continued. "Find out what drove him to kill, what life was like in the slammer, whether there was some big come-to-Jesus moment that helped him repent and get back on the right track.

"We blow the whole thing up!" I went on. "Make it a five-part series! 'Man commits heinous crime, pays his debt to society, gets right with the Lord, seeks atonement in a humble Baltimore gym helping others feel good about their bodies and themselves."

I leaned forward in my chair.

"Tommy, readers eat that stuff up! You *know* that! They'll be blubbering in their morning Cheerios. When's the last time this rag won a Pulitzer? When cars had running boards? You put the right writer on this – and that would be *me* – this baby's a shoo-in for every big award there is."

But it was no use.

Tommy drummed his fingers on his desk. He squirmed in his seat. He looked at the clock on the far wall.

My God! I thought. *The Guinness is practically screaming his name!*

Finally, I threw up my hands in frustration.

"Well," I said," at least you're open-minded about it. At least you're the kind of discerning editor who values input from his staff. And isn't afraid to act on their suggestions."

Halloran sighed wearily.

"Jackie, I can't spare you to write about something that happened three decades ago. I need *columns* from you, man! *Hard-hitting* columns. About what's happening *now.* Maybe you haven't noticed, but the homicide rate in this city is through the roof. Sixteen killings in the last two weeks alone. Bodies are turning up in the streets like ISIS has taken over."

I rolled my eyes.

"Not exactly breaking news, Tommy. This is the Big Crab. When *isn't* the homicide rate skyrocketing?"

Ignoring me, he continued. "Plus the mayor's race is heating up. There's what, six candidates running for office? And each one seems more brainless and corrupt than the other."

"Stop the presses!" I said dryly. "'City Hall mired in incompetency! Voters hold their noses, head to polls as scandal envelopes leading hopefuls to replace the Honorable Fucking So-and-So, who'll be lucky to escape an extended jail sentence.' Don't we run that story every couple of years?"

I started to rise, but Halloran held up his hand.

"Here's the other thing, Jackie. Have you looked around the newsroom lately? We're down to what, 80 reporters and editors?

To cover a metro area of 2.8 million people? And I'm gonna let you go off on a lark? To do a puff piece – no offense – on some old guy who snuffed out his wife a hundred years ago and is now some kind of a cult hero at a local gym?"

He shook his head emphatically.

"Sorry, pal. We need you here. It's all hands on deck all the time."

He reached for his coat, signaling the meeting to a close.

Moments later, from the window of my office on the fifth floor, I looked down in time to see him hustling across the loading dock toward McGuirk's. He looked both ways before crossing the street, a bit of pedestrian caution that was, as we all knew, strictly an act.

Tommy Halloran wouldn't care if an out-of-control 18-wheeler was barreling down on him. Nothing would stop our brave and noble editor from his appointed rounds with a pint or two of dark, tasty Irish stout.

I watched as he yanked the tavern door open, waved merrily to someone inside and slipped into the cool darkness, a big shit-eating grin plastered on his fleshy puss.

The man was in his element at last.

13.

The gym was busy the next morning, so I herded the Big Five into the empty spin cycling studio. There, I briefed them on my visit with Lt. Barnwell and the latest sordid revelations about Alejandro Maldonado

My buddies were, of course, properly horrified to learn of the defiling of Carmen Maldonado's corpse through the ghastly use of produce. The killer's flippant insistence in turning part of the police interrogation into a mini-symposium on carpet fibers also elicited disgust.

"That is one twisted motherfucker," Harvey said.

"A total head case," Mikey agreed. "They should have thrown away the key when they locked his ass up."

Courtney glanced around nervously and said: "This whole conversation is creeping me out. Think he's here yet?"

Jamison peered out the door. "Oh, he's here, all right. On the mats in the back." Suddenly he stiffened. "Whoa! You gotta *see* this."

We filed out in time to catch Oven Mitts bent over in a reverse U, feet on the ground in front of him, back arched and hands on the mats behind him. Perched on his sculpted abs, now facing the ceiling, were two of the Oven-ettes.

They grinned wildly while a half-dozen other members cheered and snapped pictures with their cell phones.

Courtney's jaw dropped.

"See what he's doing? It's called a Chakrasana," she said. "The Wheel Pose. I remember it from a yoga class. I couldn't do it when I was 25. And this guy's old enough for assisted living!"

We were still buzzing about Oven Mitts' latest freak show when two men and two women, all wearing matching navy polos and pressed khakis, sauntered through the front entrance.

As they fanned out and began distributing flyers, Harvey made a face.

"Uh-oh, Dildo Alert," he murmured. "EFC's in the house."

Elite Fitness Center was the ultra-modern gym that had opened a few years earlier a mile down the road from Ripped! I had driven by it many times. You couldn't miss the place. It was as big as a NATO air base, the roof covered with large aquamarine solar panels that gleamed in the sunlight and lent it a shimmering Oz-like quality.

Within its walls were a state-of-the-art strength and conditioning facility, Olympic-size swimming pool, two full-sized basketball courts and a half-dozen squash and racquetball courts. Encircling all this was a synthetic track featuring a polyurethane surface that made your feet feel as if they were gliding on water when running laps.

It also had a kick-boxing studio, lemon-scented steam rooms, executive locker rooms and a spacious cocktail lounge with upholstered leather armchairs, plush carpeting and a fully-stocked bar. There, the titans of finance, who comprised the bulk of the membership, could get thoroughly yet discreetly plastered after a workout before staggering out to their Mercedes and Lexuses and BMWs for the blurry ride back to their gated communities.

"Joke used to be," Jamison said, "if you didn't wear a polo with a snapped collar, or a tennis sweater knotted around your neck, they wouldn't let you in. Except I'm not sure it's a joke."

"What are they doing here?" I asked.

He shook his head.

"Not sure," he said. "But it looks like we're about to find out . . ."

Just then the EFC posse made its way over to us. An intense-looking man with dark, slicked-back hair greeted us with an oleaginous smile.

"Yo, what up, what up?" he said. "J. Kenneth Oberkfell's the name. Got a little something here for you nice folks."

Harvey took one of the proffered flyers and scanned it.

"Kenny, quick question," he said. "Who's watching over the hedge funds with all you people here?"

"Yeah," Mikey said. "Shouldn't you be back at the bank? Foreclosing on a sick widow and her special-needs kids?"

Oberkfell stiffened. For an instant, the greasy smile vanished. But it was quickly replaced by one of even more wattage.

"Ha, OK, sensing a little tension here," he said. "Let me get right to the point of today's visit. Folks, we're here to propose a little friendly competition between our two gyms."

"Big bad EFC against lil' ol' us?" Courtney said. "Kind of slumming a bit, aren't you?"

Oberkfell chuckled and looked back at his grinning side-kicks. He spread his arms wide in what was meant to be a magnanimous gesture.

"We at Elite Fitness enjoy testing our physical conditioning against all comers – at *all* area facilities," he said. "Even one as" – here he paused to look around, his gaze lingering on a large patch of peeling paint on one wall – "charmingly unselfconscious as this one."

Courtney shot me a look that said: *Do you believe this*

pompous prick?

"Let's cut the bullshit," Mikey growled. "What kind of competition are we talking about?"

Oberkfell nodded happily.

"Ah, this is why we love our 'seasoned citizens!'" he said, draping an arm around Mikey's shoulder. "They're direct. No nonsense. They hear the metaphorical clock ticking. Only so much time left on God's green Earth. And they're not gonna waste it with a lot of idle chit-chat."

He pulled Mikey close. "Am I right, pops?"

Mikey looked ready to slit his throat.

"Fine, let's get to it, then," Oberkfell continued. "The contest we're talking about involves the rigorous full-body exercise that separates the men from the boys, the women from the girls, the gym wusses from the gym warriors.

He lowered his voice dramatically. "Ladies and gentlemen of Ripped!, we hereby challenge you to a burpees contest."

At this, a collective groan went up from my buddies. I waited for someone to elaborate. But no one did.

"OK, I'll bite," I said. "What are burpees?"

"Only the single most hated exercise known to man," Jamison said.

Mikey nodded. "Instead of frying the bad guys in the electric chair, they should make 'em do burpees. They'd be *begging* for 10,000 volts within seconds."

There were murmurs of agreement all around. Seeing the confused look on my face, Harvey said: "OK, here's what a burpee looks like."

He dropped into a squat. Kicking his legs behind him, he plopped onto the floor and did a pushup. From there he tucked into a squat again, climbed to his feet, threw his arms in the air and jumped.

Then he turned to us and bowed theatrically.

"Ta-daa!" he said. "Your basic burpee!"

Oberkfell exchanged amused glances with his Dockers-clad disciples.

"OK, I…I *guess* that was a burpee," he said. "Well, *sort* of a burpee. A half-assed burpee, if you want to know the truth. But you get an A for effort, buddy."

Harvey glared at him. We could tell he was on the verge of telling Kenneth J. to go fuck himself. Before he could, Oberkfell nodded to one of his crew.

"Lars," he said, "be a good man. Show our friends at Ripped! how a burpee's *really* done."

Lars, tall and Nordic-looking, with thick arms, a 32-inch waist and a wispy blond mustache, stepped forward eagerly. He looked as if he'd been waiting for this moment his entire life.

Squaring his shoulders, he dropped into a squat with astonishing speed. He kicked his legs back and, with his back ramrod straight, dropped to the floor and did a perfect pushup – the most perfect pushup I'd ever seen.

Returning to the squat position, he stood – Marine-drill-sergeant-straight again – lifted his arms overhead and jumped what seemed to be a foot in the air before landing nimbly on his toes.

He rattled off nine more of the punishing exercises with military precision, making a big show of clapping his hands at the end of each, as if to demonstrate how ridiculously easy he found the whole thing.

When he finished, Oberkell and his EFC droids burst into applause. Lars grinned and waved happily. He looked fresh enough to do a triathlon.

"Now *that*," Oberkfell said, "is how you do burpees. At least, if you want to do them correctly. Thank you, Lars. Fabulous job."

Hearing this, Lars practically quivered with delight. Harvey gave him a death-stare.

"So here are the ground rules for our little contest," Oberkfell continued. "Three teams from each gym, OK? Your best three men against our best three men. Your best three women against our best three women. Team that does the most burpees in 10 minutes wins. Everyone following so far?"

Still awed by Lars's performance, we nodded dumbly, like five bobbleheads.

"Now here comes the fun part," Oberkfell said. "We're also proposing another category: newest member and most veteran member from each gym square off against their counterparts at the other place. This one's *always* good for a few laughs."

Really? Watching someone throw themselves to the ground and lurch to their feet over and over again until they were an aching, sweating, puking mess didn't exactly seem like a night at a comedy club to me. But what did I know?

"Anyway, there you have it," Oberkfell concluded. "If management here gives the okay to this little competition, maybe we'll see some of you at the Great Burpees Challenge next month. Assuming . . ." here he smirked, "any of you actually has the stones to compete."

Wait, us?

No stones?

Well, maybe.

He started to leave, then paused. "Oh, hell, let's up the stakes a little, shall we? Losing gym pays for a highway billboard declaring the winner as 'Best Fitness Facility in Baltimore.' Just to boost the humiliation factor. We'll see if your boy Bryan goes along with that."

He waved and cackled like a movie villain. "OK, have a nice day."

We stood there in stunned silence as the EFC crew swaggered over to another knot of Ripped! members to begin their spiel anew.

Were we intimidated? Hell yes. Even Harvey, "Mr. Kick Some MAGA Ass" himself seemed shaken.

Everything about the encounter had rattled us. Oberkfell's smarmy confidence and condescending tone, for one. Lars's machine-like, almost animatronic performance, for another. What mortal could ever out-burpee that Scandinavian monster?

You'd have to pray he gets hit by a truck the day of the contest. Even then he was even money to show up in bandages and a full-body cast and wax the rest of the competition.

And what about the two women with Oberkfell and Lars, with their eerie Stepford Wives countenances and over-the-top cheerleading? Were they burpee super-stars, too? Underneath the spray tan and hot-pink lip gloss and matching nail polish, the two-carat diamond stud earrings and tennis bracelets, were they utter savages who could hurl themselves to the mats, knock off 100 of those wretched exercises and rip the soul right out of the competition?

There was no sugar-coating it: we were feeling bad about our little gym's chances – assuming this contest ever actually took place. Just then we caught sight of an amorphous figure in the shadows in the rear hallway.

As he drew closer, we could see it was Oven Mitts. He was doing a series of grueling walking lunges, all while holding a 75-pound kettlebell chin-high in front of him.

A soft smile played across his features. None of the Oven-ettes were in sight. There was no one cheering him on, no one shouting the usual hosannas and strewing metaphorical rose petals in his path.

Yet he still seemed like a man totally content with his place in the world – that being, at least at the moment, a grimy, dimly-lit corridor where he toiled silently and with monkish devotion at a workout that would tear the knees and split the groin of any other human his age.

An unspoken thought ran through all five of us: *If he's the member who's been here the longest, maybe we've got a shot at avoiding total embarrassment at the hands of EFC.*

Otherwise, we were freaking doomed.

14.

Two days later, the gym's front desk displayed a prominent bulletin:

Attention,

As some of you may know, a contingent of the usual poseurs and dilettantes from Elite Fitness Club has challenged this facility to a burpees contest. Management has accepted the challenge. Our gym will host the event at 10 a.m. on Saturday, April 27th.

Members interested in trying out for one of the men's and women's teams that will represent Ripped! in this righteous endeavor should assemble at 10 a.m. Saturday, April 6 in the auxiliary weight room. (Serious candidates only, please.)

We remain confident that, given the commitment to fitness of our clientele and with a full month to train, we can accomplish our goal of not simply defeating the loathsome EFC minions, but of whipping their dusty asses and walking them to the very Gates of Hell.

P.S. The hot water is out in the women's showers. We apologize for any inconvenience.

"Christ!" Harvey said after we read it. "It sounds like a declaration of war! Don't the North Koreans talk like that? 'The mighty forces of the Democratic People's Republic will vanquish the imperialist U.S. warmongers to eternal fire and damnation and blah, blah, blah?'"

"That dictator of theirs?" he continued. "'Lil' Kim? This is right out of his playbook, isn't it?"

The rest of us stared at him.

"Did you say *Lil Kim?*" Jamison said. "'Lil Kim's a *rapper,* you moron! Not to mention a *woman*! Kim Jong-un is the dictator – who happens to be a man. I assume he's the one your feeble mind was attempting to summon just now."

"Whatever," Harvey answered, waving a hand. "But you get my point, right? About the over-the-top rhetoric?"

Courtney was still studying the sign, head cocked to one side, as if searching for a deeper meaning than the one the words actually conveyed.

"I don't know," she said finally. "It almost sounds...*poetic.*"

A voice behind us said: "So you like it, huh?"

We turned to find Bryan the manager peering over our shoulders.

"You didn't know I was an English lit major in college," he said with a grin.

"'Whipping their dusty asses,' was the give-away," Mikey said. "That's right out of 'Othello,' isn't it?"

Bryan went behind the counter and plopped wearily on a stool.

"I'm just so freaking tired of those pompous EFC pricks," he said. "It's not enough that they have the sickest club around, with all the best equipment and amenities. But instead of just shutting up and enjoying what they have, they keep slamming all the other gyms in the area.

"And for whatever reason," he went on, "they seem to have a particular boner for this place."

Two years earlier, he recalled, during the key winter membership drive relied on by most gyms, unknown EFC operatives had parked a battered old Jeep in the Ripped! parking lot. Sprawled against the windshield was a medical school skeleton with a banner hanging from it that read: "Waited forever to use one of the three operable treadmills here. Eventually expired from boredom."

Harvey was impressed. "They got a *skeleton*?" he asked. "Not exactly something you have lying around the hall closet."

The harassment from EFC continued last year, Bryan added. This time it involved a whisper campaign – traced back to one of their newly-hired personal trainers, whom Bryan had fired months earlier – about a supposed insect and rodent infestation at Ripped!

"So one day," he said, "a couple of Terminex guys show up at the front desk. And they're in full battle regalia: overalls, thick gloves, goggles and those big-ass chemical canisters strapped on their backs like flame-throwers.

"'We got a call about roaches,' one of them says. "'What are you *talking* about?' I say. 'ROACHES!' the other guy says, like I can't hear. 'WE'RE HERE ABOUT THE ROACHES!' 'Get the fuck outta here!' I tell them. 'We don't have any goddamn roaches!'

"The next day, it's two Orkin guys who walk in. Same deal: 'Sir, we're here about your mice problem.' I run their asses out the door, too. On the third day, it's an Ehrlich Pest Control rep yammering something about spiders and centipedes. Meanwhile, of course, anyone working out here and seeing this Macy's parade of exterminators has to be thinking: 'What kind of hell-hole did I join'?"

Jamison gave a low whistle.

"God, that's *vicious!*" he said admiringly. "I'll have to remember that one. My ex owns a flower shop downtown. Next time she gives me shit about late alimony payments, I might sic those bug people on her."

Courtney shot him a barbed look. But Bryan nodded grimly. "So you see why I can't wait to stick it to those smug shitweasels. Once we win this contest, that billboard they'll have to put up should get us a bunch of new members."

As gently as possible, we informed him that, far from sending the aforementioned smug shitweasels to a crushing defeat in any burpees throw-down, it was far more likely that Ripped! would – and again we tried to phrase this delicately – get the living crap kicked out of it.

Briefly, we recounted the amazing impromptu performance by Lars, the phenom we were now calling the Swedish Soul Snatcher. We also detailed our suspicions that the two women accompanying Lars and the oily J. Kenneth Oberkfell, despite looking as if they'd come from a Daughters of the American Revolution cookout, were probably burpees Amazons who would also destroy any and all competition.

"And God knows what the deal is with J. Kenneth himself," Jamison said. "Sure, he's a total ass-clown. But he looks pretty fit. Probably a beast at this stuff in his own right."

"Yep, these EFC folks are not fiddle-fucking around," Harvey added.

Fiddle-fucking? Where did *that* come from?

When we finished, Bryan's shoulders slumped.

"Damn," he said. "Definitely not what I wanted to hear."

He stared down at the floor for a moment. "I haven't told many people this," he said, his voice low, "but we're really hurting here. Membership's down big-time. Things are so tight the owner's telling me he might have to close the place unless we can turn it around.

"That's why it would be *huge* to beat those EFC twerps," he went on. "We'd blow it out all over social media, take out ads in all the fitness magazines, maybe do some radio and TV spots. The billboard would help too.

"We'd be the Little Gym That Could! The Little Gym of Champions! Tell me *that* wouldn't have people beating down the doors to join!"

For an instant, he seemed to brighten. But the gloom quickly returned. "Except I guess from what you're saying, we don't stand a chance."

No one spoke for several seconds. None of us knew what to say. We shuffled our feet nervously and looked around. One or two of us stared at our fingernails, as if we'd never noticed them before.

Then we did what we knew *had* to be done in this situation. We lied.

"Aw hell," Harvey said finally, "of *course* you have a chance. You *always* have a chance in these things. Take that newest member/veteran member category. If your boy Tony Maldon qualifies as the vet, that's absolutely a lock for Ripped!"

"Oh, he qualifies," Bryan said. "He's been here since the day we opened."

"Then you're in," I said. "Assuming the newbie he's paired with isn't totally lame . . ."

Bryan gave me a funny look.

"In that case," he said, "I suggest you start training. *Hard.*"

It took several seconds for that to register.

"*ME*?!" I said. "You're saying *I'm* the newest member? How could that possibly be? I've been here for months already! No one's joined since me?"

Bryan shrugged. "Look around," he said. "See a lot of new

faces? No, let me rephrase that. See *any* new faces? Goes back to the membership issue we were talking about.

"Young people today, they're not interested in a modest gym like this one," he continued. "They want these big, fancy places with all the bells and whistles so they can feel like a big shot and impress their friends. Or they want to work out in some drafty, stripped-down garage and do all that Crossfit crap.

"They want to throw around 500-pound tires and do power squats and pushups until they hurl. They want to be harnessed to a 300-pound blocking sled and drag it across a cement floor. They want everyone to see them running sprints and coughing up a lung in the parking lot at 7 in the morning.

"Then they go off to Happy Hour at some trendy wine bar and brag about how the instructor beat the crap out of them, but, oh, man, they *love* it! They never felt more *alive,* they can't wait to do it all over again at the crack of dawn Monday and blah, blah, blah! It's such a pretentious load of shit."

He shook his head sadly. "Even if we *did* beat EFC, I don't know how long this place could survive, given the way the industry's going. But I guess you're right." He seemed to perk up again. "I guess there's always a *chance.* A chance we could pull off some incredible upset for the ages.

"Anyway," he continued, "I already talked to Tony Maldon. And God love him, the old guy's psyched for the contest. But we need a newbie to pair with him. Those are the rules."

He stared at me. "So how about it, Jack? Will you give it a shot?"

I was still in shock that we were even having this conversation. My mind raced to come up with an excuse. Upcoming hernia surgery? Jury duty? Exotic work assignment in Kuala Lumpur?

Yeah, like Halloran would ever sign off on that. Are you kidding? If I tried to leave the country for a story, he'd personally show up at the airport, lumber onto the tarmac waving a pistol and stop the plane. Then after dragging me off, he'd order me to write a snappy 750 words on that night's zoning board meeting.

"Of *course* he'll give it a shot," a voice to my right said.

It was Courtney. She threw an arm around my shoulder and fixed me with a radiant smile.

"Jackie loves this gym," she said. "If there's a chance to beat the Evil Empire and help keep this place open, he'd be the first to sign up. Wouldn't you, babe?"

There it was again in that honey voice: *Jackie!* With a sultry *babe* thrown in to make me tingle even more. I stared into that pretty face, and all I could do was nod.

Looking relieved, Bryan gave me a fist bump. "You da man, Jack! I knew we could count on you."

There was nothing else to discuss. One by one we drifted off to start our workouts. A few minutes later, as I climbed onto the elliptical, Bryan tapped my arm.

"I should probably tell you something," he began. "It's about our boy Tony Maldon . . ."

"Let me guess," I said. "He changed his mind about the contest. And now I'm paired with a 90-year-old grandma with halitosis and bad knees."

"No," he said, chuckling, "nothing that bad. Tony's not backing out. Like I told you, he's fired up about competing. In fact, I just spoke to him on the phone. But get this. He says he's never done a burpee in his life."

What!? I thought. *They didn't do burpees in the slammer back in the day? So all this talk about the coddling of the U.S. prison population is true!*

"But he says he's a quick learner," Brian added. "And he says he can't wait to meet you. And he knows the two of you'll make a great team."

Sure.

An octogenarian fitness guru with an unimaginably dark past and a schlubby out-of-shape journalist reeling from the most painful emotional bludgeoning of his life – how could we *not* click?

15.

One month. That's all the time I had to prepare.

I spent the next morning at Ripped! practicing burpees for the first time in my life under the supportive gaze of my gym buddies. Except when I say *supportive*, I am, for the most part, lying.

Minutes into the session, I found myself crumpled facedown on the mat. My heart was hammering in my chest. My arms and shoulders were screaming.

"How many's that? I gasped. "Gotta be eight or nine, right?'

Mikey snorted. "Try three."

"*Three*! Geez, Jack, that's pathetic," Jamison said.

Harvey frowned and said: "Don't take this the wrong way, buddy. But you look like a dazed walrus flopping around on an ice floe."

"Thank you, Mr. National Geographic," I snarled. "And how could *anyone* take that the wrong way?"

Earlier, studying the list of names taped to the wall near the front desk, we saw that some 50 members had signed up for Saturday's tryouts. This spoke to the ultra-competitiveness we knew existed among some of our more fervent – and possibly chemically-enhanced – members. But it also reflected a generalized loathing for Elite Fitness Club, whose condescending and exclusionary TV commercials ("Where Only Baltimore's *Best* Work Out!") had infuriated members of other area gyms for years.

All around us now, pockets of sweaty, red-faced men and women were throwing themselves to the ground, kicking their legs back like agitated mules and lurching to their feet, their muttered oaths only partially drowned out by the hip-hop mix blaring over the sound system.

Each and every one of them looked miserable. But not nearly as miserable as I felt.

"You're doing fine, Jackie," Courtney said, shooting Harvey and the others a dirty look. She took a towel, bent over, and gently wiped the perspiration from my face. "Don't let these dimwits get to you."

As had become clear from the outset, the Big Five would not have a large competitive presence at the showdown with EFC. Harvey, Mikey and Jamison had quickly (and profanely) made it plain that they wanted nothing to do with burpees, which they considered a pointless form of self-torture that called into question the sanity of anyone who did them.

"Why don't I just throw myself down a flight of stairs over and over again?" Jamison said. "The total effect's the same."

Courtney had toyed briefly with the idea of trying out for the women's team. But a look at some of the incredibly fit and flinty-eyed distaff members who would be her competition had quickly disabused her of the notion.

"Instead," she announced, "I've decided my focus will be on helping Jackie get ready for the contest."

"*Awwww!*" Mikey said. "Ain't that *touching*?!"

"You two need a moment?" Harvey added with a leering wink.

Courtney shot them the bird and smiled sweetly down at me. But the truth was, having her as some sort of de facto trainer/

cheerleader was not exactly making me feel great.

Here was a woman I was growing more and more attracted to. Here was a gorgeous, smart, tough-yet-compassionate babe whose body, with all its splendid curves – and I write this knowing full-well how piggish it sounds – had me in a perpetual state of unbridled lust.

But having her watch me flail hopelessly on a slimy mat, my fish-belly-white gut heaving against the flimsy elastic bands of my dorky gray shorts each time I careened to the floor and staggered back up like a punch-drunk boxer, was embarrassing.

I didn't see how it could possibly score me any points.

On the other hand, I wasn't thrilled with the hovering presence of the rest of the Big Five either. For one thing, their inane conversations, which could break out at any moment, were incredibly distracting.

That morning, as I warmed up with some light stretching, Harvey suddenly looked at Jamison and said: "What's the R for?"

Jamison gave him a blank stare.

"Is that some sort of code?" he asked.

"Jesus, are you *thick?!*" Harvey said. "The R! In R. Jamison Winthrop! What's it stand for?"

Mikey cackled: "I bet it's something really horrible."

Jamison's face reddened. "Well, I wouldn't say *horrible.. . .*"

"Yes, it is," Mikey said. "It's horrible. I bet it's something like Robespierre or Radbourne or something. Something your parents came up with after a night of sitting around smoking Pall Malls and swilling Manhattans with their high-society pals in that fancy Guilford neighborhood where you grew up."

"For your information, we lived in Hampden, pal," Jamison said. "Working-class neighborhood, remember? My dad was a plumber. Mom was the lunch lady at Hampden Elementary."

"Sure," Mikey said. "Whatever. Deny, deny, deny. That's what you people do."

"*You people?* What's that supposed to mean?"

"People like you," Mikey said. "Privileged. Entitled. Born on third base and think you hit a triple in life. With a trust fund that daddy's just itching to sign over the minute you turn 18 . . ."

Jamison looked as if his head would explode. "Did you even hear what I just *said*? About the plumber? And the lunch lady?"

"Then why won't you tell us what the R stands for?" Harvey demanded.

"I didn't *say* I wouldn't tell you!" Jamison said, voice rising. "I'm trying to correct a serious mischaracterization here! That I'm some sort of elitist asshole! Someone who had it easy his whole life! Someone who never had to struggle for anything!"

For a moment, no one spoke. Finally Mikey shook his head sadly and looked at Harvey. "He's not gonna tell us what the R stands for. We're just wasting our time."

Jamison took a deep breath. He appeared on the verge of hyper-ventilating.

"OK," he said slowly, "if I tell you fucking idiots what the R stands for, will you leave me alone? Like, for the rest of my life?"

Mikey slapped his hands against his thighs and stood.

"Forget it, Harv. It's no use," he said. "He won't tell us the truth. He'll make up some stupid name and hope we're dumb enough to accept it. I'm going to get a coffee."

"I'll go with you," Harvey said, climbing to his feet. "You're right: this is pointless."

With that, the two disappeared, leaving Jamison sputtering in a homicidal rage.

You see the problem here. How could any sentient human being concentrate on learning a new exercise with that kind of ridiculous soundtrack playing in the background?

And when my buddies weren't making idiotic small talk, they were arguing about what the best strategy was to win a burpees contest.

"Listen to me," Harvey had said, draping an arm across my shoulders when I got to the gym that morning. "When it's show-time next month, you come out of the gate like your hair's on fire, OK? Like a freaking madman. Go as hard as you can from the get-go. BOOM-BOOM-BOOM! The EFC guys sees that, it'll completely demoralize them."

Mikey overheard this. He took me aside moments later.

"Don't listen to any of Harvey' bullshit," he said. "You gotta pace yourself, OK? Start slow, make sure your breathing's right, get in a nice rhythm and keep knocking 'em out. Keep grinding, brother."

"Said *another* guy who's never done a burpee in his life," I replied.

"What's that have to do with anything?" Mikey growled. "Earl Weaver never played a minute in the majors! But he knew *baseball*, didn't he? Pretty goddamn good manager, as I recall."

After Jamison went off in search of Harvey and Mikey, ostensibly to bludgeon them with a dumbbell, I finally pulled myself off the mat. Courtney glanced around nervously. In a low voice, she asked: "So, have you met your, um, contest partner yet?"

"Nope," I said. "And you can say his name, Court. It's not like he's gonna show up here with, I don't know, a steel-bolt-pistol. Like the bad guy in *No Country For Old Men*."

"Anton Chigur!" she said. "That was the bad guy's name! Boy, he was a creepy-looking —"

Suddenly, I saw her stiffen. She was looking at something over my shoulder.

When I turned, there was Oven Mitts, smiling broadly. His arms were outstretched for a hug.

"Jack Doherty!" he cried. "I'm telling you, those snobby EFC bastards don't have a prayer! You and me, we're gonna knock their dicks in the dirt!"

Sounds painful, I thought as we embraced.

But...who wouldn't be up for a good, old-fashioned dick-knocking?

16.

The cafeteria at The Johns Hopkins Hospital was bustling when I arrived a little after noon. Dr. Daniela Ortiz Gallegos sat at a table overlooking the colorful atrium, sipping an iced tea. Seeing me, she smiled and shot to her feet.

"Jack! God, it's great to see you!" she said, giving me a hug. "How's that crazy wife of yours?"

"Crazy *ex*-wife," I said.

"Oh?" she said, stepping back with a look of concern. "Sorry to hear. Didn't know there was trouble in paradise."

"There was," I said. "Things are better now."

"What about the kids. How are they?

"Not nearly as crazy as their mom. So that's the good news."

Some 20 years ago, Dani and I had been an item. A hot and heavy item. She was in medical school, on the fast track to a brilliant career in geriatrics helping people live longer, healthier and more productive lives.

As a young reporter at the *Herald,* I was on a far slower track, just hoping not to piss off too many editors and land my dream job as a columnist before the hedge fund vultures gobbled up every paper in the country and the entire profession imploded.

We first met at a bar in Fells Point, the historic waterfront neighborhood known for its funky boutiques, seafood joints and raucous night life. With colorful names like The Horse You Came In On, The Cat's Eye Pub and Birds of a Feather, the saloons suggested the innocent, playful ambience of another era – until you saw the hordes of drunken college students staggering down the cobblestone streets at closing time. Or the trashed office workers puking near the landmark Broadway Market (est. 1786) before lurching to their cars and praying they could avoid whatever DUI checkpoints were operating that night.

To this day, I don't know exactly why Dani and I broke up. We had a ton of fun together. The sex was awesome, lively and imaginative. And of course, as practically required by law of the young and newly-smitten, we also had the requisite deep, earnest conversations long into the night – fueled with copious amount of beer, wine and illicit substances – about what we wanted to do with our lives and where we saw the world headed.

But after a few years, the relationship seemed to run its course. I broke up with Dani and dated Beth on the rebound, marrying her 18 months later. Around the same time, Dani met a gifted Hopkins eye surgeon who turned out to be a wonderful guy, and they went on to wed and have two smart, wonderful kids.

Not long after, though, she was hearing through mutual friends about my new bride's – oh, how to put this? – *uneven* temperament and the obvious tension in our relationship.

Every once in a while, I'd get an email from my old flame with the subject line: "U OK?" But I was too embarrassed to tell her, no, I sure as hell was *not* OK. I couldn't bring myself to admit I'd made a terrible mistake marrying a confrontational woman with an acid tongue who somehow turned out to be Mom-of-the-Year material to my kids while simultaneously slicing to ribbons whatever self-esteem I had left.

Dani, in her mid-40's now, was still a dark-eyed beauty, with a body that would make a bishop break out in a sweat. But one thing was certain: sitting with her now, the two of us picking at Cobb salads and catching up on each other's lives, I wasn't about to share details about the Hiroshima event on the back deck that blew up my marriage for good.

"So," Dani said, "your phone call sounded mysterious. Something about an old guy at your gym?"

Naturally, at this exact moment, I had just jammed a huge forkful of salad into my big, fat mouth.

"If anyone can tell me what's going on with him," I said, hoping not to sail an errant chunk of masticated bacon in her direction, "it's you."

Quickly, I gave her the Cliffs Notes version of all the Big Five had discovered about the astonishing Anthony "Oven Mitts" Maldon in the last months.

I filled her in on his career as a carpet kingpin, his trial and conviction for bumping off his unfaithful wife and his long stint behind bars. I told her how he had ruled the prison weight room and morphed into a fitness deity admired by the other inmates, even the fat-guy Aryan Nation-types, whose idea of exercise generally involved bending down to fish another carton of Marlboros from under their bunk beds.

I told Dani that, decades after his release, Oven Mitts had surfaced at Ripped! looking like an octogenarian Vin Diesel, and how his incredible workout routines – many involving his worshipful groupies, the Oven-ettes – had become a freak show for the other members.

Finally, I told her how I'd been (reluctantly) paired with him for the big upcoming burpees contest against the smug rich guys from EFC. And how I hoped not to completely embarrass myself competing alongside this studly geezer as the two of us attempted to – paraphrasing the exquisite street poetry of Oven

Mitts – dirty their manhood til they cried.

"Now he wants the two of us to work out together a couple times a week," I continued. "Says he knows some" – here I threw up air quotes – "*secret techniques* that'll get me ready for next month. But Dani, the things this guy does on his own in the gym? Off...the...freaking...charts."

"What kinds of things?" she asked. Ever the curious clinician, she was listening with rapt attention.

Just this morning, I told her, I arrived at Ripped! at 6:30 to find Oven Mitts warming up for our workout. But he wasn't exactly doing a few leisurely jumping jacks. Or taking a lazy spin on the exercise bike to get the blood pumping.

"There's a vending machine in the lobby," I explained. "A big-ass monster, too. Dispenses 16-oz. bottles of Coke, Pepsi, Lipton iced tea, etc. You've seen them. Anyway, he had the machine tipped on its side. And he was on the floor doing bench-presses with it! Those things weight, like, 400 pounds, easy. I Googled it."

Dani's eyes widened slightly. But she said nothing.

"Everything he does is over the top," I went on. "He pounds away on the treadmill for a half-hour – with the thing set on max speed! – and it's like he's not even sweating. They told me he took a step aerobics class – one of those high-intensity sessions that leaves everyone so gassed they want to puke? And the instructor had to admonish him for whistling the whole time! She said he was annoying the others and making them feel bad about themselves."

I shook my head.

"*Whistling!* Who does that in a goddamn aerobics class? I swear, it's like something out of 'Faust.' Like he sold his soul to the devil. And the devil said 'OK, pal, I know this isn't much.

But I'm gonna make you a big deal at this unassuming little gym in Baltimore, where you'll wow everyone with this whole Fittest Geezer Ever thing you got going on. Play your cards right, you might even score with some decent-looking babes half your age.'"

Dani rolled her eyes.

"Why is it *always* about scoring with you guys?" she asked.

"We're all pigs, Dani," I said. "That's not exactly breaking news."

"Well, *you* definitely were," she said sweetly. "Probably still are."

"Guilty as charged," I said. "But what I want to know is: how does Oven Mitts *do* it? The man's 80! This is so over-the-top it's scary!"

Dani nodded, as if expecting the question. She put down her fork, steepled her hands against her chin and appeared lost in thought for a few seconds.

"All over the world," she said finally, "there are ordinary-seeming seniors doing the most extraordinary things when it comes to exercise. We see it all the time. For instance, there's a 79-year-old man in China who does 50 pushups in a park every day using just his thumbs and forefingers.

"After that he goes over to a tree. He grips the trunk, lifts his legs until his entire body is horizontal to the ground, and hangs there. For minutes on end! It's an incredible feat of strength. It's also on YouTube if you ever want to check it out."

"Great," I muttered. "That's all we need at Ripped! – Oven Mitts going viral on social media. He already walks around like he's starring in the next James Bond movie."

"The point is," Dani continued, "he's not alone in being a geriatric phenomenon. There are 100-year-olds running marathons. An 80-year-old man just climbed Mount Everest. An

82-year-old man crossed the South Boulder Canyon in Colorado not long ago on a 320-foot tightrope. A 96-year-old in India even fathered a baby!"

"OK, different form of exercise," I said. "But I get your point . . ."

"Are all these people genetically-gifted?" Dani mused. "Maybe. Or is their secret simply decades of rigorous exercise, plus eating right, getting plenty of sleep, not smoking, drinking in moderation and all the other stuff we physicians tell people to do that they ignore?

"Without examining your guy Oven Mitts,'" she went on, "it's hard to tell how much of a physical anomaly he is. If we did an echocardiogram, we could see if his left ventricle pumps a greater volume of blood than the average person. If we did some pulmonary function tests, we could measure his lung volume, capacity, rates of flow and so on.

"But other than that," she said with a shrug, "there's no way to say how much he stands out among his peers. If I were you, I'd just sit back and enjoy the uniqueness of what you're seeing from him. This is how folk heroes emerge! How they become part of our national mythology!"

Davey Crockett, Daniel Boone, Johnny Appleseed, Paul Bunyan and . . . Oven Mitts Maldon?

The mind reels.

"You never know," Dani said. "Years from now, maybe they'll be singing songs about this man. Maybe someone writes a book about him. Maybe that someone's even you!"

Me?

I wasn't even sure I wanted to do *burpees* with the guy, let alone serve as his biographer.

The rest of the lunch passed by much too quickly. I didn't come away with any of the answers I'd been looking for, but it was hardly a waste of time. The Cobb salads were tasty, even if they'd gone overboard on the avocado. And I'd just spent 90 minutes with a smart, knockout of a woman who was once the love of my life.

As we stood to leave, I was overcome with a feeling of nostalgia, mixed with the sadness and loneliness I'd been fighting off for weeks. It came out of nowhere. My knees almost buckled.

"God," I said, "we had fun back in the day, didn't we?"

Dani nodded. "We sure did."

"It feels like so long ago," I said. "What happened to us?"

"Oh, that one's easy," she said, smiling and giving me a peck on the cheek. "You blew it, big boy."

"Story of my life," I said.

As Dani went back to her office and I headed for the elevators, it was hard not to think back on our Fells Point days.

Maybe I didn't know what I wanted back then. Or maybe I was too anxious about my career, too demanding of the relationship, too selfish, too insecure, too needy.

Too *something* . . .

But I was a changed man now. All I was looking for was someone who was kind, intelligent, funny, great in bed, loved my kids and had the smoldering looks of a superstar lingerie model.

Oh, and someone who wouldn't feel the impulse to give head to my neighbor when she got drunk.

Was that too much to ask?

17.

The questions came flying like tracer rounds – *whoosh, whoosh, whoosh* – the minute I got to Ripped! the next morning.

Mikey: "So what's he like?"

Harvey: "He's a dick, right? You can just *tell.*"

Courtney: "Is he doing all *three* of those Oven-ettes babes? That is *so sick* . . ."

Jamison: "He say anything about prison? About getting boned by his cellie?"

Harvey again: "But he's a dick, right?"

It was the first time the Big Five had been together in a week. I'd had my first two burpees prep sessions with Oven Mitts, but he'd begged off today's workout, citing an unspecified shoulder injury. (*How'd he hurt it?* I wondered. *Dead-lifting a Chevy Suburban?*)

Instead, my buddies and I met in the child-care room in the rear of Ripped!, where a sign on the door advised: "Closed due to ventilation problems. We apologize for any inconvenience."

I read it and imagined a harried mom waking early, slipping into her lululemon yoga pants and sports bra while eagerly looking forward to her workout, then rousing her sleeping toddler, giving the cranky kid breakfast, packing a diaper bag and wrestling him into and out of a car seat as he wailed nonstop.

Then to show up here and find there's no place to park the little monster so you can have a half-hour of peace and quiet on the treadmill?

Or take in a rejuvenating Pilates class?

Yeah, I'd say that qualified as an inconvenience. The kind that could totally make you snap. And gun the car through the front doors at 90 mph.

I answered the flurry of questions about Oven Mitts as honestly as I could, in the order they were shot at me:

Re: his personality. Too early to tell.

No dick-like behavior detected thus far.

No mention of any copulation with gym groupies, either.

Ditto with amorous cellmates back in the day.

See answer 1 above.

As I told my buddies, I didn't have a great read on Tony Maldon just yet. We had only worked out together twice. And because of that, I was trying – as my sainted mother always urged – not to form snap judgments about a person before getting to know him or her.

"Yeah, yeah," Harvey said impatiently. "You're a regular altar boy, OK? I'm sure Ma Doherty is super-proud. But you're not helping us here, pal."

Mikey agreed. "Your intel sucks so far."

I shrugged and said nothing. This seemed to piss them off even more.

"OK, let's try this," Jamison said. "That first workout. What did you and Oven Mitts do?"

"Breathing exercises," I said.

"Breathing exercises," he repeated.

I nodded. "For 45 minutes."

"Breathing exercises. For 45 minutes," he said incredulously.

"Is there an echo in here?" I said. "Are we in a cave? Yes, that's what we did. Breathing exercises for 45 minutes."

The four of them glanced uneasily at each other, then back at me.

"OK, what about the second workout?" Jamison asked. "What happened then?"

"Breathing exercises," I said.

"Breathing exercises," he repeated.

I threw my hands in the air.

"*Again* with the echoes! What's with you people?!"

Now they were all frowning, like I was keeping some terrible secret from them, something they desperately needed to know in order to get on with their lives and be able to sleep at night. Something any other normal human being, possessed of even a modicum of affection for his or her friends, would have no trouble divulging.

Harvey, in particular, seemed to be trying hard to control his irritation.

"You're trying to tell us," he said, "that you worked out *twice* with this man. And all you did the entire time was stare soulfully into each other's eyes and breathe deeply?"

"Who said anything about staring soulfully?" I said. "Don't make this a gay thing, Harvey. The fact is, we were both lying on the floor – on separate mats, I might add – doing the breathing."

They traded more worried glances. No one spoke for several seconds. Finally Courtney patted my hand.

"It's OK, sweetie," she said. "You know, even if you *were* attracted to this man . . ." Her voice trailed off. "My point is, we're your friends. We don't judge."

"I'M NOT ATTRACTED TO HIM!" I shouted.

"Uh-oh," Mikey said. "Looks like you hit a nerve, Court."

"A mid-life domestic crisis that alters one's sexual orientation," Jamison said, nodding knowingly. "You see it all the time. Hey, I've done stories on it for the I-Team. Nothing to be ashamed of."

Suddenly there was a tremendous throbbing in my temples. I massaged them with my thumbs for several seconds, wondering if I was having a brain aneurysm.

"Look, you idiots," I said finally, "Oven Mitts is totally psyched about this contest with EFC, OK? He even calls it the 'Day of the Burpees.' In fact, every time he says 'Day of the Burpees,' he makes this dramatic little sound effect: *dun-dun-dun-dunnnn!* Like they do in the movies."

"Dun-dun-dun-dunnnn?" Jamison said.

I pointed at him.

"If you repeat what I say *one more fucking time*, I'm gonna show up at your next live shot. And I'll smack you over the head with a shovel."

"Oooh, you know what *that'll* do, Jaymo!" Mikey snickered. "Mess up that perfectly-coiffed 'do of yours."

Jamison winced and held up his hands. "Whoa, chill! No need to get hostile, dude!"

"Anyway," I went on, "Oven Mitts says there'll be lots of pressure on us the day of the contest. On all three teams from Ripped! There'll be a ton of spectators there from both gyms. Lots of noise, lots of cheering, lots of heckling, the whole nine yards.

"Therefore he says the two of us need to stay calm and focused if we're going to beat those EFC bozos. And the way to stay calm and focused, he says, is by controlling your breathing. And not getting caught up in the moment."

Judging by their soft grunts and lack of follow-up questions, this explanation seemed to satisfy my pals.

More than anything, they seemed relieved to know I hadn't

been reclining on a sweat-dampened exercise mat, inhaling and exhaling deeply while gazing moon-eyed at the age-defying Apollo they'd fixated on for months.

"Know my biggest fear?" I said. "I'm working out with him, right? And suddenly I slip and call him Oven Mitts. Remember, the five of us are still the only ones aware of his past. Who knows how he'd react to hearing his old nickname? The one the media mocked him with all those years ago."

"Oh, Jackie!" Courtney said. She clutched my elbow, eyes wide with alarm. "Promise you'll be careful. You think he'd get violent?"

God, how could you not love this woman! I said a silent prayer of thanks for her presence on this planet.

"I'm not worried about that, Court," I said. "The man's 80 years old. Sure, he's in great shape. And he could probably kick my ass. But my guess is his violent days are way behind him. Last thing he wants to do is to attack someone. And end up back in the slammer."

Courtney seemed reassured. And she hadn't let go of my arm, which was nice to see.

"Thing is," I continued, "Oven Mitts and I have to work as a team if we're gonna beat those elitist jerks. That means zero distractions. So I don't want my burpees partner – the guy who's gonna have to carry my sorry butt in this competition – pissed off because I used a name he hates.

"Come April 10th, I want him to love me like a brother. And have nothing on his mind except beating the bad guys."

Mikey grinned. "Sounds like you're getting into this whole thing, buddy."

I nodded and mimicked gipping a microphone. In the bombastic voice of a WWE ring announcer, I intoned:

"IT'S THE SHOWDOWN ALL OF BALTIMORE'S BEEN WAITING FOR! A GRUDGE MATCH YEARS IN THE MAKING! A FITNESS EXTRAVAGANZA LIKE NO OTHER!

"LADIES AND GENTLEMEN, IT'S RIPPED! VERSUS EFC! SO LET'S GET IT ON! IT'S THE DAY OF THE BURPEES, BAY-BEE!"

On cue, Courtney sang out: *"Dun-dun-dun-dunnnn!"*

18.

Inspirational sayings lined the walls of Ripped! These were designed as emotional balm for those poor wretches struggling with their fitness regimens and beginning to doubt themselves – enough to possibly quit and deprive ownership of another fat monthly fee.

WALK IN STRONG, WALK OUT STRONGER read a sign near the locker room entrances. Another by the snack bar proclaimed: IF YOU CAN DREAM IT, YOU CAN DO IT. Yet a third, positioned near the cardio machines so that its Day-Glo orange lettering caught the weak early-morning sunlight streaming through the grimy floor-to-ceiling windows – presumably providing a jolt of endorphins to the still-lethargic – blared: THE KEY TO SUCCESS IS TO FOCUS ON GOALS, NOT OBSTACLES.

One day a new saying went up near the free weights area.

UNLEASH, it read.

The Big Five stared at it for several minutes, trying to divine the message that surely lay within.

"Unleash *what?*" Mikey asked finally.

"No idea," Courtney said.

"Your full potential?" ventured Mikey.

"The power within?" Jamison offered.

"The dog?" Harvey volunteered.

Courtney shot him a pained look. "Every time I think you

can't *possibly* say anything dumber than the last dumb thing you said, you surprise me."

Harvey shrugged.

"It's a gift," he said modestly. "You're either born with it or you're not."

We were still parsing the meaning of UNLEASH when another cryptic sign appeared two days later, this one near the spin class studio.

FINAO, it said.

Seeing it, Harvey threw his hands in the air.

"This is bullshit!" he growled. "They put up these stupid sayings. Half of 'em, you don't even know what they mean!"

He stalked up to the front desk, the rest of us trailing behind. Bryan, buzzing from his usual four cups of morning coffee, hurried over to greet us.

Harvey glared at him. "Are you trying to fuck with our heads?"

"Why, whatever do you mean?" Bryan asked amiably. "We're not in the business of head-fucking here, Harv."

Harvey whirled and pointed a bony finger at the UNLEASH sign. "Then *what*…the *hell*…does *that* mean?"

"Oh that," Bryan said. "Unleash the new you. The new *fit* you!"

Harvey's eyes narrowed. "You couldn't put that on the sign? Couldn't add three little words – *the new you* – for clarity?"

Bryan crossed his arms and sighed. "Harvey, Harvey, Harvey…our brains need exercise, too, you know. A sign that makes you *think* for a moment, one that doesn't instantly provide all the answers, but makes you use the gray matter that even *you* possess – is that such a bad thing?"

Mikey continued to eye him warily.

"OK," he said. "What about FINAO? What's that supposed to mean?"

"Oh, *come on!*" Bryan said. "That one's *easy*! You guys should know *that* one!"

"Well, we *don't*," Courtney said with a tight smile. "So please enlighten us, hon."

"Courtney, Courtney, Courtney . . .," Bryan said, shaking his head. "If I just *give* you the answer, you'll absolutely hate yourself!"

"Bryan, Bryan, Bryan . . ." she said, eyes narrowing. "If this keeps up, it probably won't be *me* I'll be hating."

Mikey leaned over the counter until his face was inches from Bryan's.

In a low voice, he said: "I don't know whether you're aware of this, but I fought in a bloody war many years ago. This was the big one in Southeast Asia. Saw some horrible things over there. *Did* some horrible things, too. Stuff that haunts me to this day.

"In fact," he went on, "there are folks in this aging, rapidly-declining facility of yours, including some of my dearest friends" – here he nodded in our direction – "who think the memories of that awful time have rendered me, well, less than stable psychologically."

The color slowly drained from Brian's face.

"My friends fear," Mikey continued, "that one of these days, the slightest provocation – say, a cruel joke made at my expense, or someone failing to say thank-you when I hold the door for them, or even, I don't know, someone being a gigantic pain in the ass when asked a simple question about the meaning of a sign – could cause me to snap.

"In which case, they're afraid that I might possibly retrieve a weapon from the well-stocked cache in my basement and hurt someone."

Bryan's hand trembled as he reached for his coffee mug.

"You certainly don't want something like that to happen, right?" Mikey added. "I'm not a business owner. But I can't imagine a scene like that – bullets flying everywhere, the screams of frightened members as they stampede for the exits, frantic calls to 911, police sirens wailing in the distance – would be good for business. Wouldn't you agree?"

Bryan gulped and nodded.

"FINAO's an acronym," he blurted. "Stands for FAILURE IS NOT AN OPTION."

Mikey stared at him for several seconds.

"*Thank you*," he said finally. He reached out and patted Bryan on the cheek, like a Mafia don who'd just spared a screw-up underling from being whacked. "I'm glad we got that settled."

The important business of deciphering the gym's hieroglyphics behind us, my friends went off to their workouts while I headed for my third burpees prep session with Oven Mitts. He'd promised that we were done with the creepy breathing exercises, and that now the important work of "maximizing" my "full potential" in the upcoming contest could take place.

I found him in a side room where evening Jazzercise classes were conducted. He was doing a head stand on a floor mat, his skull, shoulders and elbows perfectly aligned, his entire body completely still.

"A terrific way to warm up," he grunted when he saw me. "Great for your circulation. Core stability and strength, too. It's called a *sirsasana* in yoga. Also alleviates stress and depression. Wanna try it?"

"Not unless you want your burpees partner in a neck brace." I said.

He seemed disappointed. "OK. Gimme a sec and we'll get started."

I watched as he took a few deep breaths before bending his torso at the waist and effortlessly lowering his legs. He touched the mat lightly with first one foot and then the other before springing upright.

Grinning, he clapped me on the back and said: "Ready to work?"

"Aye, aye, sir!" I said.

I don't know why I said that. Probably because Oven Mitts struck me as the kind of man – old school, disciplined, maybe even ex-military at some point – who'd appreciate the gesture.

As we headed to the mats, he said: "Did you know there was actually a man named Burpee who came up with this crazy exercise? It's true. I looked it up. Royal H. Burpee was his name. A physiologist from Columbia University. Invented the burpee in the 1940's as a way to measure a person's fitness. The army had their soldiers do them in World War II."

"Lemme guess," I said. "That's why so many GI's went AWOL back then."

Oven Mitts threw back his head and laughed. "Hey, good one! You're sharper than you look, my friend!"

Despite the dig, I breathed a sigh of relief. At least the man wasn't totally devoid of a sense of humor. At least he didn't react to my open lack of enthusiasm with a snarl and some kind of exotic roundhouse kick to the scrotum that he learned in the slammer.

After we did some light stretching, he explained that today we'd be practicing two key components of the burpee: the squat and the kickback into the pushup position.

"You want to drop to the ground like a baseball catcher," he advised. "Then hands in front of you and kick your legs back. *Hard.* Like a zebra kicking a lion when it's threatened."

Wait...*what?*

Did zebras really have that kind of thunder in their hooves? Sure, we've all heard about mules and their powerful kicks. But zebras? And if they got into it with the King of the Jungle, could they really lay him out, Mike Tyson-style, with a mighty flick of a hoof?

To be honest, I wasn't 100 per cent sure of this. But I wasn't sure Oven Mitts knew, either. After all, for much of his adult life, he'd been a guest of the state in a large, forbidding-looking lockup in Western Maryland ringed by chain-link fences and razor wire where, to the best of my knowledge, no zebras – never mind lions – had ever been spotted.

It was doubtful he'd gleaned a lot about them from the prison library, either, books on nature and exotic wildlife tending not to be in high demand among the incarcerated. Nor was it likely he'd learned about zebras from any TV programs in the slammer.

I couldn't picture him sauntering into the dayroom on an autumn Sunday afternoon, say, and asking his fellow cons if they minded forgoing the Ravens-Steelers game in favor of the National Geographic Channel, where an excellent special on the African equines known for their distinctive black and white stripes was airing.

But OK, I thought, *don't get hung up on the zebra stuff. Focus on the larger message: the need to be quick and efficient at the beginning of the exercise.*

For the next 40 minutes, we practiced this sequence side-by side. Does this sound boring to you? It was boring to me, too. Oh, you have no idea.

The whole time, Oven Mitts studied my form with Talmudic

intensity, quietly offering tips – "Bend the knees more. Athletic stance" – and occasional snippets of encouragement. ("That's it, now you're keeping that core tight.")

By the end of the session, he pronounced my movements as "significantly improved."

"I gotta tell you, buddy," he said as we cooled down. "You looked like shit when we started. But you might be getting the hang of it."

At this, a warm glow came over me. *Yayyy, I don't look like shit anymore!* But then I caught myself. *Jesus! Was I becoming an Oven Mitts fanboy? An OM groupie?!*

Was this how easy it was to be charmed by this guy? Simply by being fed a tiny morsel of back-hand praise? Would I start hanging with the Oven-ettes now, becoming their first male member, swooning and slobbering over every new age-defying feat performed by our Glorious Leader?

God help me if that were the case . . .

Yet the other thought that occurred to me was this: maybe, as he'd told Bryan, Oven Mitts had never done a burpee in his life before the contest was announced. But he sure had done his homework on them since.

You could tell he'd watched many of the dozens of instructional videos on the Internet – a confession: I'd looked at some of them, too --and broken down every facet of the loathsome exercise from beginning to end. He was looking to master it and gain any edge possible against the EFC dweebs.

One thing was sure: he wasn't treating this competition as a lark. Far from it. He was in it to win it.

We parted ways with a fist bump and a pledge to again practice together in a few days. But after slinging his gym bag over his shoulder, he turned and looked at me.

"I know people here talk about me," he said softly. "Maybe you'll tell them I'm not a complete asshole. Sure, I've done some stuff. But I'm not a bad guy."

19.

"So when are you gonna ask me out?" Courtney said.

It was 7:30 a.m. a couple of days later and both of us were pounding away on the elliptical machines. OK, I say *pounding*. But only one of us was reaching that level of intensity. I had been out until closing time the night before, swilling beers in Fells Point at yet another going-away party for a *Herald* staffer leaving for greener pastures, which in this case meant anywhere with a paycheck and a work environment free of the overbearing, stressed-out frauds who were our supervisors.

Massively hung over, I was unprepared for wherever Courtney was going with this line of questioning. Instead, my thoughts were mainly centered on whether or not I might puke.

"What makes you think I want to ask you out?" I wheezed.

Courtney smiled and glanced up at the bank of TV's. The one directly overhead was tuned to "Fixer Upper," where Chip and Joanna Gaines were studying a giant termites nest on the exterior wall of a clapboard house.

The close-ups of the slimy, translucent little critters wriggling about weren't helping my roiling gut.

"I've seen the way you look at me," she said finally. "You think you're pretty cool at hiding it. But you're not."

"Listen," I said, "if I've ever ogled you – and I'm not copping to anything here – it was strictly a courtesy ogle. A woman your age needs that kind of reaffirmation, needs to feel she's still vibrant and attractive and —"

I didn't get to finish the thought. Because just then, she reared back and smacked my head.

I almost toppled off the machine. Now, in addition to fighting off waves of nausea, I wondered if I had a concussion.

"OK, OK," I said. "If I ever *were* to ask you out – like a regular *date* date – and I'm not making a commitment here —"

"A *commitment?*" she cried. "Oh, God forbid! That would be horrible, wouldn't it!?! I mean, you men, you'd rather hack off your arm with a jagged shard of glass than *commit* to anything, right!?"

"A total stereotype," I said. "A tired trope repeatedly trotted out by members of your gender simply to make us feel bad."

"Commitment! The C-word!" she went on. "You guys hear it and you're like" – here she pretended to shudder uncontrollably.

"Sarcasm does not become you," I said. "Anyone ever tell you that?

"All the time," she said sweetly. "But it's my default mode when dealing with all the chicken-shit men I come across."

She turned her gaze back to the termites on TV, which were now under a vicious chemical bombardment by one of the Gaines' exterminator henchmen.

"If I ever *did* ask you out," I said again, "what do you think your response would be? Just for curiosity's sake. . . "

She seemed to mull this over carefully.

"Well, I don't know," she said at last. "Before that crack about my age, I would have probably said sure, I'll go out with you. Then when you came to the door, I would have greeted you in a skimpy negligee and smothered you with deep, passionate kisses, including lots and lots of tongue action.

"Then I would have ripped off your clothes and thrown

you on the carpet for some hot and nasty love-making before we headed off to whatever fine dining establishment you had picked out."

She shrugged. "But now…guess I'm just too old for that stuff."

I stared at her slack-jawed. Then I lunged for the STOP button on my machine.

"OK, OK, maybe we got off on the wrong foot," I said. "How about dinner tonight? Pick you up at 7?"

She flashed another enigmatic smile and turned back to "Fixer Upper," where the termites were already deep into their agonizing little death throes.

"I'll think about it," she said. "But, hey, that's not a *commitment*. You understand that, right?"

Um, sure. Moments later, she went off to the locker room to get ready for work, saying she'd let me know one way or the other later that afternoon. I drifted back to the free weights area where Harvey, Jamison and Mikey were taking turns doing bench presses.

Mikey had just finished spotting Jamison – 12 reps of 185 pounds, not bad for the I-Team's middle-aged lead investigative reporter – when out of nowhere, Harvey said: "It's a simple question. And yet no one seems to know the answer."

"What's the question?" Jamison asked.

"Oh, there are all sorts of theories," Harvey continued. "Yet you'd think by now there'd be a definitive answer."

"OK, I'll try this again," Jamison said. "What's the question?"

"Understand, I'm not saying it's *the* existential question of our time," Harvey said. "But it's an *interesting* question. Especially in a place like this, you'd at least like to have a consensus of opinion on it."

Jamison jumped to his feet and glared at him.

"YOU SKINNY, HEAD-GAME-PLAYING SON OF A BITCH!" he roared. "WHAT IS THE FUCKING QUESTION?"

Harvey smiled innocently. "Thought you'd never ask. OK, here it is. How many times are you required to say hello to someone in the gym?"

Mikey was incredulous. "*That's* the question?"

Harvey nodded. "Like, say you pass someone in here, right? Maybe they're coming out of a spin class or you see them at the barbell racks or the coffee station or wherever. And it's the first time you've seen them that morning. So naturally you say hi, right?"

The rest of us nodded dutifully.

"You say hi," he went on, "because you're not one of these rude shitheads who looks down when they pass someone and never says hello. But now, what if you pass that same person again? Like, I don't know, 10 minutes later. And the two of you make eye contact. What do you do there?"

For a moment, no one spoke.

"Head nod," Mikey said finally.

"Head nod?" Harvey said. "That's it?"

"Mikey's right," Jamison said. "Head nod. A simple, effective, yet not overly-time-consuming acknowledgement. You're simply saying: *Yep, I see you again.* Look, you can't keep saying hi every time you pass a person. You'll come off like a Walmart greeter. People will think there's something wrong with you."

Silence descended on us once more.

This, apparently, was one of the weightier issues they'd been discussing since I'd been off doing cardio with Courtney. And they were now thoroughly engaged with the subject, and determined to come up with a solution.

Finally, Jamison said: "You could always give them one of these." He pretended to point an index finger at an imaginary passer-by.

"The finger-shoot?!" Harvey said. "I don't know. That's so . . . *Sinatra* isn't it? So *Rat Packy*. Why don't you go ahead and wink at the person at the same time? Make it even *more* cheesy."

"Let me offer this," Mikey said. "Why do you even *have* to acknowledge the person a second time? Or a third time? Isn't there already a tacit agreement between the two of you? Like: 'Look, we've already said hi to each other. We've demonstrated that we're not a couple of ill-mannered, anti-social d-bags. Now let's get on with the business of why we're here. Let's get back to the workouts.'"

At this point, I had to walk away.

Here was yet another example of why I couldn't practice burpees around those knuckleheads. How do you focus on the proper form for the exercise – and the correct technique – with that kind of vapid soundtrack playing in the background?

By 4 that afternoon, I still hadn't heard from Courtney. It was the same at 4:30. Finally at 5:45, my cellphone dinged.

Her message read: *Re: your vile ageist slurs this morning, I'm willing to assume that was a boorish one-off. So yes, I'll go out with you. But the ER is nuts right now. Must be Bring-Your-Own -Glock Day in Charm City. Can we make it 8 tonight instead of 7? If so, meet at the Naughty Leprechaun? SHN.*

Well. So much for being welcomed by a smoldering vixen in a Victoria's Secret getup, with all the torrid face-sucking and sexual hijinks to follow.

Sure, all that was probably said in an ironic sense, designed to be equal parts flirty, hyperbolic and humorous. And to see how I'd react. But it would have been nice to ring her doorbell and find out for sure.

I texted back: *Sounds good. BTW, what's SHN stand for?*

Smoking Hot Nurse, she replied.

Already I could feel my feet starting to sweat.

20.

The Naughty Leprechaun was the kind of Irish pub determined to bludgeon you with its Irish-ness from the moment you walked through the heavy wooden doors until the moment you stumbled out with a wedge of Shepherd's pie and a few Guinness's sloshing around in your gut.

Located in Baltimore's trendy Harbor East neighborhood, it had all the requisite touches its customers demanded: the Pogues blaring over the sound system, dark floors, dark paneling, dark tables and chairs, the Irish "tricolour" hanging in one corner to remind you, as if you needed reminding, of the exalted nationality on display here.

And of course, every centimeter of wall space was crammed with Gaelic traffic signs, tiny faux Celtic harps, miniature mirrors advertising all manner of Eire-made whiskeys, postcards from the windswept Aran Islands and an exhausting amount of other Fenian bric-a-brac.

It even had the obligatory friendly Irish bartender, one with an ever-present smile plastered on his puss and the hint of a brogue, although one that sounded suspiciously more Dubai than Dublin.

God help us, but this was what passed these days for an "authentic" Irish pub. My sainted mother, resting peacefully all these years in the loamy ground of a quiet cemetery in County Roscommon, was surely spinning in her grave.

I found Courtney perched at the end of the bar, happily sipping a Cosmopolitan. The sight of her nearly took my breath away. After a long, frantic day in the ER, I expected her to show up in drab medical scrubs and sneakers, the standard uniform of the profession. Instead, she was dazzling in a low-cut silk blouse, tight black pants and high-heel boots.

"Wow," I said, adding a low whistle. "New dress code at Shock Trauma? If so, it's a definite upgrade."

She laughed and gave me a playful peck on the cheek.

"You like?" she said. "We got off work early, which almost never happens. I had time to run home and slip into this old thing. I call it my nun outfit."

"I can see why," I said, "It just screams Sister Courtney Mancini. All you're missing are rosary beads. The Cosmo's a nice touch, too."

"*What?*" she said, glancing at her cocktail. "Vodka, triple sec and cranberry juice – that's not the national libation of Ireland?"

"I'm surprised they didn't toss you for ordering it," I said.

She nodded and pointed to the bartender. "I had to beg Colin to make one. At first, he said he'd only do it if the lights went out and no one could see him."

I ordered a Guinness. Just then an overhead speaker crackled to life and the Dropkick Murphys' shrieking peg-leg anthem "I'm Shipping Up to Boston" blared, making all conversation impossible.

We grabbed our drinks and adjourned to an outdoor table.

"So how was work?" I asked.

"Oh, you know," she said. "The usual cavalcade of gunshot victims. Plus two homeless guys with stab wounds courtesy of some nutcase who went on a rampage at their shelter on North Mount Street. Plus your routine over-doses, poisonings, pit bull attacks – one of those psycho mutts practically tore the groin out of a 60-year-old man . . ."

"Ouch! Just another day at the office, eh?" I said.

She sipped her drink and nodded.

"Pretty much. Although this was new. A young guy, maybe 16, came in complaining about headaches and confusion. He'd also been having seizures. They rushed him into surgery. Guess what they found?"

"I'm almost afraid to," I said.

"How 'bout an eight-inch tapeworm in his brain?!" she said. "And people wonder why I drink .. . ." She raised the Cosmo and took another sip, a longer one this time.

Our server was hovering nearby, displaying the universal body language of the profession that signaled: WILL YOU FUCKING PEOPLE PLEASE ORDER SO I CAN MAKE SOME MONEY HERE?

"All this talk of brain tapeworms and eviscerated groins is making me hungry," I told Courtney. "You?"

"Famished," she said. "Remind me to tell you about the man who came in with a knife embedded in his head."

"Oh, let's save that one for dessert," I said. "In the meantime, how do you feel about bangers and mash?"

"Totally approve," she said.

As I waved over our bored waiter, Courtney added: "Order me a Tullamore Dew and Coke, too. I can't torture poor Colin with another Cosmo request."

There is something alternately thrilling and terrifying about a first date, especially for a broken, overweight and desperately horny divorced man in his mid-40's. On the drive to the pub, I tried to remember the last time I had sex. It was many months ago, just before the infamous Night of the Hummer that caused everything to go to shit.

On this particular evening, Beth and I had gotten smashed, me after drinking enough beer to float an aircraft carrier and her after copious amounts of Sauvignon blanc. Our love life had cooled considerably by then, due in no small part (I realize now) to her getting regularly shagged by Friendly Neighbor Dan Henson.

But on that night, with both of us at home, drunk and bored and with nothing on TV, a silent thought stirred in both of us: *Oh hell, let's see what happens ...*

The results were, to say the least, depressing.

My enduring memory of the feeble rutting session on the couch that followed was of Beth staring blankly up at the ceiling as I attempted various thrusting maneuvers, throwing a grunt or two into the mix and a moaned *Oh yeah, baby!* to signal the heroic effort being undertaken on her behalf.

It was over quickly – yes, I was not exactly a porn star on this occasion. And Beth had the good sense to not even *try* to fake an orgasm. Afterward we both skulked away in different directions, me to the bedroom to sleep it off and her to toss a slice of pizza in the microwave and stare at her phone.

So much for the spontaneous intimacy that can spice up a flagging marriage . . .

Yet sitting in the Leprechaun with Courtney, the two of us talking and laughing and enjoying dinner, I dared to think for the first time in ages about the possibility of emerging from my monk-like existence and actually...*getting laid*. With the added bonus of it happening with a smoking hot nurse! And someone I was starting to have feelings for!

Yet just as quickly, my Irish fatalism rose up to strangle that thought, set it on fire, and fling it in a shallow grave.

Whoa, slow down, Big Guy, I told myself. *You're setting yourself up for a world of disappointment. Keep the bar low. That way you don't leave here wanting to put a gun to your mouth.*

Even more than being sex-deprived, it was the crushing loneliness of my pitiful existence that was most upsetting. To come home day after day to an empty house, with no one to talk to, no one to touch or hug or kiss, facing another long night of watching another crappy movie on Netflix before shuffling off to bed and tossing and turning for hours – juts shoot me.

Did I mention the combo of chronic lustfulness and abject isolation had led – predictably – to a third condition? Insomnia? I should probably mention that. Then to shuffle off every morning in a fog of exhaustion to my crappy job at the crappy newspaper where the next round of layoffs was always around the corner and my bosses were salivating to get rid of me. . . no wonder I was such a joy to be around these days.

Yet mercifully, at least for one blessed night, Courtney and the Guinness had had taken my mind off all that.

Inevitably, the conversation got around to Oven Mitts, with Courtney wanting to know how the burpees training was going.

"Look," I said, "you know I thought he was full of shit when we started working out together. I mean, he'd never even done burpees before, right? Then we spend two sessions doing that Zen breathing stuff and I'm thinking: *What's next? Is he gonna break out the sappy Mr. Miyagi quotes like 'We make secret pact. I promise teach you burpees, you promise learn?'*"

"An all-time classic," Courtney agreed. "My favorite Karate Kid quote of his was: 'A lie becomes truth only if person chooses to believe.' Think I used that on my ex when I threw his cheating ass out."

"But now," I went on, "I'm seeing Oven Mitts in a different

light. He's really studied up on burpees, broken the whole exercise down to a series of intricate movements. Like some kind of elaborate *flamenco*. He's a patient instructor, too. And it's not easy to be patient dealing with a complete schlub like me."

She leaned across the table and took my hand.

"Now listen," she said, "I am *not* going to sit here and let you run yourself down like that. You are *not* a complete schlub. Do you have schlub-like tendencies? Yes. Most definitely. But your quasi-schlubiness is endearing, too. At least to me."

A confession: at that moment, between her touch and her smile, I was just about the happiest quasi-schlub on the planet.

As we finished our meal with after-dinner drinks – a Baileys for me, a Nutty Irishman for Courtney – I also felt compelled to share the curious remarks Oven Mitts had delivered at the close of our last practice session.

"He said that? That people think he's an asshole?" she asked.

"Yep. And he had this pained look on his face. Like it cut him to the bone to be perceived that way. I actually felt sorry for him."

Courtney frowned and shook her head.

"The guy murdered his *wife*, Jack! The mother of his *kids!* Left her body to be picked over by wolves and vultures and God knows what else. Pretty hard to muster sympathy for someone like that."

"Understood," I said. "It's something I think about a lot. So far I've managed to push it out of my mind when we work out."

We drained our drinks and Courtney let me reach for the check without stabbing me with a fork. Outside, the streets were still bustling. Across the water, we could see the sun setting over Federal Hill, a dull yellow ball with a hazy orange halo dipping below the horizon.

For a moment, we stood on the sidewalk in awkward silence

"The night's still young," I said finally.

"Very true," she said.

More silence.

"We could go for a nightcap somewhere," I said. "I mean, if you're up for it."

"Isn't your apartment close by?" she replied. "We could probably get a nightcap there, couldn't we?"

"Definitely," I said, my heart racing. "There just happens to be a bottle of first-rate amaretto on the coffee table, too. Straight from Saronno."

"Sounds heavenly. Did I mention I don't have to work tomorrow?"

"I don't think you did."

She rummaged through her purse and pulled out a toothbrush.

"Now how did *this* silly thing get in there?" she said with a grin. "Oh, well. Be prepared. That's what they taught us in Girl Scouts."

"I thought that was the Boy Scouts motto?"

"Whatever," she said, hooking her arm around mine. "Let's not get bogged down with details, Mr. Hotshot Columnist. Let's just go with the flow."

21.

It was a little after 1 the next afternoon when Courtney and I arrived to watch the tryouts for the teams that would represent Ripped! in its holy war – hadn't Brian alluded to something like that? – against EFC in the Great Burpees Challenge.

Our entrance did not go unnoticed. Maybe it was the loopy ear-to-ear grin that seemed permanently affixed to my face. Maybe it was the familiar way Courtney kept touching my elbow and leaning in as we talked. Maybe it was some sort of post-coital afterglow we projected, the fabled firing of the dopamine and oxytocin receptors that results in an air of exalted well-being among the recently-boinked.

Look, I don't know what it was.

But as soon as we walked in, the rest of the Big Five descended on us. They seemed to sense that some grand tectonic shift had occurred in our relationship, likely involving some sort of heated sexual shenanigans after our date.

"Well, well, looks who's here!" Harvey sang out. "And don't we look *extra* happy today!"

"Yeah," said Mikey, winking lasciviously at Courtney. "Good thing Jack doesn't have to try out today. Bet he'd be a little, um, *drained*."

Pretending to grip a microphone, Jamison lapsed into his classic TV newsman's voice: "I'm here at Ripped! where members Jack Doherty and Courtney Mancini have just put in an appearance. The I-Team has confirmed the couple had an intimate dinner at a Baltimore bistro last night. What is *not* clear is what exactly transpired behind closed doors when the two lovebirds, no doubt a bit tipsy at this point, opted to continue their canoodling at an undisclosed location.

"Observational evidence suggests they sampled from a full buffet of carnal delights until the wee hours this morning. Did the earth move for them? Did the heavens part and a choir of angels descend singing the 'Hallelujah Chorus'? We hope to have those details for you later in the broadcast. In the meantime, live from North Baltimore, this is I-Team lead investigative reporter R. Jamison Winthrop."

"Guys, guys . . ." I said, attempting to nip this juvenile – yet all-too-predictable – inquisition in the bud.

Courtney, bless her heart, took a more direct approach.

"SHUT IT, PIGS!" she snapped. Naturally, this set off a round of leering guffaws, which only intensified when she added: "NO WONDER YOU IDIOTS NEVER GET ANY!"

Yet the truth was, she and I were both in too good of a mood to stay irritated for long. The previous night had indeed been glorious. We had barely settled on my sofa and taken the first sips of the pricey (yet totally over-rated) amaretto touted to me by a friend before we were all over each other.

A spirited discussion took place later over which of us had initiated the feverish love-making, with her claiming I had gently – but firmly – pressed her down onto the cushions while simultaneously delivering deep kisses, clearing the amaretto glasses and unzipping her pants.

"You don't usually see that level of multi-tasking from a guy," Courtney had noted dryly.

"Plus I'm out of practice," I reminded her. "In the old days,

I might've thrown in a little juggling, too."

"Now *there's* an image I can't un-see," she said. "Who knew you were such a romantic?"

After moving further activities to the bedroom, we slept late that morning. When I finally awoke, it was to find Courtney gently writhing on my hip, a big smile on her face.

"Rise and shine, Mr. Writer," she murmured.

"I don't know about the shine part, Nurse Mancini," I said. "But I have *definitely* risen."

"I'll be the judge of that," she said, slipping a hand beneath the covers to investigate. Then, in a delighted voice, she cried: "By God, the man speaks the truth!" before climbing on top of me again.

When we finally roused ourselves an hour later, I whipped up a breakfast of bacon, scrambled eggs and toast, the only meal I could prepare without fear of inflicting gastric distress on this lovely woman.

Hoping now to get my nosy buddies to focus on something other than our hookup, I glanced around the gym. It appeared to have been transformed into some kind of weird burpees performance art space.

With David Bowie blaring over the sound system and green and red lights flashing, dozens of men and women were flinging themselves about and offering their singular interpretation of the world's most reviled exercise – all under the watchful gaze of Brian and his lieutenants.

"How're the tryouts going?" I said.

"Don't ask," Harvey said. "We're totally fucked."

"Can you say 'bloodbath?'" Jamison added.

"EFC's gonna smoke us," Mikey agreed. Then, looking pointedly at me: "Only way we avoid a shutout is if, by some miracle, Oven Mitts carries your fat ass to a win."

Courtney sighed and shot them a blistering look.

"That's what I love about you three!" she said. "That relentlessly positive outlook. Always sunny and upbeat. The glass isn't just half-full, it's *overflowing!*"

Mikey shrugged. "See for yourself, Court. None of our guys has a prayer against the Swedish Soul Snatcher. Compared to that freak, they look like they're doing burpees in quicksand."

"The women aren't much better," Jamison said. "Only one who looks like she has a shot is Colleen Stupak."

"Colleen Stupak, Colleen Stupak . . ." I murmured, mentally searching for a face to put with the name.

"Annoying little gal who fast-walks around the gym to warm up?" Jamison said. "Always gets in everyone's way? Seems to jump out of her skin if you so much as say hi?"

"*That's* Colleen Stupak?" I said.

"The one and only," Jamison said. "And she's a burpees dynamo! She's out there *killing* it! But let's face it: EFC might have a dozen women as good or better than her."

"Colleen Stupak," I repeated, dumbfounded. "Who knew?"

Harvey nodded. "Not me, buddy," he said. Then, jerking his head in the direction of the tryouts: "But go ahead, you and Court walk around. Check out the, ahem, *talent* for yourself."

The format for the competition was simple: two members were paired against each other in each round. Whoever completed the most burpees in three minutes moved on to a second round. When it was over, the three men and women with the highest total scores would represent Ripped! against the evil cross-town financiers.

Right away, Courtney and I could see why our buddies were so down on the men's chances. Mostly it was a bunch of weight-lifters trying out. These were beefy, pumped-up guys who could barely squat without snapping a hamstring and who dropped to the floor with all the grace of a drunk decked in a bar fight.

"What we need are some Navy SEAL types," I muttered. "Strong and lean and agile. Not built like a stand-up freezer."

We studied the two men on the mats now. One, at least 6-foot-8, burly and heavily-tattooed, appeared to be in his late 30's. The other we recognized as a man named Tony Barbato, in his mid-40's, who pulled up to the gym each morning with a handicapped parking permit dangling from the rearview mirror of his fire-engine-red Toyota Supra.

Invariably, he would angle his car so as to claim two parking spots, then leap out with a satisfied grin and practically skip to the entrance, the very picture of vim and vigor.

"Maybe he has a wife or a girlfriend who's disabled," Courtney said charitably the first few times we witnessed this act. But after it went on for weeks – and after we found out his name and other salient facts about his marital and employment status – the verdict was in.

No, Tony Barbato didn't have a wife with serious orthopedic or neurological issues, a poor hobbled soul who required a wheelchair or crutches or a cane, someone for whom every step was a slow and agonizing journey.

Nor did Tony Barbato have a girlfriend with, say, a debilitating respiratory issue, or a lung or cardiovascular disease, someone for whom obtaining a parking spot close to a store or business was absolutely essential.

No, the truth was, Tony Barbato was a dick. A single, narcissistic mope known for hitting on dozens of women at Ripped! in the most coarse and inartful manner – and getting shot down each time.

"I got buddies who were wounded big-time in 'Nam," Mikey growled as Barbato waltzed into the gym one morning weeks earlier. "One has a prosthetic leg and limps so bad you think he'll fall over any moment. The other has grenade shrapnel in his spine and uses a walker. But neither one would stoop to the level of this guy and get a handicapped parking sticker. Now ask me why."

"Why?" we asked.

"BECAUSE THEY'RE NOT DICKS!" he roared, staring hard at Barbato as he slinked past on his way to the locker room. "THEY WON'T TAKE A PARKING SPACE AWAY FROM SOMEONE WHO ACTUALLY NEEDS IT!"

After silently rooting against Barbato and somehow stifling our glee when he got smoked by the tatted giant, we watched a few more of the men stumble in their tryouts before turning our attention to the women.

The scouting report on Colleen Stupak proved to be accurate. She was indeed amazing. Her lithe, compact body seemed specifically designed for burpees greatness. And she was apparently a lot stronger than she looked. We watched her effortlessly dominate her second round, blowing away a woman in her 20's whose face was contorted in agony from the moment she first took the mat.

Everyone could see Colleen was a lock to make the final cut. You'd think this might have infused her with some degree of swagger, or at least help her take a deep breath and relax a little. Instead, with legs jiggling non-stop and eyes darting everywhere as the competition continued, she looked like someone who expected to be hit in the head with a bottle at any moment.

Suddenly, a pair of familiar-looking women strode onto the

mats.

"Oh, my God!" Courtney gasped. "It's the Oven-ettes! Well, two of them anyway."

"This is weird," I said. "Like seeing two-thirds of the Supremes in concert."

"Or Destiny's Child and no Beyonce," Courtney said.

A murmur of recognition rippled through the on-lookers. The Oven-ettes, after all, had achieved almost the same celebrity status as Oven Mitts among the early morning workout cognoscenti. Now, some in the boisterous crowd began cheering them on.

"C'MON PAMELA!" a voice bellowed. Another voice whooped: "LET'S GO, TAMARA! YOU GOT THIS!"

So the Oven-ettes had actual names! At least these two did. It was the first time we'd ever heard them. They were Pamela and Tamara! Or Pammy! and Tammy!, as they undoubtedly called themselves during their daily workouts-cum-worship-sessions with Oven Mitts.

"How much you wanna bet the third one's named Samantha and they call her Sammy?" Courtney cackled. "Pammy, Tammy and Sammy – that would be perfect."

She gazed around the room. "Speaking of your pal, the Oven Master Himself, shouldn't he be here coaching up his cuties? And dispensing all those icky lingering hugs and back-rubs? The ones that conveniently end – TA-DAA! – with his hands all over their asses?"

"*Meow*!" I said. "Ladies and gentlemen, the claws are coming out . . ."

Yet as soon as their round began, it was clear that no amount of instruction or encouragement from anyone – even the Bill Belichick of burpees, if there was such a thing – would help

Pammy and Tammy, who appeared completely out of their depth.

Their squats and kick-backs were slow, listless movements. Their jumps lacked tempo and energy. They were a hot mess. When their three minutes were up, they embraced before collapsing in a sweaty, exhausted heap.

Somehow, both had managed to do exactly 24 burpees each, a dismal score that effectively eliminated both from the competition.

"Oh, your boy Oven Mitts is *not* gonna like this," Courtney chuckled. "Wait 'til he hears his protégés totally spit the bit."

The tryouts ended a half-hour later. Soon after, Bryan's voice boomed over the sound system, inviting us to gather near the front desk.

"We want to thank everyone who came out today, both the participants and the folks here to cheer them on," he said. "So without further ado, here are your winners . . ."

But we knew better. With Bryan, there was always further ado-ing.

"OK, sorry, a few quick notes first," he began before letting us know about a new spin class being offered on Thursdays, about the side walkway that would be closed to repair cracked and shifting concrete, and about a men's wedding band, black tungsten, found hear the picnic table behind the building.

"Claim it if it's yours," he added. Then, to knowing chuckles. "No need to furnish details of how it got there."

Finally: "OK, without *further* further ado, your men's winners who will represent us in the Great Burpees Challenge are – drum roll please! – Rusty Quaranta, Matt Lito and Collin Terwilliger! Let's give them a big hand!"

We gave them a big hand. Collin Terwilliger turned out to

be the elaborately-inked behemoth who had eliminated Tony Barbato an hour earlier. (To no one's surprise, the ever-classy Tony B. did not stick around to congratulate the winners, having roared out of the parking lot in a cloud of burnt rubber and exhaust fumes seconds after Terwilliger waxed him.)

"Your women's winners today," Bryan continued, "are Lisa Goldstein, Marion Westfeld and Colleen Stupak! Give it up for them too!"

We gave it up for them, too.

"I'd be remiss," Bryan went on, "if I didn't say: How *about* that Colleen Stupak?! Isn't she something? Best overall score on the day! If you missed Colleen's performance, you missed quite a show! So a special round of applause, please, for Colleen!"

We gave her a special round of applause. All eyes cut to her. Nearly crimson with embarrassment, Colleen bowed her head and clasped her arms in front of her, as if praying for the roof to collapse and bury her in the rubble.

"Finally," Bryan continued, "as you might already know, the tandem of Tony Maldon and Jack Doherty will represent us in the oldest member/newest member flight. Tony has been coming here since the gym opened and his incredible workout routines are legendary – for a man of *any* age, never mind someone 80 years young."

More spirited applause.

"And Jack . . ." Bryan said. Here he paused, his brow furrowed, as if desperately searching for something positive to say about the useless amalgam of flesh Oven Mitts would need to hoist over his shoulder and lug to the finish line against the EFC whippets.

". . . well, Jack is a gamer," Bryan finished. "We know he'll give it his all."

As a noticeably more subdued round of applause followed, Courtney purred in my ear: "And you *will* give it your all, won't you, Jackie? Just like you did last night."

Was I offended by Bryan's remarks?

Not in the least.

I knew my place. Of the eight of us who would represent Team Ripped! in three weeks, I was by far the weakest link, on the roster simply due to a fluke – *lucky me!* – in the date I joined a once-middling fitness club now in steep decline.

"So congrats again to all our winners!" Bryan said in conclusion. "Now let's go beat those pompous EFC – wait, any kids in here? If so, cover their ears, parents – ass-wipes! So long everyone!"

The microphone went dead. It clicked on seconds later.

"One more bit of business," Brian intoned. "For those who asked about smoothies, the blender is out of order. It looks like a problem with the coil. A replacement part has been ordered. We apologize for the inconvenience."

22.

I'm a glutton for punishment. I know this.

If you whipped me across the legs with a car antenna, I'd probably grit my teeth and grunt: "Harder!"

If you wheeled me into surgery, I'd tell the anesthesiologist: "Go grab some lunch, doc. We don't need you here today."

It's a deep and profound psychological flaw, one I'm loathe to confess to too many people lest they think there's some kind of depraved sexual component to it (there isn't) or that I'm a total whack job (still up for debate.)

But there's definitely a screw loose somewhere. How else to explain that the very next day, I drove to the Herald and hovered outside Mark Minske's office, waiting for the right moment to burst in on our feckless managing editor and lobby again for a big take-out on Oven Mitts.

Sure, Tom Halloran had shot me down, big-time. But there were new developments in the story. Maybe I could make Minske, Tommy's faithful lapdog, see the light. And maybe if I groveled enough, he'd go to bat for me with the big guy.

Yes, it was a long shot, especially after our last tete-a-tete about my West Coast hotel spending spree. But as a new sign on the walls of Ripped! so aptly put it: "You miss 100 per cent of the shots you don't take."

This would be the equivalent of a 30-footer with Kevin Durant's hand in my face and .01 on the clock. But something told me I had to take it.

Yet gaining entrance to Minske's inner sanctum would be no easy task. For one thing, the ever-vigilant Debbie Nesbo was at her desk directly adjacent to his glass-enclosed lair, ready to head off anyone who'd dare disturb the great man as he awaited his next marching orders from Halloran.

As always, Minske's desk was piled high with papers, suggesting a crippling workload and an unmatched devotion to the job. Head down, brow furrowed, reading glasses perched on the end of his nose, he appeared perpetually enmeshed in one weighty matter after another that could decide the very fate of the Herald and its hard-working, yet ever-shrinking, staff.

Unlike Halloran, Minske wasn't much of a drinker. You didn't have to worry about him disappearing for hours in the middle of a workday, then returning in a beery haze to doze fitfully on his couch until multiple cups of black coffee brought him back to life.

But Mark Minske had another demon clawing at his soul: he was a degenerate gambler. The man would bet on anything. A casino was his personal Disney World. Poker, blackjack, roulette, slots – the game didn't matter, only the action.

He wagered on baseball, hockey, NBA and college hoops. He was a sucker for the dumbest NFL prop bets: time of the National Anthem, what commercial would air immediately after the coin toss, what color Gatorade would be dumped on the winning Super Bowl coach's head, etc.

One year at the company picnic – this was back when we *had* a company picnic, which now feels like the Nixon Administration – he pulled out a wad of cash and put $50 on Toby Ellison to beat Nate Monroe at ping-pong. (Nate crushed Toby 21-9. "Rematch!" screamed Minske, pulling out another

$50. This time Nate won 21-6.)

In the immortal words of grizzled copy editor Leo Ranzone: "Minske would bet on two squirrels fucking."

We had no idea how you'd make such a bet. But it sounded about right. At the moment, I was willing to wager that at least one of the papers Minske studied was *The Daily Racing Form,* to see what horses were running at Pimlico.

The moment I saw Debbie Nesbo headed down the hall toward the vending machines, I popped my head in Minske's office.

"Begging Your Worship's pardon," I said, "might I have a moment?"

Our industrious ME – surprise, surprise – did not seem overjoyed to see me.

"Well, well," he growled, "if it isn't Mr. Four Seasons himself."

"Thought we'd moved past that little misunderstanding, Marko," I said, plopping in a chair across from him.

He pushed back from his desk and stared at me.

"That *little misunderstanding* cost the paper $4,000 fucking dollars, Doherty," he said in an icy tone.

I nodded gravely.

"The Hollywood suite with the balcony, that was a mistake on my part," I said, trying to appear contrite. "In fairness, that was only a $200 a night upgrade. They were pretty booked up that weekend, Marko. I didn't have much of a choice."

A vein on the side of his neck began to throb.

"Now," I went on, "could I have done without the full marble bathroom and *porte cochere?* In retrospect, yes. And I apologize for that. Sometimes I let my dedication to this newspaper and my zeal for getting the story overwhelm my better judgment when it comes to the company's money. That's just the way I'm wired, buddy.

"But if my actions in California caused you and Tommy any consternation or embarrassment – and it sounds like they have – I'm here to tell you how sorry I am. And I promise to be more careful with expenses when it comes to future assignments.

"No, check that," I continued, pounding his desk for emphasis. "I'll be *more* than careful. I'll be positively frugal. Parsimonious. *Miserly*, even! You have my word on that."

Minske stared down at his hands for a moment.

Finally he looked up. "What the fuck do you want, Doherty?"

I gave him a big, shit-eating grin. Then I launched into my spiel about why Oven Mitts (nee Alejandro Maldonado, Tony Maldon), the wife-murdering ex-con who had morphed into the age-defying fitness hero of a small and dying gym, was worth a 100-inch takeout.

I told him about the Great Burpees Challenge, how the two of us were now paired together against the odious EFC bankers, how the former prison yardbird-turned-exercise-savant was teaching me things about movement and physiology I had never known.

Just that morning, I went on, the two of us had put in another punishing workout, this one an intense vivisection of how to drop into the push-up position, hop into a squat and jump.

"This guy's a genius, Marko!" I said. "He's like the Stephen Hawking of burpees! Today he brought along a spreadsheet that broke down every facet of what we were working on, each move choreographed for maximum efficiency."

This was not exactly true. It was more like a print-out from a web site. But I was on a roll. If it took a massive shitstorm of hyperbole to convince Minske of the terrific tale within our grasp, then by God I was going to make it rain.

"But here's the thing, Marko!" I said. "The story really isn't about burpees or any stupid contest. Don't you see? It's about a man's *life!* The dark secret he holds! The tragic past that haunts him! Like I told Tommy a few weeks ago: I can get this guy to open up! About *all* of it!"

At this, Minske arched an eyebrow. "Oh? You already pitched this to Tommy?"

Uh-oh.

Somewhere in the dim recesses of my brain, warning lights flashed and klaxons sounded: AHH-OOO-GAH! AHH-OOO-GAH! DANGER! DANGER!

"Fine, I *did* pitch it to Tommy," I said. "But Tommy doesn't have your feel for great narrative journalism, Marko. Don't get me wrong, I love the guy" – somehow I kept a straight face – "but Tommy's got other stuff on his mind. He's trying to keep this dumpster fire of a newspaper from imploding once and for all. Besides, Tommy's not an ideas guy – everybody knows that.

"Now *you,*" I continued, "you *get* good writing. I've seen some of your old reporter clips. That five-part series on the over-weight serial killer in Essex. What was it called? 'Super-Sized Psycho?' You wrote the *shit* out of that, Marko!

"And your profile of the gun nuts who owned the Asian restaurant in Pikesville? 'Locked and Loaded for Lo Mein?' Riveting. Seriously, that's the only word for it."

I was sucking up as hard as I could, harder than I'd ever sucked up in my life. And I've done plenty of sucking up in this business.

Minske waved a hand impatiently. "So when you pitched this to Tommy, what did he say?"

Damn. I felt my armpits getting damp.

"Well," I said," with Tommy...I don't know...I'm not sure he appreciated the universal theme to this story: old man seeks redemption for a heinous crime committed in a long-ago moment of insanity, a senseless act he's still paying for to this very —"

"Tommy said no, right?" Minske said.

He seemed to be trying to suppress a grin. The corners of his tiny, rodent-like mouth quivered. The outline of his pointy gray teeth came into view.

"If Tommy said no," Minske said, "then the answer is no." He looked at his watch. "I got a budget meeting in 10 minutes."

Why, the officious son of a bitch! For an instant, I was afraid I'd lose it and rake an arm across his desk, sending his stupid papers and his precious *Racing Form* flying everywhere. But that would have been suicidal. They were already trying to get rid of me. Security would be escorting me from the building within minutes. Probably in handcuffs.

Instead, I stood and stuck out my hand. He looked at it uncertainly before finally shaking.

"So the rumors aren't true," I said.

"What rumors?" he said.

"That you'd grown a spine," I said. "Here we've got some of the top reporters in the business. And they can't even get that story straight."

I turned on my heel and left. Debbie Nesbo was back at her desk. She smirked as I passed by.

"Oh, Jack," she called out, "Mark's a very busy man! Next time you want to see him, please make an appointment with me first. As you know, that's newsroom protocol."

"*As you know, that's newsroom pro-to-col!*" I said mimicking her grating, schoolmarm voice.

As I stomped away, I might have also muttered a fervent wish – not proud of this at all – that she choke on her vanilla latte.

Halfway down the hall, I could still hear her chortling: "NOW *THERES* THE JACK DOHERTY WE ALL KNOW AND LOVE!"

23.

"Let me get this straight," Beth said. "You're in a burping contest?"

"Burpees," I said.

"Jesus, Jack! Is this really how you and your low-life buddies pass the time now? Sitting at the bar swilling beer and seeing who can make the most disgusting sounds? And then what? Everyone laughs hysterically and buys that halfwit a beer? And you do it all over again?"

"Beth, look at me. Read my lips. It's a *burpees* contest."

"I don't care what kind of cutesy name you call it. It's repulsive."

"Actually, it's not," I said. "Burpees are an exercise that —"

"And why would you tell your *kids* you're in a burping contest? Is that something to be proud of?"

"I *didn't* tell my kids that," I said.

"So you're saying they're lying? Your own flesh and blood? What has *happened to* you, Jack?"

"No," I said. "I'm *not* saying they're lying. I'm saying they misunderstood what I said. It was near their bedtime when I called the other night, remember? I could hear the TV on in the background. Plus they were tired. For whatever reason, I guess they just didn't hear me."

Beth stood there with her hands on her hips, glowering. As usual, another discussion with my lovely ex had run off the rails. Not only had it run off the rails, it had also careened off a cliff, plunged into a canyon and burst into flames, killing all aboard.

"Hmmm," she said. "Two children who just had their hearing checked by the pediatrician. Yet suddenly they're rendered semi-deaf. Well, according to *you*, anyway."

I let that one go. It was a beautiful Friday afternoon, sunny and spring-like, and I was in a great mood, having just spent a series of wonderful days with Courtney.

Beth returned to her Volvo to retrieve the kids' backpacks. Both Emmie and Liam were already inside my apartment, laughing and crashing about the place, which always seemed a bit less forlorn when they stayed the weekend.

As Beth handed me their overnight stuff, I thought: *Wait for it, wait for it…*

Right on cue: "Emily hasn't been sleeping well. Apparently she had a big fight with her friend Jessica. You know the bossy little girl with the blonde hair? Who takes over every game they play? She can be *such* a little bitch! Her mother's the same, by the way. She has some big job with the Chamber of Commerce, which apparently makes her think she's the Empress of the Universe or something. Talk about pushy broads…

"Anyway, you might want to let Emmie stay up a little later. Let her get good and tired before you put her to bed. Oh wait, what am I saying? You let these kids stay up 'til all hours anyway, right? They'll be lucky if they're in bed by midnight."

There it was, another quick jab, this one with a little more *oomph!* behind it. Now I wasn't just a liar, I was also an irresponsible parent. I was – *maybe* – a cut above the dad who passes out on the couch after guzzling a fifth of Jack Daniel's while the kids run around with sharp knives.

God bless this woman, I thought, *she never disappoints…*

"Liam got in trouble in school today . . ." Beth continued.

"*Trouble?!*" I said. "What kind of trouble could he get into? He's in first grade! What, the teacher caught him smoking during Story Time?"

Beth sighed and looked slowly up to the heavens, silently conveying the immensity of the burden she carried in having to deal with a parenting partner who was also a full-fledged simpleton.

"Actually, he hit one of the other children," she said. "Well, maybe *hit* isn't the right word. Mrs. Knight said another boy took Liam's crayons. And when he grabbed them back, he left the boy with a nasty scratch on his arm."

"Ooooh, a nasty *scratch!*" I said. "They Medevac the kid to Johns Hopkins?"

Beth threw up her hands.

"You're hopeless, you know that?!" she said. "Why don't you try being a good dad for once? Why don't you try sitting down with Liam and letting him know violence is never the answer? And that if he has a problem with another student, he should let the teacher know so she can handle it?"

Ah, there it was, the knockout punch, the uppercut to the jaw – *For chrissakes, Jack, one time, do the right thing!* - after the two set-up jabs.

"That's it, I'm outta here," she said, jiggling her car keys. "Have the kids back on time Sunday. And whatever you do, don't do any of that stupid burping crap with them."

She was halfway down the walkway when I sang out: "Nice talking to you, Bethie!"

She turned and smiled sweetly. Then she mouthed: *Fuck you, Jack.*

Ahhh, was there a better way to start the weekend? I missed her already! Often, when I thought of my ex these days, the great

H.L. Mencken quote about Puritanism came to mind: "The haunting fear that someone, somewhere, may be happy."

Yep, that was my Bethie, all right.

The kids and I spent the rest of the afternoon at a nearby park until it was time for dinner. After the disaster with the chicken tenders and a subsequent fiasco with a chili dish that also didn't go over well, I decided to play it safe. I grilled burgers and baked fries in the oven.

Both menu items were greeted with an absence of sullen looks and simulated retching sounds, which I took as a positive sign. We were halfway through the meal when Emmie said in a soft voice: "Mommy thinks you have a girlfriend."

I almost choked on my iced tea.

Liam nodded gravely. "Mommy says she can tell because you're in a good mood these days."

"She said you're not as much of a, um… *jerk*," Emmie said.

Liam shook his head vigorously. "Uh-uh! Mommy didn't say jerk! She said *a-hole*! She said Daddy's not as much of an *a-hole!*"

"*Li-amm*," Emmie said reproachfully. "That's *not* a nice word."

"But thanks for clarifying, buddy," I said. "Accuracy is important."

Liam looked down at his plate and giggled. Then both kids stared at me.

"So?" Emmie pressed. "Do you? Have a girlfriend?"

I didn't know how to answer that. The kids deserved honesty, of course. Their mother, fancying herself as some sort of emotional empath, had just lobbed a metaphorical hand grenade in their midst: your dad's just too damn chipper these days. He must be getting some. (Although thankfully she didn't put it quite that way.)

The thing was, I wasn't sure how to characterize my relationship with Courtney just yet. Yes, we'd been seeing a lot of each other. I loved being with her, loved talking with her, loved lying next to her at night and listening to her gentle breathing before I fell asleep. And yes, the sex was other-worldly, especially to a starving man who felt like he hadn't had any since Obama was in the White House.

But was she my *girlfriend*? Hard to say. Maybe. Possibly. Unspoken between us was the sense we had no intention of rushing things. At the risk of sounding overly dramatic, both of us were still traumatized.

I was coming off a 15-year marriage that had been stale for some time and then blew up like the Hindenburg after the infamous New Year's Eve BJ. Courtney had spent years catching her sleaze-ball husband in one infidelity after another, tracking his movements in sketchy bars and hook-up chat rooms, alternately weeping and seething with each new "gotcha."

The clueless dipshit couldn't even cover his tracks. Courtney kept thinking he would change, a form of insanity she now recognized as peculiar to many wronged spouses. But finally she reached a point where she couldn't take it anymore. And so, when he pulled into the driveway at 2 a.m.one morning after another night of chasing booty, she opened an upstairs window and sailed two Samsonite hardshell suitcases crammed with his clothes onto the hood of his Audi Q5, causing sizable dents.

She followed this up with an edict, delivered with gritted teeth, that he was never to darken the door of their home again. And *this* was followed up with a bulletin announcing that she'd retained the services of a renowned (and cutthroat) divorce lawyer who would not only take him to the cleaners financially, but would also no doubt demand the forfeiture of his penis and testicles in any final settlement.

As Courtney would later relate, Donny – that was the dip-shit husband's name – seemed far more upset about the body damage done to his precious luxury SUV than he did about the dissolution of his marriage.

So we were both still working out stuff, Courtney and I. In the meantime, though, we were enjoying each other's company, not worrying about how long this little fling – or whatever it was – might last. Or what it might lead to.

With Emmie and Liam eyeing me like a pair of junior fed-eral prosecutors, I took a deep breath.

"Guys, a part of me will always love your mom," I began. "And *all* of me will *always* love you two. But I've been lonely since your mother and I split up. And you don't want your dad to be lonely, do you?"

They both shook their heads somberly. Although you could also see them thinking: *Can we get on with it? Do you have a new squeeze or what?*

"So, yes," I continued, "Daddy is dating a nice woman I met at the gym. But right now we're just friends. It's nothing serious. You understand that, don't you?"

All in all, I thought it was a decent answer, one that would at least satisfy their curiosity enough so we could move onto another topic. And it did, but only temporarily. For the rest of the weekend, as we rode the roller-coasters at Six Flags America and I tried not to hurl, and as we enjoyed a picnic lunch at Loch Raven Reservoir the next day, I was peppered with random ques-tions about my new boo, as the kids say. ("What's her name?" "Where does she live?" "When can we meet her?")

Knowing Beth would grill the kids like the interrogation team at Guantanamo, I kept my answers strategically vague.

Well, all except one.

As I dropped the kids off at my old house Sunday afternoon, Emmie turned to me and, with all innocence of youth, asked: "Is she pretty? Your new, um, friend?"

I kissed her on the forehead and said: "I'm not gonna lie to you, sweetie. She might be the prettiest woman I've ever seen."

Emmie nodded and smiled. It was almost as if she expected my answer. Best of all, she seemed happy to hear it.

In about 30 seconds, right after the kids charged through the kitchen door, that nugget of information would be passed on to Beth.

I doubted she'd be thrilled to hear it.

Which wouldn't exactly break my heart.

24.

A new inspirational saying had gone up at Ripped!, where the walls were now so crammed with inspirational sayings you got whiplash reading them all. This one read: "RE-RACKING YOUR WEIGHTS BURNS FAT FASTER THAN CARDIO, ACCORDING TO A STUDY WE JUST MADE UP.

Bryan had just finished putting it up when Courtney and I walked in. He stepped back to admire it the way you would a fine painting in a museum.

"What do you think?" he asked.

"Love the tone," I said. "Whimsical. Droll. With just the right touch of self-mockery."

"Yet conveying a serious message," Courtney added, nodding thoughtfully. "The need for orderliness. For a sense of communal responsibility. For the notion that – even on the micro level of a small, unostentatious gym – one should be skeptical of the so-called research being conducted into so many aspects of physical fitness."

Bryan shot us a blank look.

"Whatever," he said finally. "I just want these fucking slobs to pick up after themselves."

He went behind the counter, gulped down some coffee and slumped dejectedly on a stool.

"What's the matter, hon?" Courtney asked. "You look like someone ran over your dog."

"You didn't see it yet?" Bryan said.

He grabbed his laptop and turned it so the screen faced us. There at the top was the source of this morning's gloom-fest, a Twitter post that blared: EFC POISED TO DELIVER HISTORIC BEAT-DOWN! COME OUT AND WATCH US DESTROY THE HAYSEEDS FROM RIPPED! THE GREAT BURPEES CHALLENGE IS TWO WEEKS FROM TODAY! BE AFRAID, RIPPED! BE VERY AFRAID!

Accompanying it was a photo of a grinning J. Kenneth Oberkfell and the same merry band of EFC leg-humpers who had sauntered into our gym with him weeks ago. Pointing menacingly at the camera, like a WWE villain about to clobber someone with a folding chair, was Lars, the burpees automaton who had so freaked us out.

"Wow," Courtney said. "Classy bunch, aren't they?"

Bryan moaned: "They're gonna put that crap all over social media to make us look like losers – even *before* they beat our ass in the contest." He looked at me. "I'm surprised they didn't take out an ad in that rag you work for, too. Or maybe they did and I missed it."

No, I assured him, nothing like that had run in my rag. Although the *Herald* was so starved for revenue, the advertising folks would break out the champagne and party hats for a full-pager of one gym taunting another.

"But why so worked up?" I said. "It's just trash talk. They're just trying to intimidate us. Get in our heads."

"Well, they're definitely in *my* head," he muttered. "It's like they moved in, destroyed the place after an all-night rager, and now I can't get rid of them."

We left Bryan to wallow in his misery. I had an off-day from my prep sessions with Oven Mitts, so we went looking for the rest of the Big Five.

Jamison, we knew, would not be posting today. He had a rare early-morning assignment for WBGB at a petting zoo in Carroll County. Apparently, the station was under the assumption that what viewers crave most at 7 a.m. as they dash around getting ready for work, wolfing down breakfast and seeing the kids off to school, is footage of cuddly baby goats, pigs and lambs, as well as an overly-enthusiastic interview with the animals' owners.

Why the station had tapped its lead investigative reporter for such puffery was another mystery. The assignment editor had told Jamison it was simply due to a manpower shortage. But Jamison had hinted darkly at a feud between him and the station manager, who apparently took out his revenge by dispatching a Peabody Award-winning member of the I-Team to do a mindless feature on juvenile farm animals.

We found Harvey and Mikey near the cardio machines. There, Mikey was busy sending silent hate waves toward a skinny young woman 20 feet away who, lost in the music pulsating through her cordless headphones, bopped blissfully atop the gym's only functioning stair-stepper.

"What is this, 'Dancing with the Stars?'" he growled. "You don't need a stair-stepper for that shit! She can do that anywhere!"

Radiating telepathic loathing toward those tying up the machines was not an uncommon practice for the Big Five. Some of us believed we could actually penetrate the groggy subconscious of these equipment-hogs, at least enough for them to become dimly aware that: *OK, someone's waiting on me ....*

The problem with Mikey was that he rarely left it at that.

Instead, if the person on the machine failed to vacate in a timely fashion, Mikey would saunter over and park himself uncomfortably close by. Then he would make a big show of tapping his foot, checking his watch and sighing audibly.

Subtle he was not.

This had earned Mikey a reputation as a cranky – and possibly demented – senior citizen, one other members should approach with caution. Even the young muscle-heads with their bulging biceps, backward ball caps and cobra neck tats tended not to dally on a piece of equipment if Mikey lurked nearby.

The price of a confrontation with him – either verbal or physical – was deemed too high. After all, how would it look to be seen berating or punching the crap out of a codger with thick glasses, baggy sweatpants and a "World's Most Awesome Grandpa!" T-shirt just because he was a bit of a pest?

For his part, Mikey seemed totally comfortable being tagged as the gym's crazy old coot, someone who could ruin your workout in a heartbeat. In fact, he was about to go thermo-nuclear on the dancing queen atop the stair-stepper when Jamison suddenly appeared in our midst.

"Well, well, if it isn't Edward R. Murrow!" Harvey sang out. "Just back from Lil' Paws N' Hoofs! My, that was some hard-hitting journalism this morning!"

"Hey, Jaymo," Mikey added, "the station just called. Looks like a baby alpaca escaped from its pen. They need Baltimore's 'Most Trusted 24-Hour News Source' back out there for an update."

Jamison scowled and loosened his tie. He was still wearing his pricey Cole Haan wing-tip oxford shoes and navy Bonobos suit, which seemed a particularly bad wardrobe choice for traipsing around a sodden enclosure in the middle of nowhere filled with skittish animals and their droppings.

"All of you," he said, "can go fuck yourselves. And here I'm about to deliver some good news. For which you buttheads will thank me profusely."

"Let me guess," Harvey said. "You got us free tickets to the baby chicks exhibit?"

Jamison ignored him.

"Gather 'round, folks," he said, lowering his voice and looking around furtively. "How'd you like to visit Oven Mitts' old stomping grounds? That's right: I'm talking the Big House in Hagerstown."

OK, he had our attention.

"How do we do that?" I asked. "We have to murder someone first? 'Cuz I got a pain-in-the-ass exec editor I'm willing to ice. If that's what it takes."

"Easy, big guy," Jamison said. "No need to ice anyone. This is courtesy of a good buddy of mine, the chief flack for the Department of Corrections. He said he could arrange a tour for us. Not only that, he said the warden – who's apparently been there forever – remembers Oven Mitts from back in the day. And he'd be willing to talk to us, too."

As we gaped in astonishment, Jamison chuckled.

"Didn't all you, ahem, *detectives* say you wanted to learn everything possible about Oven Mitts? Well, here's your chance. What's better than visiting the locked-down hellscape of violence and sodomy where he spent years as a guest of the state?

"Now I ask you," he continued, smiling broadly, "did your boy Jaymo come through or what?"

We had to admit he had. For all his smug, self-congratulatory bullshit at times, WBGB's lead investigative reporter – and foremost chronicler of petting zoos --had *definitely* come through.

It took a minute to sink in: the Big Five were going on a road trip!

To one of the most notorious lockups on the East Coast!

Filled with some of the worst bad guys in the country!

Whoo-hoo!

Were we lucky or what?!

25.

Harvey shivered involuntarily as he stared at the massive stone walls ringed with coils of lethal razor wire and the twin guard towers manned by hard-eyed men in drab uniforms toting shotguns. Bathed in shadows, the Maryland Correctional Institution-Hagerstown, with its Gothic-looking clock spire jutting into the sky like the angry finger of God, seemed even more forbidding in person than it did in photos.

The total effect was like something out of "The Shawshank Redemption."

"Oh, man," Harvey said, "I'd last 10 seconds in this place. First time someone said 'Yo, white boy, got a smoke?' That's it, I'm dead of a heart attack."

He shook his head and took a long pull off a Heineken.

"Little early for that, isn't it?" Courtney said.

"Oh, excuse me," Harvey sneered. "I didn't know this was a church outing."

"It's 10 in the morning!" Courtney said. "Can't you at least wait 'til we leave to get hammered?"

Harvey rolled his eyes.

"Know what, Sister Courtney? You're right. I'm ashamed of myself. I have *sinned*, Sister! I'm drinking a *beer!* What was I thinking! Now if you'd please summon a priest, I, as a good Catholic boy, will seek immediate absolution to save my soul."

Courtney shook her head and walked away, although not

before murmuring: "A good Catholic jackass, maybe" under her breath.

"Guys, *please!*" Jamison said. "Could we continue this scintillating conversation later? They're waiting for us inside."

"No, no," Harvey said, "Sister Courtney's right! I've seen the error of my ways! In fact, priest or no priest, I'm checking myself into rehab as soon as we get home."

He drained the last of the Heineken and tossed the empty bottle in the car trunk before issuing a long, ungodly belch that echoed across the parking lot.

"Great!" Jamison said, throwing up his hands. "Why don't we just make an announcement: 'Hey folks, the cringey hillbillies from Ripped! are in the house!'"

The sniping between various members of the Big Five had started early on our two-hour car ride from Baltimore to rural Washington County. A report on the radio that the Powerball jackpot had reached a record $750 million triggered an animated discussion on what effect such a haul might have on the winning ticketholder's psyche.

"It'd be disastrous!" insisted Jamison, our driver for the day. "People can't handle that kind of instant, inconceivable wealth. It screws up the hard-wiring in their brain. Throws off their moral compass, too. Pretty soon it makes them *miserable*. I read one study that says 70 per cent of lottery winners are broke within seven years."

"Well, I'd like a shot at that kind of misery," Mikey piped up from the back seat. "You give me that payday, I'm shacking up somewhere in the Caribbean with a hot, young senorita. And you'll never hear from me again."

Courtney snorted. "What would a hot young thing see in an old goat like you?"

"She'd see $750 mil for starters," Mikey said. "I got a little something else for her too, Court." He gazed down at his crotch before giving her a lecherous wink. "Actually, from what women tell me, it ain't so little, either."

"Oh, *please*," Courtney said. "I think I'm gonna be sick. . ."

"I'm telling you, Mikey," Jamison said, "these huge jackpots are nothing but trouble. Look at all the nightmare stories about people pissing the money away on luxury cars and yachts and big-ass mansions.

"Plus now everyone the lottery-winner knows has their hand out: family, friends, neighbors, ex-wives, etc. They come out of the woodwork. And if you just won $750 mil, now you don't know *who* to trust. Are people being nice because they like you? Or are they just angling for a slice of that loot?

"No, believe me," Jamison concluded gravely, "money can't buy happiness."

Hearing this, Mikey feigned astonishment.

"Is that right?" he said. "Gee, I never heard that before! Let me write that down." He pretended to scribble in the palm of his hand. "Money...can't buy...what was that last part again, Jaymo?"

As Jamison turned crimson with rage and stomped on the accelerator, sending us off the shoulder of I-70 at 85 mph, Mikey cackled madly. Mercifully, that killed all conversation until we pulled up to MCI-H. Once the dust-up between Harvey and Courtney finally settled down, it was agreed that we'd go inside and get on with our visit, if for no other reason than to prevent more bickering – and possibly even bloodshed – in the parking lot.

This was not my first time in a max-security facility. Over the years, I had done many columns on bad guys behind bars.

But as we made our way through the various security check-points – including a body scanner and a room where we locked away our cell phones – it occurred to me that you never get used to the oppressive atmosphere of prison.

The sounds of heavy metal gates buzzing open and clanging shut, the din of noise and the wave of heat, body odor and industrial-strength Lysol everywhere, the skeptical glances of world-weary corrections officers wondering if you're another delegation of clue-less do-gooders bent on lobbying for more reforms that will only make their jobs even more dangerous and terrifying – all of it can be unnerving.

At one point, as we made our way to the warden's office, Courtney reached for my hand and squeezed it. But after taking a quick glance at her, I could see she was fine. Hell, this was a veteran trauma nurse who saw more harrowing sights in a day than most people do in a lifetime.

This was a woman who'd seen legs snap in half like kindling and brain tapeworms and near disembowelments caused by enraged canines. A woman who saw a man walk –under his own power! – into a trauma unit with Bowie knife lodged in his skull like a spatula blade in a cheeseball.

No, she wasn't about to become unglued here.

Warden Otis T. Rackley turned out to be a genial, ruddy-faced man in his mid-60's. The rheumy eyes, the broken blood vessels that spider-webbed his nose and the prodigious gut spilling over his belt suggested he enjoyed a drink or two on occasion – possibly on many occasions.

Yet who could blame him? The job was a pressure-cooker: overseeing a dank 75-year-old penitentiary housing some 2,300 tortured souls, many of them hardened cons seething over past injustices, present-day beefs, the overall unfairness of life and the daily threat of violence they faced. Not to mention the shitty food they were forced to consume daily.

"Every one of 'em is innocent, too" Warden Rackley said with a phlegmy chuckle "'Least, that's what they tell me. They're in here 'cuz the prosecutor set them up. Or their lawyer wasn't worth a shit. Or the witnesses at their trial lied their asses off. Or the evidence was planted."

But Alejandro Maldonado was different, the warden recalled.

"That fella was filled with remorse for what he'd done. You could read it in his face from the get-go. Ended up doing so many good things in here. Might have saved some lives, too."

Saved some lives?

But before we could explore that fascinating tidbit, he stood, reached for his hat and said: "C'mon, I'll show you around."

26.

Warden Rackley proved to be the ideal tour guide, fearlessly plunging us into the steady stream of inmates mopping hallways and polishing floors, going off to various treatment programs or headed for jobs in the laundry, wood-working shop or library. All the while, he regaled us with fascinating details about the prison and folksy anecdotes about some of the notable criminals housed there over the years.

"Arthur Bremer was a guest of ours, did you know that?" he asked as we passed the medical wing.

Arthur Bremer?

The Arthur Bremer?

The nutjob who tried to assassinate George Wallace back in the 70's? And left the then-presidential candidate paralyzed for life?"

"Yep," the warden said. "The shooting was at a campaign stop in Maryland. In Laurel, I believe. I was a young CO when Bremer arrived. He was here for many years, too. Finally got out in 2007."

So the sentences of Bremer and Alejandro Maldonado had overlapped at some point! How interesting!

I had seen plenty of photos of Bremer in the *Herald* archives. With Laurel practically in our back yard, the newspaper had done a ton of stories on the 21-year-old, unemployed busboy with the creepy, enigmatic smile who had stalked Wallace for weeks before finally pumping three bullets in him with a .38.

Now I wondered if Bremer and Oven Mitts had ever crossed paths in the can. If so, were they buddies? Did they lift weights together? Shoot baskets? Watch TV?

Did they share a lunch table and bitch about the chow?

As we made our way around the prison, we attracted curious glances from everyone we passed. It was Courtney, to no one's surprise, who received most of the attention, although Warden Rackley's presence kept the leering and wolf whistles to a tolerable level.

In a pre-visit phone call with an aide in the warden's office, the basic fashion advice given to her had been: dress like a Quaker.

This turned out to be a bit of hyperbole. But the list of prohibited clothing for women was extensive: no tube tops, tank tops or halter tops. Nothing see-through. Ditto anything form-fitting, such as mini-skirts, spandex, leggings, etc. No shorts. No tops with revealing necklines. No dresses with slits up the side.

"So a teddy from the Love Connection boutique is out of the question?" she'd asked, deadpan. The aide, Courtney reported, failed to find the humor in this. ("Not even a courtesy ha, ha!") Instead, he quickly hung up.

Yet even dressed in a demure navy suit, white blouse and sensible pumps, Courtney was still a show-stopper. Hell, I felt like leering and wolf-whistling myself. But there was no time for that. The warden kept us moving at a brisk pace.

After we visited the gym and exercise yard, Warden Rackley announced: "Next stop, the meat-processing plant."

Wait, *what?*

A meat-processing plant?

In the middle of a prison?

Who knew?!

Yet a short walk took us to a low-slung building that was one of the true marvels of MCI-H: a 12,000-square-foot packing-house, staffed by scores of inmates, where thousands of pounds of meat were butchered and processed each week and sold to state entities like prisons and universities.

"Uh, Warden," Mikey whispered as we gazed around, "I don't know whether you've noticed. But many of these men seem to be brandishing very large and very sharp knives. Which – I'm just guessing here – could be used to, um, stab someone."

Rackley smiled and draped an arm around Mikey's shoulder.

"Can't do much butchering without big ol' knives, right pardner?" he said. "But everyone pretty much behaves. There's a waiting list a mile long for these jobs. The pay's good – well, for prison, anyway. And it's good training for when they get out."

"Good *training?*" Harvey said incredulously. "For what? Their next gang fight?"

The warden didn't answer. Instead he pointed to a tall, scowl-ing inmate with a shaved head, multiple piercings and elaborate face tattoos who was energetically attacking a slab of beef with a cleaver.

"See that guy there? He's doing 10 years for manslaughter. Got in a street fight outside a strip joint and killed the other guy. Stomped his head against the curb. Anyway, I talked to him a few months ago. Guess what he wants to do when he gets out? Open his own butcher shop. With the skills he learned here."

"Great," Jamison said. "Just the kind of solid citizen I want taking my order for a half-dozen porkchops."

Warden Rackley nodded wearily, seeming to anticipate this reaction.

"Thing is, people change," he said. "You may not believe that, but it's true. God knows we see it every day in here. Sure, a

lot of these knuckleheads will leave here just as vicious and igno-
rant as the day they shuffled in in shackles.

"But for some, prison is their Road-to-Damascus moment.
Remember the story of ol' Saul? In the New Testament?"

"Of course!" Harvey chirped. "It's my favorite."

He said it with such sincerity and conviction that anyone
could see he was full of shit. Harvey, we were certain, wouldn't
know the New Testament from the new iPhone.

The story of ol' Saul? Harvey would think: *What's that, a porn
flick?*

"So Saul saw that blinding light on the road to Damascus,
right?" the warden continued. "Heard the Lord cry out from the
heavens 'Why are you persecuting me?' And just like that, Saul
repented his evil ways. It's *the* classic redemption story.

"Well, this job can give you moments like that. Keeps you
from thinking all of society's headed straight down the crapper."

Our next-to-last stop was the prison kitchen. There we were
engulfed in a cacophony of banging pots and pans, trays being
slammed onto stainless-steal counters and clouds of hissing
steam rising to the ceiling as the dishwashers were loaded and
unloaded.

The place looked clean and well-run, and whatever was
cooking smelled delicious. Nevertheless, we had already declined
the warden's gracious invitation to stay for lunch, citing a press-
ing need to return to Baltimore post-haste.

This, though, was a little white lie. The truth was that a day
earlier, vaguely recalling something about contaminated food in
the Maryland prison system, I had again called on the most brilliant (and sullen) newspaper librarian in the country, Benjamin
A. Parisi.

Sure enough, Benny had found clips in the *Herald's* archives detailing massive outbreaks of E. coli at the Cumberland, Jessup and Hagerstown lockups in recent years. (This time he didn't flash the finger during my attempts to goad him into conversation. Instead, he rolled his eyes and made a thrusting up-and-down motion with his fist, the universal sign for: Dealing with a jerk-off here.)

After seeing Benny's research, the Big Five had decided unanimously to dine elsewhere. Yet exactly where remained a mystery. The only place near the prison that served food appeared to be a dingy biker bar off I-70, where the fear of contracting a vicious gastro-intestinal infection was outweighed by the fear of getting our asses kicked.

Our tour ended in the cafeteria, just as the first lunch shift for the inmates was ending. Warden Rackley directed us to an empty table in the corner. After we sat, he removed his hat, ran a hand through his thinning hair, and regarded us gravely.

"Back in my office," he began, "I said your man Alejandro Maldonado might have saved some lives in here. I'll tell you about that. But first, let me give you some background."

Maldonado, the warden said, was one of the rare inmates who, over the years, had earned the grudging respect of all three of the prison's largest factions: blacks, Hispanics and whites. He did this largely by being open and charitable to all, rare qualities in an environment where emotional distancing and knee-jerk reactions of violence are the norm.

"But he wasn't like that right away," Warden Rackley said. "He came here a broken human being. Most of the men in here don't talk about the crimes they committed on the outside. Alejandro was the opposite. He told whoever would listen – you couldn't shut him up --about the horrible thing he'd done to his wife in a moment of madness, how he hoped it wouldn't define him forever, but he knew it would."

Wracked with shame and guilt, the warden went on, Maldonado lapsed into a depression that lasted months. But when he finally emerged from it, he was a new man. Driven to atone and desperate for a new start, he threw himself into the study of Eastern philosophy, eventually earning a master's degree from a top university in Europe.

"He once told me 'Warden, the self is an illusion.' I don't pretend to know what that means. He talked about how we were all connected. 'Part of a universal whole,' he said. A lot of it was deep stuff. *Way* too deep for me."

A fitness nut even then, Maldonado also spent hours learning about nutrition, holistic methods of fighting anxiety and depression, Mindfulness and other ways of reducing stress. He was generous in sharing his new-found knowledge with other inmates, patiently answering all their questions, talking those in distress off the ledge and encouraging those on the verge of exploding to open up about their feelings and let some of the anger out.

"Sounds like a regular Dr. Phil," Mikey said, rolling his eyes.

"You're being snide, I know," Warden Rackley said, not unkindly. "But in a lot of ways, he was. And Lord did we need him that September afternoon 20 years ago."

For weeks leading up to that fateful day, the warden continued, prison staff had sensed tension growing between the black and Mexican inmates.

"What you need to understand, is that absolutely *anything* can trigger a disturbance in here. Stealing from another inmate. Ratting out someone to the guards. Moving in on someone's drug operation.

"Or little piddling stuff. Accidentally stepping on someone's foot. Walking across someone's personal space. This incident started over soup."

Soup?

It happened in a flash, the warden said. A black inmate in the food line accused the Mexican inmate server of spitting in his soup. The Mexican server snarled the n-word and told him to shut the f up and keep moving.

"I'm a Christian," the warden said, "so I'll spare you the other stuff that was said. But all of sudden you had a group of blacks and a group of Mexicans ready to kill each other. Half of 'em had shanks, too. You know, homemade knives. They make 'em out of sharpened toothbrush handles, razor blades stuck in pieces of wood, metal pieces torn from fans – whatever they can get their hands on. Make 'em so fast, we can't confiscate them all."

Suddenly, into this roiling mass of enraged inmates, strode Alejandro Maldonado.

"I was there and I'll never forget it," Warden Rackley said. "The guards were just about to move in. Instead, he got in the middle of the two sides. He stood there with his arms spread wide, like a boxing referee keeping the fighters separated before the bell rings. And all he said was: 'Please . . .don't.'

"That's it, two words. *'Please…don't.'* And just like that, it was over. Oh, there was still some cursing and muttering back and forth. But almost immediately, both sides started backing down, eyes lowered, almost as if they were *embarrassed* to be fighting in front of this decent, upstanding individual. Damndest thing I ever saw."

When the warden finished, we sat there in stunned silence. It was almost too much to take in. Oven Mitts Maldonado as the Great Peacemaker! The Gandhi of the Guardhouse! The Mandela of MCI-H!

The Mob Whisperer!

Our heads were spinning.

We left a few minutes later, after thanking the warden profusely for his time. No one was in the mood for lunch so we blew off the biker bar, where at least 20 Harleys were now parked outside, their owners glowering at us as we passed.

On the long ride home, we couldn't stop thinking about Oven Mitts.

"So what, this guy was some kind of hero back in the day?" Harvey asked. "Is that what we're thinking now?"

"Kinda looks that way," Jamison said.

Even Courtney's icy disdain for the man seemed to crack a bit. "He was probably working some angle. But, OK, that was a pretty courageous act. Pretty self-less, too."

Suddenly, Harvey leaned forward in the back seat and cleared his throat.

"Speaking of heroes," he began, "a great man once said: 'When your time comes to die, be not like those whose hearts are filled with fear of death, so that when their time comes, they weep and pray for a little more time to live their lives over again in a different way. Sing your death song, and die like a hero going home.'"

We stared as if he'd lapsed into Mandarin Chinese.

"*What?*" Harvey said, looking around the car. "Tecumseh. Everyone knows that quote."

"*Nobody* knows that fucking quote!" Courtney roared. "The question is: how does a certifiable nitwit like *you* know that quote?"

Harvey didn't answer. Instead, he sat back, crossed his arms and spent the rest of the trip wearing a satisfied smile.

Not until we reached the Baltimore Beltway did he speak again, this time to ask the existential question now on everyone's mind: "So...do we still think he's a dick?"

27.

With the Great Burpees Challenge fast approaching, I was getting lots of comments about my weight-loss "journey."

The latest to mention it was Tami, the front desk ingenue at Ripped! Studying me as I walked through the doors one morning, she flashed her most luminescent smile. All 32 teeth, incisors and canines, premolars and molars and wisdom, came together in perfect harmony, sparkling like white mosaic tiles.

"Looking good, Jack Doherty!" she sang out.

"Feeling good," I replied. "Down almost 15 pounds so far."

Hearing this, she jumped up and down and squealed with excitement, as if she'd just won Beyonce tickets. Springing from behind the counter, she pulled me into a tight hug.

"Whoa!" she said, stepping back to appraise me. "Are those six-pack abs I'm feeling?"

"Not a chance," I said. "You're talking to Mr. Zero Abs. A fact confirmed each time I walk past a mirror with my shirt off."

Undeterred, she fixed me with an earnest look and said: "It's been a long journey for you, hasn't it?"

Oh, you have no idea, I wanted to say. *In my quest for even a semblance of fitness, I have traversed many continents, sailed across countless seas, climbed the highest mountains, all to achieve this slightly-less-flabby-than-before bod upon which you now gaze...*

But all I said was: "Yes. Yet the journey never really ends, does it?"

"It never does!" she chirped. "But remember: you're not alone on the journey! We here at Ripped! are with you every step of the way."

"I can't tell you how reassuring that is," I said. "To have that kind of support on this long, strange trip…it's almost impossible to put it into words."

"*Awww*," Tami said. She reached for a tissue and dabbed her eyes.

I reached for a tissue, too, but mainly to ward off another hug, which seemed imminent.

Was I being cruel?

Yanking her chain like that?

Probably. In which case I fully expected the day to come when, upon realizing said chain was yanked, she'd mutter an angry oath, pick up a machete and come looking for me.

Tami wasn't the only one remarking on my physical transformation. A few days earlier at the *Herald,* Debbie Nesbo and I found ourselves in the snack room at the same time, in front of the same vending machine, gazing at row after row of the depressing fare it offered.

When I made my selection and a granola bar whirred from its little storage coil and dropped with a thud, she asked: "Are they any good?"

"They're horrible," I said. "But it's a *good* kind of horrible. Dry. Tasteless. Tremendously unsatisfying. You should try one."

She smiled knowingly. "Three months ago, you would've never bought one of those. Not only that, you would've mocked anyone who did."

"People change," I said. "I'm practically a Nature Valley spokesman now."

"How much weight have you lost?"

"I'm not at liberty to say, Deb. Doctor's orders. You know how they are."

"Minske says you're having a classic mid-life crisis. He says you're a walking cliché."

"Minske's a walking dickhead. So we're even."

"The fire-engine red sports car, the hair-plugs, the 25-year-old girlfriend with the fake boobs – he says that's who you are now."

"Fake boobs? Is that a shot at the less well-endowed, Deb? I thought the Sisterhood was supposed to stick together? Besides my girlfriend's boobs are real. Trust me, I checked."

Realizing the futility of further conversation, she turned back to the vending machine.

"Well, good luck on your weight-loss journey, Jack," she said. Patting her mid-section, she smiled ruefully. "Sure wish I had your discipline."

As she left, I couldn't help noticing that her choice of a late-afternoon snack was a pack of Frosted Strawberry Pop Tarts. The damage: 420 calories. 10 grams of fat. Plus enough sugar to leave the average human vibrating like a gong.

Does it sound like I was being judgy? Maybe a tad.

But I *wasn't* being hypocritical. Months earlier, if those had been the last Pop Tarts in that machine, I would have tackled Deb from behind and gnawed off her hand to get at them. But now I was a changed man.

Now I had joined a gym. Now I worked out diligently (well, sort of) and watched what I ate (kind of) and limited my beer-swilling to weekends. Now I was determined to get in the best shape possible, if for no other reason than to avoid total embarrassment in the upcoming burpees tong war with EFC.

Even my ex-wife felt compelled to deliver a commentary

on my changed appearance, although, in classic form, she was unable to pinpoint exactly what had changed.

"Is it the hair? Is that what's different?" Beth asked after dropping the kids off at my apartment one day.

We were standing in the tiny patch of weed-filled vegetation that constituted my front lawn. She looked me up and down, straining to determine why her former husband – the pale, pudgy physical wreck of her memory – no longer looked quite as pale, pudgy and physically wrecked.

"I've lost weight," I said at last.

"No, that's not it," she said dismissively. "You're back on Just for Men, aren't you?"

Unbelievable. Only Beth could make a simple hair-coloring product used by millions sound like a dangerous narcotic.

"I'm telling you I've lost 15 pounds," I said.

She regarded me suspiciously, as if lying about my weight was something I routinely did throughout the course of our marriage, another thing that led to the break-up.

I threw up my hands.

"Should I get on the scale for you, Bethie? Is that what you need to see?"

"No, that won't be necessary" she sniffed. She gave me a last lingering look before heading back to her car.

"Too bad you didn't look that good when we were together," she said over her shoulder. "Maybe if you had . . ." The car door slammed as her voice trailed off.

Maybe if I had what? I wanted to shout.

Maybe if I had, you wouldn't have carried on a sleazy back-door affair with sterling neighbor Dan Henson? (Who, by the way, was no Jason Momoa himself.)

Maybe if I had you wouldn't have rung in the New Year on your knees in the shadows of our back deck, the pressure-treated wood creaking rhythmically as you went about your appointed task with a penis that a) was not mine and b) was a sight so shocking that, when captured by the powerful beam from my trusty tactical flashlight, simultaneously took my breath away, made me sick to my stomach and broke my heart for a nifty physiological trifecta?

Maybe if I had I could have avoided the weeks of crying jags, sleepless nights and searing, self-lacerating introspection that followed?

Sure. Me being overweight caused all that.

After successfully avoiding another smothering embrace from Tami, I went off to meet Oven Mitts.

This was to be one of our last training sessions before the big contest. As usual, he was already slick with sweat and deep into another personalized warm-up session: lifting a 30-pound medicine ball over his head, bringing it down to chest level, slamming it to the floor, bending over, picking it up again, and doing the whole routine over again.

This, of course, would rightly be considered a full workout in and of itself by 99 per cent of the human race. But not my man Tony Maldon. To him, it was merely "getting loose."

Looks like fun, I thought, watching the veins in his neck bulge hideously and his face contort with the effort. But to Tony, apparently, it *was* a good time.

"Be right with you, partner," he said with a grunt. After five more reps, he tossed the ball in a corner and dried his face with a towel.

"The theme of today's workout is 'Stamina, Stamina, Stamina,'" he announced. "The all-important key to winning a burpees contest. So this'll be a conditioning workout, OK? We'll do 15 burpees, followed by 30-second wall-sits, another 15 burpees, more wall-sits and so on.

"We'll go for 40 minutes. Or as long you can stand it. How's that sound?"

"Awful, Awful, Awful," I said.

He flashed a wan smile and clapped me on the back. The good thing about working out with Oven Mitts was that whenever he proposed a grueling new exercise and I bitched and moaned about it, he assumed I was kidding.

On the other hand, I tried to keep the bitching and moaning to a minimum. Even though we were both warming toward each other, I still didn't want to get on the wrong side of a guy who'd done serious time for murder. Even if he *was* a big peacenik in the slammer and now seemed about as threatening as the old fella grinning and nursing a Bud Light at the bar in the VFW hall.

"No, this is good for you," he said. "Really builds up your endurance. It's great for the quads, glutes and calves. Great for your whole core, really."

"OK, fine," I said. "Let's do it."

Once again, I reminded myself of how anxious I was to not totally suck in the Great Burpees Challenge, and of how much stronger and fitter I felt since starting these prep sessions with Oven Mitts.

Trust this guy and put in the work was my new mantra. I pulled off my sweats and we dragged a couple of floor mats to the center of the room.

"By the way," he said casually, "heard you and your buddies were out in Hagerstown."

28.

I froze.

For maybe 15 seconds, I wasn't sure I could speak. My mouth felt like sand and my throat constricted, as if it had collapsed inwardly and now no sound could escape except for a high-pitched, panicky squeak.

Even if I could find my voice, what would I say?

Why, yes, Tony, we were out in Hagerstown. But not to visit the prison or anything. See, we're all big into agriculture. So we drove to bucolic Washington County to check on this year's soybean crop. The alfalfa crop, too. Turns out it was a banner year for both.

Or:

Sure, we were out there. But it was to tour the famous Civil War battlefields. No, we're not reenactors or anything – those people need to get a life, don't they? But we spent a lovely day at the site of the 1863 Battle of Hagerstown. It's very impressive. You really should check it out.

Or:

What?! Hagerstown? I don't know what you're talking about. I've never heard of the place. Is that even in Maryland?

Each response seemed even more ludicrous than the next. On the other hand, the idea of telling him the truth seemed even more fraught than any bullshit story I could concoct.

How to explain that a bunch of fellow members at his gym were, in essence, playing a silly-ass game of detective and snooping into his dumpster fire of a life, going so far as to visit the notorious penitentiary where he was locked up all those years?

And that we were doing all this simply for a few laughs and a vicarious thrill – *Hey, can you believe it? There's a guy at our gym who knocked off his wife!* And for something to talk about whenever we were bored out of our minds with our workouts?

How freaking juvenile and petty would that sound?

Not only was I speechless but, still hunched over while unfurling my mat, I was afraid to even look at him. Was he rip-shit pissed? Stupid question. Of *course* he was ripped-shit pissed! But *how* ripped-shit pissed was he?

Enough to renounce his pacifist ways and whip out a shank and stick me right then and there? With some sneaky prison move he learned from the Salvadoran MS-13 gang-bangers or the Baltimore Nine-Trey Bloods?

Enough to mount a vicious campaign of psychological terror against the Big Five? One that ranged from slashed tires and poisoned house pets to ominous letters stuffed in our mailboxes, with words cut from newspapers and magazines and pasted together in the manner of a ransom note that read: I KNOW WHERE YOU WENT LAST WEEKEND?

But when I finally glanced over at him, what I saw on his face wasn't anger at all. Instead, there was only sadness – maybe the deepest sadness I'd ever seen. He looked so forlorn, I felt like hugging him.

"So I guess you know," he said.

I nodded dumbly.

He was silent for a moment. Finally he said: "Ah, hell, it was just a matter of time. Sooner or later someone in here was bound to find out."

I still hadn't said a word. I was afraid to move, convinced my knees would buckle and I'd collapse in an embarrassing heap, like a man who'd been bashed in the head with a brick.

"If you're wondering how I know about your visit," he went on, "I still have friends out there. Stayed in touch with a couple of officers, too. They let me know when strangers show up asking questions."

Hearing this, I suddenly felt even dumber than usual.

Well of *course* he still had contacts in Hagerstown! Of *course* he'd find out if a lone woman and four men – whose descriptions eerily matched five knuckleheads he saw regularly at his gym – had been led around the prison by a chatty warden who might as well have held a sign that read: Alejandro Maldonado Info Tour.

"Tony . . ." I blurted at last, still unsure of exactly what I'd say. But he cut me off with a wave of his hand.

"No, it's OK. Let's get on with the workout."

Um, excuse me?

A good-sized nuclear device had just been detonated here – at least metaphorically speaking. The flash of blinding light was still visible, the shock waves could still be felt, the acrid smoke and radiation still spewed.

And we were going to pretend like nothing happened?! That it was business as usual?!

We return you now to our regularly-scheduled workout . . .?

Yet that's pretty much what we did.

What followed was the most surreal workout I had ever experienced. Side by side on our cobalt-blue mats, we did one grueling series of burpees and wall-sits after another, all completed in silence except for our muffled groans and labored breathing.

Still appalled by our earlier conversation, I also found myself strangely adrenalized. Normally I would have been flailing by the second or third set without a break. My lungs would have been burning, my arms aching, my legs feeling weak and rubbery.

But not this time. This time, somehow, I pushed through the pain, determined not to quit and disappoint Oven Mitts even further with a display of congenital wussiness just days before the showdown with EFC.

The truth was, I felt terrible for him, horrified that he'd discovered our stupid little pastime, our mindless adolescent entertainment – even though (thank God) he didn't know the full depth of our shameful prying into his personal life.

Had he suffered enough after spending so much time behind bars for the shocking crime he'd committed as a cocky rug merchant with an unfaithful wife? That wasn't for me to say. But what right did my buddies and I have to add to his misery all these years later?

Some 40 minutes later, when the workout had mercifully ended, I slumped against one wall, gasping for breath. Oven Mitts, as usual, barely seemed winded. He paced around the room before gazing restlessly out the window, as if hoping he might spot a 10-K race he could enter.

"You're getting more and more fit, Jack," he said quietly. "It's great to see."

When he turned around, he wore an even more sorrowful look than before.

"Can I tell you something?" he asked. "I'm not who I used to be. You and your friends need to understand that."

Before I could say anything, he slung his gym bag over his shoulder and headed for the door.

"But those pretentious EFC blowhards?" he said over his shoulder. "We're still gonna knock their dicks in the dirt."

29.

The Golden Saucer was busy the next morning when Courtney and I arrived, the signature smell of stale coffee and burnt bacon wafting everywhere. I had already filled her in on the latest workout with my superstar octogenarian partner and the bombshell he'd dropped. Now it was time to brief the rest of the Big Five.

We commandeered a table in the back, wiping up twin smears of grape jelly and cream cheese somehow missed by the busboy, who looked brutally hungover.

I got right to the point.

"Oven Mitts is on to us," I said. "He knows we were out at the prison asking questions."

As expected, my friends greeted this news with the innate equanimity for which they were known.

"That's it, we're all dead!" Harvey moaned. "D-E-A-D!"

"When he comes for us," Mikey said, "it'll probably be at night. Well, I'll be ready for the bastard. Starting this evening, I'll be doing armed re-con patrols around my property. Dusk to dawn. I suggest the rest of you do the same."

We watched with growing alarm as he poured an entire bottle of syrup over his short stack of blueberry pancakes until only the top was visible, like a small coastal island nearly consumed by rising seas.

Jamison's eyes darted nervously around the room.

"Maybe I should stay off the air for a few weeks," he said.

"Let Oven Mitts calm down. The easiest thing in the world to do is take out a reporter when he's doing a stand-up on a desolate street in, like, West Baltimore.

"What's my photographer gonna do?" he continued. "'Yo Jamison, some old guy with a .357 is creeping up behind you? Oh, and by the way, the studio's coming to you in 15 seconds, so stand by?'"

I pointed at Harvey and said: "What happened to you, Mr. Tough Guy? What happened to 'Bring on those juiced-up MAGA muscleheads, I'll kick their asses from here to Mar-a-Lago?'"

Harvey shook his head. "This guy's different. He's practically a trained assassin. Let's face it: by the end of your first day in the slammer, you've already learned 20 ways to kill a man. Within a week, you could wipe out a Navy SEAL team. I have this on very good authority, by the way."

As she stirred her tea, Courtney rolled her eyes

"You guys are *such* pussies!" she said.

"Easy for you to say," Harvey replied. "He probably won't *kill* you."

"Yeah," Mikey agreed, "he'll probably just make you his sex slave. That's how guys like him operate. Pretty soon you'll be part of the Oven-ettes, squealing and jumping up and down and getting the vapors whenever he's around."

"*Getting the vapors*?!" Courtney exclaimed. "Did you really say that? What century are we in? Who's the president, Millard Fillmore?"

She looked at me pleadingly.

"Jack, for God's sakes, tell these lamebrains the rest of the story. So we don't have to listen to any more of this stupidity."

"OK," I said. 'The rest of the story is that Oven Mitts didn't seem angry we were out there. Or that his secret was out. If anything, he seemed defeated. Depressed. Somber."

Mikey snorted derisively. "C'mon! That's the oldest trick in the book! The Indians – I guess we're supposed to call 'em Native Americans now, right? – played those kind of head games in the Old West, remember?

"They'd sit around a fire with the U.S. soldiers and break out the peace pipe and act like, 'OK, you guys are an indomitable force, you have way too many troops, we could never beat you. So let's bury the hatchet, OK?'

"Then five minutes after the soldiers left thinking 'Well, that was a nice visit, I don't think we'll have any more problems from those folks,' the Sioux or the Apaches or whoever would be whooping and smearing on war paint and jumping on their horses to attack another wagon train."

He shook his head emphatically. "Uh-uh, sorry. I don't buy that 'defeated' business he's peddling. Not for a minute."

"Me either, Jack," Harvey said. "Oven Mitts is setting you up." (*For the kill,* he mouthed silently to the others.)

I looked at Courtney, who shrugged as if to say: *It's useless. There's no getting through to these imbeciles.* She pulled a compact mirror from her purse and proceeded to touch up her lipstick, a tacit signal that she was done with the whole discussion.

But I was on a mission, determined that my three cynical friends see that Oven Mitts no longer posed a threat to anyone. Maybe they hadn't seen what I'd seen yesterday in his mournful hound dog visage, the weary resignation in his eyes. But hadn't the trip to Hagerstown convinced them of *anything?*

"Didn't you guys listen to Warden Rackley?" I asked. "Did you even hear a *word* he said? He told us Oven Mitts was a changed man, didn't he? That he'd had some kind of jailhouse conversion, some come-to-Jesus moment?

"Look at the guy's legacy! Never gave the guards a problem. Was like a human Xanax around the other inmates. Single-handedly stopped a riot. Are you kidding me? When his sentence was up, I'm surprised they didn't bake him a cake and order a limo to drive him home."

Progress!

Suddenly the looks on my buddies' faces were a little less hostile, a tad less skeptical. Their collective paranoia had diminished, if only slightly. Harvey and Mikey exchanged hopeful looks. Jamison's right leg, which had been jiggling furiously, slowed to a less manic tempo.

I pressed on, convinced of the righteousness of my cause.

"Look at it from a practical standpoint, too. We *talked* about this! Does anyone *really* think Oven Mitts would be dumb enough to come after one of us? And risk spending whatever time he has left on this earth back behind bars?"

Now the sense of relief at the table was palpable. Harvey and Mikey exhaled audibly. Jamison's annoying lower body gyrations stopped. Tentative smiles appeared. Fist bumps were exchanged.

Within seconds, all three seemed almost giddy, like you'd feel after missing a flight that crashed into the side of a mountain. I knew I could rot in hell for what I was about to do next. But I couldn't resist.

"In all honesty," I added, "the only one Oven Mitts *really* seemed pissed at was Harvey. I'm paraphrasing here. But at one point in the workout, I remember him practically shaking with anger and muttering: 'That skinny son of a bitch, he'll get his.'"

The color drained from Harvey's face.

"*SEE?*" he wailed, standing and tossing down his napkin. "This is what I'm talking about! The guy's a monster! A killing machine! But why's he mad at *me?* What did *I* ever do to him?"

"Harvey, he's *kidding!*" Courtney said. "Jack, tell him you're kidding . . ."

"I wish I could, Court. But what Oven Mitts said he'd do to Harv, that business with the shears and the testicles – that came from a pretty dark place."

"JACK!! STOP THAT THIS INSTANT! THE POOR GUY'S GONNA STROKE OUT!"

She was right. Harvey's eyes were wide with alarm. Sweat was beading on his forehead. He looked as if he wanted to hurl himself out a window.

"OK, fine," I said. "Harv, I'm just messing with you."

He looked at me, then at Courtney, then back at me, still shaken and confused, trying to determine if we were telling the truth this time. Finally convinced that we were, his body seemed to go limp. He sank back down in his seat, although not before pointing at me and whispering: "You motherfucker! I'll get you for this!"

My work at the Saucer was done. I had called the Big Five together simply as a courtesy, so they wouldn't be startled if Oven Mitts ever hinted in their presence that he knew we were poking around in his private life.

With that discussion over, we turned our attention, with morbid fascination, to the eating habits of Mikey.

He had ordered another short stack of pancakes – banana-walnut this time, topped with great, puffy clouds of whipped cream and sprinkles. These he assaulted noisily, smacking his lips and licking his fingers to corral any errant sprinkles on the plate before shoving them back in his mouth.

"That's disgusting!" Courtney said.

"You don't have to watch me," Mikey growled.

"I can't *not* watch you! You're like the gastronomic version of a 10-car pile-up."

"*Gastronomic?*" he said. "Is that even a word? Or some arcane term you learned at that fancy college you went to? What was it again? Sarah Lawrence? Vassar?"

"Try community college for two years. Then nursing school at the University of Maryland."

"Whatever," Mikey said, stabbing another forkful of pancakes and chewing with clamorous gusto.

Listening to this biting, ceaseless squabbling, the new soundtrack of my life, it occurred to me, not for the first time, that I had fallen in with the perfect band of soulmates, each of them seemingly as traumatized, resentful and aggrieved as I seemed to be.

Everywhere we went, you could feel the love.

Now we needed Oven Mitts to feel it, too.

30.

When I showed up at my old house to pick up the kids for the weekend, Beth was at the kitchen counter, eyes glued to the Weather Channel.

"There's a cold front coming in," she announced. "Lots of dense air. My God, look at the Doppler radar! We're really in for it now."

There was a huskiness to her voice that I recognized instantly. Even before we were married, she'd been an avid consumer of so-called "weather porn." Reports of torrential rain, tornados, hurricanes, typhoons, thunderstorms, blizzards, massive flooding on a Biblical scale – all of it stirred something in her that bordered on the sensual – if not the outright sexual.

Video of rain-swollen rivers washing away houses in Arkansas, giant mudslides wiping out multi-million-dollar mansions on the West Coast, hellish wildfires raging across Northern California and threatening Lake Tahoe, cars hitting sheets of black ice and skidding off the Beltway before banging off guardrails in a shower of sparks – there was no end to her lust for this stuff.

A friend of hers once told me: "Extreme weather is erotica to Beth. That may be difficult for you, as the husband, to deal with."

For me, as the husband, it was.

Locally, nothing aroused her more than the prospect of the

dreaded "wintry mix." The mere mention of the triple whammy of freezing rain, ice and snow caused her to bound around the house in a frenzy, eagerly peering out the window every half-hour to see if the terrible event had begun.

When bad weather hit, she devoured coverage of panicked shoppers at the supermarkets stocking up on bread, milk and toilet paper and exchanging worried glances in the long checkout lines. The jittery hordes descending on The Home Depot and Lowe's excited her, too, as they scrambled feverishly for snow shovels, snow blowers, sidewalk de-icers, ice scrapers, portable generators and anything else that might stave off serious injury and/or death during this perilous time.

As for the meteorologists who forecast these "weather events," the men and woman in nicely-tailored suits and fashionable floaty dresses talking and gesturing in front of brightly-colored maps that showed the latest high-pressure system sweeping down from Canada and low-pressure system pushing up from the Gulf of Mexico – why, she regarded them as practically gods.

How blessed they were to be able to divine what was coming for us from the heavens! Sure, they were aided by the latest technology, powerful super-computers and dual-phase radars and weather satellites overseen by the National Oceanic and Atmospheric Administration. She knew this, of course.

But Beth had also convinced herself that these well-dressed, well-coifed men and women also had intuitive powers. Even without all the sophisticated tools at their disposal, they would, she was certain, instinctively know the answer to the question always foremost in her mind: when should she and her family take shelter?

"Are the kids ready?" I asked.

She shrugged.

The shrug said it all. Who could think about stuffing back-packs with freshly-laundered T-shirts, shorts, underwear and pajamas – plus whatever toothbrushes, inhalers, vitamins and medications were needed – when a fresh weather calamity might be on the horizon?

"If it's gonna be as bad as you think," I said, "I better get them to my place right away. We'll hurry down to the basement and crouch in a corner with our arms over our heads 'til we hear the all-clear siren."

It was only then that she turned to look at me.

"There you go, making fun of me again," she said, frowning. "And anyway, you live in an apartment. A very *modest* apart-ment, I might add. So you don't even *have* a basement. Although at times like this, I wish you did."

She made my lack of a basement sound like a moral failing on my part, another example of me dropping the ball as a father, much as I had as a husband.

The truth was, I had become more and more worried about Beth's weather fetish affecting the kids. Would they grow up freaking out every time they saw a dark cloud overhead?

Would a few flurries falling from the sky trigger panic attacks and frantic trips to the ER, followed by years of intensive (and expensive) psycho-therapy?

Would the children start wearing Weather Channel gear – sweatshirts and windbreakers and ball caps with the company's prominent blue-and-white logo – to school, drawing stares and derisive laughter from classmates, who would surely find their outfits mega-dorky?.

And what would the teachers and administrators think? Would they red-flag Emmie and Liam as being the possi-ble victims of parental abuse, forced to attend class in junior weather-person costumes their mom and dad *knew* would draw ridicule on both the school grounds and social media?

So far I saw no signs of this happening. But I remained cautious. If either child ever let drop in casual conversation their admiration for, say, NOAA's new Tornadic Vortex Signature, the algorithm that detects the likely presence of tornado activity, I knew I'd have to take action.

"I'm sorry you find my living conditions to be sub-par," I said. "The kids seem to like it just fine."

"They're *kids*," Beth said. "If you lived in a cardboard box under a sidewalk grate, they'd think it was cool."

"I feel like I've done a lot with the place," I replied. "The living room furniture is all new. Modern. Sleek."

She smirked. "Sorry, but I close my eyes and picture Ikea. A particle-board palace."

"No, no. Think rich earth tones. Sophisticated."

"Said the man about to participate in a burping contest . . ."

"We've been over this, Beth. It's not a *burping* contest."

"I know, I know. So you say. So who picked out your furniture? Please tell me it's not your new" – here she paused, as if the next word was almost too inconceivable to utter – '*girlfriend.*'"

"Why? You'd have a problem with that?"

"Jack, Jack, Jack . . ." She shook her head solemnly. "OK, consider this scenario. Your girlfriend – what's her name? Cody? Cory? The kids told me, but I forgot already."

"Courtney. She's very nice."

"Anyway, let's say she gets you to plunk down thousands to update the dreary, hopelessly out-of-date stuff at your place. Gone is the avocado green couch, the torn bean-bag chair, that stupid singing-fish plaque, the moose-head over the fireplace."

"I don't have a fireplace."

"Silly me. Of *course* you don't." Beth said. "Anyway, you go into debt to modernize the place. Make it just the way she wants it. But a year later, as invariably happens, she dumps you."

"That's the over-under for this relationship? One year?"

"Yes. Now what do you do with the new furnishings?"

"Um, continue to enjoy them?"

"Ha! Impossible! This was Coby's dream living room, not yours."

"Courtney's."

"But she's gone now, remember?! Now let's say you take up with someone else. And this new floozy walks into your place for the first time, sees the new look and goes 'Oh my God, what a train wreck!' See what I'm getting at?"

"Not really."

She shook her head and sighed, finding my mental incapacity as wearying as ever.

"My point is, if you're going to let every skanky 'girlfriend' you're diddling re-decorate the place, it becomes a vicious cycle: buy new stuff, get dumped. Buy new stuff, get dumped. Can't you see that?"

Suddenly a voice behind us said: "What's skanky mean?"

"What's diddling mean?" asked another voice.

Whipping around, we came face-to-face with a grinning Emmie and Liam, who had somehow crept up behind us with Ninja-like stealth.

"Yeah, Bethie," I said. "What *do* they mean? Enlighten us.""

Looking mortified, my ex shot to her feet and said: "C'mon kids, let's get your backpacks ready. You dad needs to get going."

It fell to me on the drive back to my apartment to explain – with lots and lots of linguistic tap-dancing – what those two lovely terms meant.

Apparently, it wasn't my finest effort. Because on a trip to the zoo the next day, Emmie, in a voice that could be heard in Wyoming, observed: "That polar bear's really *skanky*."

The remark drew quizzical looks from the parents of other children nearby, which I handled deftly by staring down at my shoes.

Mercifully, though, there was no talk of diddling from either kid, and we made it out of there without further incident.

31.

When the Big Five arrived at the gym the following morning, all we could do is gawk.

With the Great Burpees Challenge now two days away, the place had been radically transformed. Red, white and blue bunting hung everywhere. Martial music blared over the sound system. Large banners dangled from the ceiling proclaiming "GO RIPPED! BEAT EFC!" and "WE DON'T NEED NO STINKIN' HOT STONE MASSAGE!" and "TAKE YOUR INFINITY POOL AND SHOVE IT!"

"It's like a combination Trump rally and Occupy Wall Street protest!" Courtney marveled.

We found Bryan at the front desk looking happier than we'd seen him in weeks.

"The new look's aggressive," Jamison told him.

"*Super*-aggressive," Courtney added.

Bryan nodded. "Good. I want a hostile environment for those dickweeds. And I don't care if we get waxed anymore. Or that we have to pay for some stupid highway billboard. I'm over that. Long as we go down swinging."

Suddenly he smiled. "Did you see Intensify yet? No? Follow me."

The Intensify Studio was a large, dingy, little-used room in the rear of the gym. It had a heavy boxing bag suspended from the ceiling on a chain and a speed bag under a heavy board fastened to the wall with steel brackets. Both looked as if they hadn't been touched since the last time Muhammad Ali climbed in the ring.

A few exercise mats and orange speed cones languished in one corner. Finally there was something called a TRX, which consisted of a couple of heavy-duty straps and handles suspended from on high for resistance exercises "designed to meet the demands of high-volume training."

Except no high-volume training ever took place there. Nor did much low-volume training. The joke was that the only thing the Intensify Studio intensified was the need for a nap.

Yet on this day, it, too, had metamorphosed into something vastly different than before. Over the door in big block letters was a sign that read: THE SHOWDOWN IN CRABTOWN: WHO BLINKS FIRST?

"Tastefully understated as always," Courtney murmured.

Gone was the dusty boxing and TRX paraphernalia, the mats and cones. Instead, the room was brightly lit, the floor polished to a high gloss. And everywhere there were photos of celebrities – Hollywood actors, musical artists, sports stars and politicians – clad in colorful workout gear and doing burpees.

"The stars! They're just like us!" Harvey sang out.

"Well, sort of," Courtney said. She pointed at a photo of Justin Timberlake. "See his Hermes sneakers? They're called Defis. They go for $1000 a pair. Just saw an ad for them in *Vogue*."

"The stars! They're *not* like us!" Harvey sang again. "We buy $60 Nikes! At Dick's!"

All the celebs in the photos seemed to be having a wonderful time, too. Their eyes danced, their skin looked radiant and they wore bright, confident smiles, in stark contrast to the pain, exhaustion and regret normally seen on the faces of those engaged in America's most hated exercise.

In defiance of the natural laws of physical exertion, none of the celebs appeared to be perspiring, either.

True, Demi Lovato and Serena Williams seemed to have something of a "glow" about them. But Shaquille O'Neal, who sweated like a pack mule on the court throughout his long NBA career, appeared as fresh as if he'd just stepped off a yacht. So did former New Jersey governor Chris Christie, a man you could reliably envision working up a lather just brushing his teeth.

Then again, I imagined a retinue of hair-stylists, make-up artists, manicurists, pedicurists and gofers bearing fresh towels lurking just off-camera, ready to swoop in and buff up the VIPs at the first sign of exertion marring their appearance.

Bryan pointed to a shot of Drake in the push-up position and said admiringly: "Hell, we all know *that* guy does burpees."

"Uh, not really," Mikey said. "I have no clue who that is."

"He's a famous rapper, Mikey. Look how jacked he is! I read he once did 100 burpees without a break. Likes to work out to 'Shaky Shakey' by Daddy Yankee."

"Who doesn't?" Mikey replied, deadpan. "That's always been my go-to tune in here."

Jamison, who had been studying the photos intently, suddenly whirled and said: "Wait a minute! *Helen Mirren* does burpees?"

Bryan looked sheepish. "OK, I photo-shopped that one. The face, anyway. I think that's J-Lo's body. Or it might be Sofia Vergara's."

"Oh, great!" Courtney said, frowning. "That's not unethical at all, is it? What's next? Mitch McConnel's turtle puss on Hugh Jackman's torso?"

"Hey! Not a bad idea, Court!" Bryan said. "Lemme see what I can find on the Internet."

She shot him a disgusted look. As she and the others wandered off to look at the photos of other personalities fake-loving burpees, Bryan pulled Jamison and me aside.

"I need to talk to you two, ahem, media superstars," he whispered. "Any chance of getting some coverage for Saturday's event?"

"Doubtful from our station," Jamison said. "The president's in town this weekend. He's giving a big speech to his GOP donor stooges at the Marriott Waterfront. Then he's going to Fort McHenry to present some fallen hero award, which you *know* he'll screw up somehow. Anyway, it's all hands on deck for the Angry Orange Creamsicle's visit."

Bryan sighed. He turned to me. "What about that fish-wrap you work for?"

"Not a chance," I said. "I already pitched two stories about our boy Tony Maldon that were promptly machine-gunned down. The executive editor hates me. His lapdog, the managing editor, hates me even more. They'd both love to push me down a flight of stairs.

"So I'm real popular in the building. I've fallen so out of favor, even my colleagues avoid me. There are lepers in Calcutta that get more lunch invitations than I do."

Now Bryan looked seriously bummed. We understood why, Jaymo and I did, because we could almost see the gears turning in his pointy little head. Like P.T. Barnum and Oscar Wilde, Bryan had convinced himself that any publicity was better than no publicity for a fitness center clearly emitting a death rattle these days.

If, as seemed certain, the Great Burpees Challenge turned

into a towering dumpster fire for Ripped! and we got smoked by the evil EFC bots, Bryan knew the gym would be ridiculed unmercifully on social media.

But he wanted it to be ridiculed unmercifully on legacy media, too, on TV and in print, on the theory that if the debacle attracted enough eyeballs, maybe folks would feel sorry for the poor downtrodden facility taking so much abuse.

Maybe then people would feel compelled to check out the place, at which point they'd see it wasn't such a bad gym at all. And maybe *then* they might be induced to slide a credit card toward Tami the Molar Queen and become members, which might juice the pitiful revenue stream enough to keep the lights on another month.

Pure and simple, Bryan was playing the sympathy card. Sure, it was a long shot. A Hail Mary pinging through the synapses of his over-wrought brain the last couple of weeks. But it was his way of coping with the ugly prospect of impending humiliation.

Who were we to question that?

Yet by the time we finished looking at all the photos – was that really a shirtless, Speedo-wearing William Shatner leaping to his feet like a hyper Labradoodle? – Bryan had regained his usual good humor.

Escorting us out, he snapped off the lights and cried: "EFC VS. RIPPED! IT'S GONNA BE A WAR, BAY-BEE!"

I often wondered what people like Mikey, who had fought in a real war – who'd seen buddies killed and maimed and others haunted from what they'd done on the battlefield – thought of how loosely we toss around the word "war" for any kind of competition.

The Super Bowl was America's very favorite "war," of course. And conveniently enough, it was fought every year! In the middle of winter, too, when we needed an escape from our doldrums, lest we start attacking each other with snow shovels.

But the Super Bowl was hardly our only "war." *Everything* was a war now. Politics was a war. We had Culture Wars, the War on Crime, the War on Drugs, the War on Cancer.

Comcast versus Verizon was a war.

Coke vs. Pepsi was a war.

Toyota vs. Honda was a war.

Now Bryan was making The Great Burpees Challenge into a similar existential conflict. Yet doing some burpees and going out for pizza and beer afterward didn't exactly call to mind the Battle of the Bulge or the Tet Offensive or the Invasion of Iraq.

Not that burpees weren't their own special kind of hell. Which was a thought that again needed to be suppressed as I headed off to the final prep session with Oven Mitts.

32.

The man never ceased to amaze me.

This time I found him in the empty spin cycle room doing tai-chi, the ancient Chinese martial art known more for its health benefits than its effectiveness in warding off a meth-crazed attacker after your wallet.

He was in the midst of a series of languid, rhythmic movements – some with feet pointed in different directions, some with knees bent, others with arms raised or legs lifted – each flowing into the next without pause.

Did I mention he had his eyes closed the whole time? I should probably mention that. I kept waiting for him to bang into one of the stationary bikes and unleash a torrent of violent curses that would peel paint off the walls. But that never happened.

It made me wonder if he'd somehow developed a form of echolocation similar to that of bats, whales and dolphins. Good God, was he, like them, able to emit sound waves that bounced off objects and alerted him to their proximity?!

Sure, it sounded far-fetched. *Ridiculous.* But the guy was such a freak of nature, I was ready to believe anything.

I watched in awed silence as he made his way slowly and purposefully through the movements. Finally, I could hold it in no longer.

"Tony," I said, clapping, "you are too much!"

As if emerging from a trance, he opened his eyes and grinned.

"Started doing this years ago, back when I was in . . ." he said before his voice trailed off. Then: "Aw, hell, you know where I was."

With his usual Gumby-like flexibility, he hurdled a couple of the bikes and made his way to me.

"Did the warden tell you we did tai-chi back then? It's true. I started a class. There were maybe 30 of us doing it at one time. Man, you should have seen it."

I tried to envision dozens of hardened cons at Hagerstown taking to the exercise yard and eschewing touch football and weight-lifting and full-court hoops to perform such movements as "white crane spreads its wings" and "hand strums the lute" and "snake creeps down."

I then tried to envision them sitting around afterward and discussing whether their *qi*, the energy force adherents believe flows through the body, was now unblocked and flowing properly, and whether their *yin and yang* were in harmony.

But the images wouldn't come.

Maybe that was because I'd heard enough stories of inmates who were ridiculed unmercifully for something as innocuous as wearing goofy Thanksgiving-themed socks. Or for checking out cheesy romance novels from the prison library. Or for requesting almond milk for their coffee and gluten-free meals. Or for anything else that stamped them as weirdos and misfits in the hard-ass world within a prison's walls.

So I couldn't imagine the shitstorm of abuse that would rain on someone who copped to enjoying a "foreign" and "sissy" exercise created by a Taoist monk over 700 years ago.

On the other hand, if Oven Mitts insisted that a large bloc of his fellow prisoners jumped out of their bunks each morning eager to do "parting the horse's mane" and "repulsing the monkey" and "maiden working the shuttles," who was I to doubt him?

One thing was clear: the man's mood had done a 180-degree reversal since the last time we worked out.

Gone was the hangdog expression and slumped shoulders brought on by the Big Five's prison visit. As we moved to the gym for our prep session, his eyes were lively again and there was a bounce in his step.

The old Oven Mitts swagger was definitely back.

"Are we ready to do this, partner?!" he said, clapping me on the back. "Ready to kick some butt on Saturday?"

There was something new in his voice, too. A different timbre, a new intensity. I'd heard it in the voices of dozens of athletes I'd interviewed over the years. Simply put: Oven Mitts was stoked to be competing again.

Apparently, it was one thing for him to show up at the gym every day to school the Oven-ettes on fitness techniques, bask in their adoration, then go off to do his own super-human workouts, these free-weight/cardio marathons that could go on for hours. But the prospect of going mano-a-mano against a bunch of entitled ass-wipes from the EFC Death Star had him super-excited now – even if it involved an exercise he'd never done until a few weeks ago.

Seeing him bursting with energy as he dragged the mats out for our workout, I grew more and more confident of our chances. After all, what were the odds that anyone in their oldest member/newest member duo was a total beast like Oven Mitts?

Unless Lars, their fearsome Norse automatron, had an elderly blood relative with the same demon-seed gift for churning out ungodly amounts of burpees, I was pretty sure Oven Mitts would crush anyone they threw at us. As long as I didn't muck things up with an absolutely abysmal showing, I was certain he'd carry us to a win.

"Ok, let's get started," he said. "We probably should have done this weeks ago. But today we're doing something new. Today we're gonna work on what might be the single most important element in a burpees contest."

Huh?

To my mind, we had gone over every conceivable aspect of the burpee for weeks now. We'd dissected – ad nauseum – the squat, leg kick-back, push-up/plank position, leap to the feet and jump.

We'd watched dozens of YouTube videos of buff-looking men and women demonstrating the most efficient ways to do burpees. We'd studied the average time it takes to do a single burpee (3-4 seconds) and extrapolated from that the overall calorie-burning potential (100 burpees = 50 calories) of the exercise

We'd perused glowing stories in medical tracts extolling the muscle-building, metabolism-boosting wonders of burpees. We'd read teary first-hand accounts in health magazines about enormous fatties, men and women, with coronary-heart disease, hypertension and Type-2 diabetes who had finally slimmed down by doing burpees, and who credited the exercise with saving their lives.

God knows we'd done enough breathing exercises. What more was there to learn?

Or work on?

"The single most important element in a burpees contest?" I repeated. "OK, I'm intrigued. Let's hear it."

Oven Mitts looked around furtively, as if EFC operatives with cameras and recording devices lurked nearby.

"The smile," he said in a hushed voice.

Excuse me? The what?

"The smile," he repeated. "Think about it. Burpees are the most hated exercise in the whole world, right? We hear it all the time. So what better way to intimidate your opponent than by appearing to *enjoy* the physical and psychological torture of it all? You follow me?"

"Um, not really," I said.

"Think about some of your most celebrated boxers, Jack. Muhammad Ali, Joe Frazier, Mike Tyson. Roberto Duran, Sugar Ray Leonard, so many of the greats. They'd get hit with a thunderous right hook to the temple, right? Or a brutal uppercut to the jaw or whatever. And what would they do?"

"Topple to the canvas?" I guessed. "Lie there twitching and moaning until the ref counted them out? Wait for the trainers to climb in the ring and drag their sorry ass off on a stretcher?"

"NO!" Oven Mitts said. "Nine times out of 10, they'd *smile!* It was like 'Ho-hum, OK, you caught me with a good shot there. Maybe your *best* shot. But I'm still here, pal. Didn't faze me at all.' Do you realize how demoralizing that was to their opponents?"

"So we're gonna *smile* as we do burpees?"

"Exactly."

"And this will intimidate our opponents?"

"How could it not? OK, let me see what you got."

"You want to see what I've got *smile-wise?*"

"Right. I want to check out your form."

"The form of my *smile?*"

"Yes. As you're doing a burpee. Everyone's form is different, Jack. Some people can hold their smile in place a long time – even in the midst of rigorous exercise. Others let it dissipate too quickly."

This was possibly the most surreal request anyone had ever

made of me. Dutifully, I plastered what I thought was a pleased expression on my mug, dropped and did a burpee. The whole time I felt really, really…oh, what's the word here? – *stupid.*

When I finished, Oven Mitts frowned.

"Okay, we need a *way* better smile out of you," he said. "We need a kid-opening-gifts-on-Christmas-Day smile! A landed-the-big-promotion smile! A just-got-laid-after-a-long-drought smile!"

That one I can do, I thought.

"What you gave us there," Oven Mitts continued, "was a kind of bored, senior-class-yearbook smile. Like 'Can we get this over with? I'm supposed to meet the guys to smoke some weed.'"

He patted my hand sympathetically.

"Try it again," he said.

This time I tried to give my smile some extra oomph by summoning a particularly happy memory from my past.

What I came up with was a scene in Tischler the Lawyer's office during the divorce proceedings with Beth. Tischler had just studied the final settlement terms proposed by my attorney when he turned to Beth and said glumly: "This is probably the best we can do . . ."

Recalling how her face fell always brightened my day.

"Better," Oven Mitts said. "Not to nitpick, but what I saw from you there was a smile of *relief.* We don't *want* a smile of relief. That defeats the purpose. What we want is a smile that signals *confidence!* And *joy!* A smile that says: 'I'm on my 60th burpee, bitches! And I can do this all day!'"

I did a few more smiling burpees, with Oven Mitts taking note of such factors as how much of my teeth showed, how far my eyebrows shot up, how much the corners of my eyes wrinkled.

He still wasn't satisfied.

"What we're looking for is *authenticity!*" he exclaimed. "Genuine delight! We have to sell those EFC wankers – God, how did the Brits come up with *wankers?* – on the idea that we're happy 'cause we're *indomitable!* We *know* we're going to win!"

I said a silent prayer that no one else would stumble on this deranged tableau, a grown man jumping up and down and smiling like a fool while another man critiqued the degree of pleasure his expression showed. Outside of an orthodontist's office, the whole thing would be too creepy for words.

Finally, after a half-dozen more burpees, Oven Mitts pronounced himself satisfied with my smile.

It was the one I flashed while remembering the terror in Good Neighbor Dan Henson's eyes a few days after the Night of the Hummer, when he spotted me in an aisle at Costco, turned to flee and smacked into a 6-foot pallet of Deer Park water bottles, nearly knocking himself out.

"*That's* the one!" Oven Mitts said excitedly. "You smile like that, it'll rip the very *souls* out of those elitist schmucks!"

Thus ended our very last prep session, by far the most bizarre one of them all. This time, instead of my lungs burning and my legs and shoulders aching after a workout, it was actually my face that hurt. My lips, stretched nearly to the point of bleeding, were killing me.

We left the gym and traded fist-bumps in the parking lot, psyching each other up, telling each other how bad-ass we were and how we were going to crush EFC and, yes, knock their dicks in the dirt – a phrase I was beginning to embrace more and more.

It reminded me of my high school football days, me and my buddies whipping each other into a frenzy the night before a big game. The only problem was that my high school football team sucked and we'd invariably get our asses kicked the next day, something I tried not to think about during this impromptu pep rally.

"But what about you?" I asked Oven Mitts. "How come we didn't see *you* practicing that all-important psychological weapon today?"

He nodded, seeming to anticipate the question.

"Don't worry about me, kid," he said. "I spent 26 years in a place where you didn't see a whole lot of smiles. Sometimes you forgot what they looked like. But I knew how important they were. I knew a good smile could be the difference between a guard doing you a favor or telling you to shut the fuck up and get lost. Or between walking the yard safely or getting your ass kicked by someone with a beef.

"Know what I used to do?" he continued. "True story. I used to practice smiling when I was alone in my cell. I know, I know... how *pathetic* was that? I'd stand there holding my little mirror and pretend I had an upcoming hearing in front of the parole board, or a sit-down with the warden about a class I wanted to start. Something where I needed to bring my A-smile."

He tossed his gym bag in his car and turned back to me.

"Don't worry," he said, "when it's our turn to rock and roll Saturday, I'll be smiling like a motherfucker. Just pray my dental plate stays in."

He threw back his head and laughed uproariously.

I couldn't tell if he was kidding about the plate or not. Nevertheless, I vowed to say a prayer in case he wasn't.

33.

At 7:30 on Friday night, Buffalo Wild Wings had all the calm of a camel auction in Tangier.

An army of servers carrying steaming platters of food wove around the 40 tables, dodging wayward toddlers, beered-up frat bros regaling each other with dumb jokes and befuddled seniors looking for the rest rooms.

The multiple big-screen, high-def TV's, each tuned to a different channel, offered a non-stop, migraine-inducing buffet of seemingly every sport known to man. The Orioles-Red Sox game appeared to be the marquee event. It was shown on the largest screen, one that wouldn't seem out of place at a local multiplex.

But for those with ADHD and other concentration issues, their eyes could flit back and forth to a dozen other screens showing everything from golf and martial arts to women's softball and Australian rugby.

Over the din, diners inhaled fried pickles, mozzarella sticks and beer-battered onion rings. They raked carrot and celery sticks through puddles of bleu cheese and ranch dressing before moving on to the main event: mounds and mounds of chicken wings drenched in every conceivable sauce, from the exotic (Thai Curry, Asian Zing, Caribbean Jerk) to the scorching (Blazin' Carolina Reaper, Desert Heat, Jammin' Jalapeno) to the mundane (Original Buffalo, Honey Garlic.)

It was an astonishing spectacle, an unholy melding of

commerce, our national obsession with athletics and All-American gluttony.

I was thrilled to be a part of it.

"Nervous about the contest tomorrow, Jack?" Mikey asked.

Me? *Nervous?* What was there to be nervous about? The prospect of falling on my face and letting down my octogenarian superman partner? Stinking it up so badly that Ripped! loses all three burpees divisions and a humble gym fallen on hard times – one that that desperately needs a shot of positive publicity – has to pay for a demeaning highway billboard? And might be forced to close for lack of members?

"No, I'm not nervous," I lied.

"You *look* nervous," Harvey said. "Doesn't he look nervous?"

Taking my hand, Courtney barked: "Why don't you butt-heads leave him alone? He *said* he's not nervous. What do you want him to do, pinky-swear?"

Jamison stared at me and shook his head. "Sorry, Court, but he looks jangly to me. And I know just how to fix that."

Windmilling his arm, he caught the attention of our waiter. "Another pitcher of Bud Light, stat!" he cried. "We've got a medical situation here!"

I was there, in the midst of all this madness, because the other male members of the Big Five had insisted on taking me out for dinner. What better way to prepare for the Great Burpees Challenge, they reasoned, than by gorging on greasy poultry and swilling cheap beer?

The fact I might develop raging heartburn and show up for the contest bloated and hungover apparently didn't concern them. Harvey, Mikey and Jamison just wanted a night out. My small role in the Challenge was just the excuse they needed to get away from their wives and blow off steam by engaging in their favorite pastime: bitching and moaning about life.

That started right after the second pitcher arrived.

"Know what I hate?" Mikey asked.

"Pretty much everything?" Harvey volunteered.

"And everyone?" Courtney said.

Mikey grinned. "OK, you got me there. But what I really hate is when people call you 'Chief' or 'Boss' because they're too lazy to learn your name. Happens to me at the gym all the time."

He banged his fist on the table. "I'VE BEEN WORKING OUT IN THAT FUCKING DUMP FOR YEARS! EVERYBODY KNOWS ME, RIGHT?! AND THEY CAN'T GIVE ME THE COURTESY OF CALLING ME MIKE?! IS THAT REALLY TOO MUCH TO ASK?!

The beer was kicking in. The couple at the next table shot us nervous glances.

You folks might want to move, I thought. *This'll go on for a while . . .*

"Think that's bad?" Jamison said. "How 'bout the guy at the gym who *salutes* everyone? You know who I'm talking about, right? Dark-haired guy about 40? Always wears Clemson gear? Never says a word when he passes you, right? Instead he snaps off a salute! Like we're in the fucking army or something!"

Right on cue, Harvey said: "With me it's the weight-loss cultists." Jabbing an index finger at an imaginary former chunker bragging about his newly-slimmed-down bod, he continued. "Dude, I don't want to hear about your stupid diet, OK? I don't *care* how many pounds you're down. I don't *care* if you're going paleo, vegan, macro, low-carb or gluten-free.

"I don't *care* if you're doing Weight Watchers or Mediterranean. Or bending over the toilet and sticking two fingers down your throat to purge. What makes you think the whole world's focused on your unholy obsession to drop tonnage?!"

All three were impressive rants.

I gave each an 8 out of 10 for both passion and topicality alone. Harvey's hammering of the word "care" and his use of "unholy obsession" as a coda were very effective. Jamison's targeting of "The Saluter," a dork we all found super-annoying, was spot on. But Mikey's semi-hysterical tone and pounding of the table was a nice touch, too. (I noticed the couple next to us was now hurriedly paying their bill.)

As the Hate Fest rolled on, Courtney and I looked at each other and smiled. There would be no griping and whining from either of us. No, we were in too good of a mood, having just spent a wonderful afternoon with my kids.

Emmie and Liam had been clamoring for weeks to meet Courtney. Finally I had arranged an outing for the four of us to the big Shriners Fair, where we could spend some time together and the kids could get to know her.

At first, Courtney was clearly nervous about the prospect.

"What if they don't like me?" she said. "What if they see me as some evil interloper out to crush their last flickering hopes that dad and mom get back together?"

"They'll *love* you," I told her. "And if they don't, I'll disown them. Plus I'll raid their college funds. And you and I'll blow it on a Paris vacation."

Yet the afternoon got off to somewhat of a rocky start as we walked amid the booths featuring carnival games. We stopped at the basketball shoot, where I fished a $20 bill from my pocket.

"Dad, put your money away," Emmie said.

"You don't want to play this?" I asked. "You used to *love* this game!"

She crossed her arms and sighed. In a world-weary voice, she said: "*Da-a-a-d*, you can't win at this. They put too much air in the basketballs. And the hoop's too small, so the ball can't fit. It's a scam. Everybody knows that."

Wait, it's a *scam*?!

And *everybody* knows it?!

Good God! I thought. *Was this more of the fallout from the malignant Imposter-in-Chief? Trump had already convinced millions of dopes in this country not to trust the Supreme Court, the FBI, the CIA, the IRS and the military, among other once-revered institutions*

Had this corrosive cynicism even filtered down to carny games? If so, you might as well lock the doors and turn off the lights on this country.

We moved on to the ring toss booth, which I hoped was still uncorrupted.

"How about this one?" I asked.

Liam shook his head mournfully.

"It's a con game," he said. "Ahmad's dad says the rings are too small. They don't fit over the bottle."

Ahmad's dad? Who's he with, the Attorney General's office? How does HE know what's rigged and isn't rigged?

"Plus the rings are made out of super-hard plastic," Emmie added. "So when they hit the bottle, they just, like, bounce off."

Unbelievable. It was like attending the fair with a crew from "60 Minutes." Or with Jeff Rossen, NBC's dogged wizard of consumer rip-offs.

On and on it went, with these junior curmudgeons offering their assessments of the other carny games we passed, complete with blistering commentary.

The balloon dart throw? *Puh-leeze!* The tips of the darts were dull. The balloons were so underinflated you needed a speargun to pop one.

The milk bottle pyramid? Ha, even more of a swindle! The bottles were weighted down, the softballs filled with cork. Justin Verlander couldn't win a stuffed teddy bear.

Shoot the star? Good luck, sucker! You could fire that air gun at that paper star 'til the cows come home. But the rifle's sight was off. And the BBs were so tiny your trigger finger would go numb before they hand over that plushie monkey you've been eyeing.

Thankfully, the kids' moods perked up with an infusion of hot dogs and cotton candy and a successful trip to the arcade's claw machine, all of which Courtney insisted on paying for – a strong move for someone determined not to be seen as a wicked marriage disruptor. After that, we moved on to the rides, which I was happy to hear were (as yet) not rigged.

A confession: there are carnival rides I am simply too chicken to go on. My fears are two-fold. I fear throwing up on someone if there's too much spinning involved. On the rides that go very fast and high, I fear the bolts holding my seat will suddenly loosen, the seat itself will detach, and I'll be sent catapulting into orbit before I crash to the ground and die.

That crashing and dying business is by far the greater of the two fears. So the Ferris Wheel and the Pirate Ship were both doable with Courtney and the kids. But it was up to her to take them on the Zipper and the Scrambler, two rides that would have left me whimpering and vibrating like a ceiling fan.

Neither Liam nor I had any interest in going on the Swing Ride, which involved centrifugal force, tiny seats and uncomfortable elevation changes. But Courtney stepped up again, going on it with Emmie, the two of them alternately laughing and shrieking in terror as the hellish swings sped round and round.

All in all, the day was a big hit with the kids. So was Courtney, apparently. After we dropped her off at her place, the kids couldn't stop gushing about her.

"She's *so-o-o* pretty!" Emmie said.

"And *so-o-o* nice, too!" said Liam. "Look what she bought me!"

From his pants pocket, he pulled out a brown lump that appeared, at first glance, to be the days-old remains of a tiny woodland creature, the torn tail of a chipmunk maybe or the hind leg of a squirrel. Instead, it turned out to be a partially-melted Mounds bar encrusted with dust, lint and God knows what else, which he happily gnawed on for the rest of the ride.

As I pulled into the driveway of my old house and the kids clambered out, I wondered how Beth would react to this latest intel regarding Daddy's new squeeze. "Pretty" *and* "nice?" Oooh, that wouldn't go over too well with ol' Stoneface.

Suddenly, I was jolted out of my reverie by another fist banging the table and a voice shouting: "WHY CAN'T THEY PARK BETWEEN THE FUCKING LINES?! WHY DO THEY HAVE TO TAKE UP TWO FUCKING PARKING SPACES?! IF YOU CAN'T DO A SIMPLE THING LIKE PARK YOUR CAR CORRECTLY, HOW THE FUCK DID YOU GET YOUR LICENSE?!"

This time it was Jamison in the midst of a harangue. It was getting late and the crowd at BDubs was finally starting to thin. My buddies, on the other hand, had ordered another pitcher and seemed in no hurry to wrap things up.

After Harvey started in on a fresh tirade about the interminable waits at doctors' offices ("IS THEIR TIME ANY MORE VALUABLE THAN MINE? HUH? NO, TELL ME THE TRUTH! IS IT?!) Courtney and I took it as our cue to thank the guys for dinner and escape.

The minute we walked into her house, I smothered her with deep kisses and attempted to deftly steer her into the bedroom. (Oh yeah, you talk about *smooth* . . .)

Yet somehow she resisted my charms and pulled away. After planting a chaste peck on my cheek, she pointed me to the guestroom.

"No action for you tonight, Romeo," she said, smiling. "Big day tomorrow. You need to conserve your strength."

"You know that's an old wives tale, right?" I said. "The idea that sex before a big game hurts your performance? It's been totally debunked for years."

Courtney shrugged. "I read somewhere Muhammad Ali wouldn't have sex within six weeks of a fight," she said. "Seemed to work pretty well for him."

She handed me a pillow and blanket. "I'll make it up to you tomorrow night, sweetie."

"Promise?"

"Promise," she said.

Only after I shuffled dejectedly off to the spare room did the thought occur to me: *Damn, I should have made her pinky swear.*

Just then my cell phone pinged. It was a text from Beth, along with a photo of a smiling Emmie and Liam.

"Know it's late, but your two beautiful children asked me to wish you good luck tomorrow. I would wish you the same – if I only knew what the hell you were doing."

Ah Bethie, I thought. *You are truly one of a kind.*

34.

At precisely 9:15 the following morning, the first vanguard of EFC supporters marched through the doors of Ripped! They did not go unnoticed.

Dressed in Vineyard Vines polos and breaker shorts, Lily Pulitzer skorts and leggings, Ralph Lauren white jeans and gingham Oxford shirts, they were a riot of pastel and plaid, stripes and polka-dots, tassel loafers and popped collars.

They held signs that blared "WE'RE EFC AND YOU'RE NOT!" and "R.I.P. RIPPED!" Two of them carried a banner with photos of crying babies and a caption that read: "HEY RIPPED! THIS IS YOU REAL SOON!"

Thrusting fists in the air, they chanted "TWO, FOUR, SIX, EIGHT, WHO WILL WE OB-LIT-ER-ATE?!"

As the Big Five stared slack-jawed at this spectacle, Mikey muttered: "RACS. One of the worst cases I've ever seen . . ."

"I know I'll end up regretting this," I said, "but what's RACS?"

"Ralph Principio was among the first to identify it," Mikey said. "He was a buddy of mine back in 'Nam. What a character! One time we were in Saigon for a little R&R – rest and recuperation, the generals called it, but we called it I&I, intoxication and intercourse . . ."

He gave Courtney a libidinous wink. "Anyway, Ralphie ended up jumping out the third-floor window of this brothel.

Turned out these two pimps were after him for —"

Courtney cut him off. "Could we skip the back-story? Even though I'm sure it's super-fascinating?"

"Yeah," Jamison said, "get to the point, dude. What's RACS?"

Mikey glared at the two of them.

"OK, fine," he said. "RACS stands for Rich Assholes Congregating Syndrome. Ralphie's theory is that rich assholes, when they're around normal, everyday people, are always trying to show they're just normal, everyday Joes and Janes, too. That they're polite, modest, self-effacing, blah, blah, blah. But when they get around *other* rich assholes . . ."

He swept his hand to indicate the preppy mob assembling before us.

" . . .well, you see what happens. Their true colors come out. The assholery quotient goes through the roof." He shook his head and smiled ruefully. "Tell me ol' Ralphie wasn't an astute observer of the human condition."

Behind their obnoxious fans came the eight men and women who would compete for EFC in the Great Burpees Challenge, all clad in white Lacoste T-shirts and white tennis shorts.

"Oooh, look how matchy-matchy!" Courtney murmured. "*Very* impressive."

"It's like they missed the flight to London for the Wimbledon Finals," Jamison said. "And due to some tragic mistake, they've been transported to this squalid, no-name bunker, where you can't even get a decent sapphire martini."

Like a general leading his troops into battle, J. Kenneth Oberkfell strode at the head of the column with Lars, his Dark Prince, behind him. Their erect bearing, squared shoulders and confident smiles said it all: *This'll be a cake-walk. Someone call the Prime Rib. Tell 'em to start setting up for the victory party.*

I went off to find Oven Mitts and do some stretching. My nerves were kicking in, big-time. I felt a tap on my shoulder and turned to see Harvey.

"I need to talk to you," he said. "You know El Chapo? The Mexican drug lord?"

"Yes. Where is this going, Harve?"

"He used to kill his rivals, chop up their bodies and feed them to his tigers," Harvey said.

"Why are you telling me this now?"

"Thought it might calm you down."

"CALM ME DOWN?! How would it do that?!"

"You know. Like, OK, you're feeling a lot of pressure, right? But at least you're not getting chopped up and fed to jungle animals."

"THAT'S THE BEST YOU GOT?! WELL, IT DIDN'T WORK!"

"OK, OK," he said. "I'll come up with something else."

Next I spotted Colleen Stupak, looking pale and drawn as she came out of the women's locker room.

"Good luck today," I said. "How you feeling?"

"Like I'm about to puke," she said. "Like a big, goddamn wolverine is skittering around in my gut. You?"

"Same," I lied. Why make her feel bad?

In five months at Ripped!, this was the most I'd ever heard Colleen speak. But: *a big goddamn wolverine skittering around in her gut?* What was *that* all about?

Oven Mitts was nowhere to be found. Given his status as gym royalty, I assumed he planned on being fashionably late for the contest. Maybe he wanted to show up at the last minute and bask in a hero's welcome from the Oven-ettes and his many other admirers.

Which was fine with me. If there was one member of the Ripped! team we didn't need to worry about, it was Oven Mitts. He'd show up whenever he showed up. And when he showed up, he'd be his usual indomitable force of nature. Of that I was absolutely certain.

Twenty minutes later, the PA system crackled to life and Brian announced that the women's burpees contest was about to start. We filed into the Intensify Studio, the partisans from both gyms lined up against opposite walls, cheering and jeering and creating an unholy din.

Here in a nutshell was what Oven Mitts had warned about: a chaotic atmosphere and the need to keep calm and focused as a competitor. I was already failing miserably on that point, even as a spectator. Just taking in the latent hostility of the EFC fans, their angry scowls, the veins in their necks bulging like ripcords as they shouted insults at the Ripped! team, I felt a pounding in my chest.

Boy, I thought, if these *people get this worked up about burpees, what are they like at a Ravens game? They probably need straitjackets by the second quarter.*

Minutes into the contest, however, two things became readily apparent.

First, EFC had none of the burpees goddesses we feared they might have. Their three women were stolid, if unspectacular, competitors. One turned out to be Lars's wife, which we cleverly deduced by his exasperated cries of "CHRIST, HONEY! YOU GOTTA PICK UP THE PACE!" as she gasped and struggled to her feet like a punch-drunk fighter around her 20th burpee.

"That should make for an interesting conversation when they get home," Courtney said. "Can you picture it? 'Honey, no offense, but you absolutely sucked out there today.' 'Oh, Lars, you insufferable pain in the ass, go fuck yourself!'"

She cackled with delight. "What do you want to bet the big guy's sleeping on the couch this week?"

Yet the greater revelation was that Colleen Stupak, despite whatever was skittering in her gut, was again in absolute Beast Mode.

We stared in fascination as this tiny, mournful-looking creature cranked out burpee after burpee with metronomic precision. Her movements seemed effortless, her breathing controlled and never labored. There was a far-away look in her eyes, as if she were operating on autopilot, oblivious to her frenzied surroundings.

Had she been studying some form of self-hypnosis to calm herself in the heat of battle? (If so, I wanted in on that action. By now I was shaking like a cement mixer.) Even the EFC supporters seemed impressed, nudging each other and pointing at her in wide-eyed amazement.

I felt sorry for her teammates. Lisa Goldstein and Marion Westfield, bless their hearts, were gamely putting on a yeoman-like performance. But they could have been doing their burpees in a broom closet, for all the attention they received.

No, all eyes were on Colleen the Magnificent. She was in the zone and kicking ass. By the seven-minute mark, she had already done an incredible 120 burpees. None of the other women were anywhere close to that figure. And Colleen showed no signs of slowing down

The three EFC women, on the other hand, seemed thoroughly gassed. Lars's wife's face had turned an alarming shade of red and it was painful watching her moaning and struggling to her feet after each burpee.

Lars seemed to take her exhaustion as a personal affront, one that appeared to be sending him over the edge. As he alternately crouched awkwardly and rose again to maintain eye contact with the poor woman, he bellowed: "HONEY, IF YOU'RE NOT FIRST, YOU'RE THE FIRST *LOSER!* CAN YOU LIVE WITH THAT? HUH? BECAUSE I'M NOT SURE I CAN!"

When the 10 minutes were up and the horn sounded, the Ripped! supporters, whooping and clapping, rushed Colleen and her teammates. It was a rout. Final score: Ripped! 321, EFC 235.

Colleen, true to form, looked as if her dog had just been run over. But the significance of what she and Lisa and Marion had accomplished was huge. Even if Lars and his fellow droids blew out our men's team, Ripped! still had an excellent shot of winning the overall competition – as long as I didn't spit the bit alongside my 80-year-old wonder of a partner.

The unthinkable was suddenly, well, thinkable.

I wasn't the only one daring to hope. Bryan strutted around with a big shit-eating grin, hugging Collen over and over again to her eternal chagrin and high-fiving Lisa and Marion. When he finally tore himself away from the three women, he did a victory jig around the room while flashing the thumbs-up sign to the jubilant Ripped! backers.

Dancing over to us, he said: "Did I tell you there's a keg of Shiner Bock icing in my office? I thought we'd be drowning our sorrows. But now…my God! This could turn into a celebration!"

When he was out of earshot, Courtney said: "Why do I have a feeling there'll be an announcement that says: "Attention members: due to a faulty keg pump, the post-burpees party has been cancelled. We apologize for the inconvenience.""

As the disconsolate EFC women shuffled off, Lars, who had finally calmed down, tried to drape a consoling arm around his wife, which she angrily shrugged off. Watching this, I couldn't help wondering if Tischler the Lawyer was about to get another client.

Just then Harvey beckoned me from the other side of the room. He wore a worried look.

"Your boy Oven Mitts just got here," he whispered. "He doesn't look too good."

35.

I found him slumped on a bench in the back of the men's locker room. He had his shirt off and his arms and shoulders were covered with dark bruises. As he struggled to pull on a pair of sweatpants, I could see an ugly swath of cuts and scrapes on his legs, too.

His cheeks were puffy and his eyes were bloodshot. A deep gash on the side of his forehead oozed a brownish liquid.

Staring at him, I thought I might be sick.

"Jesus, Tony!" I gasped. "What happened?"

"I'm fine, kid," he said softly.

"*Fine?* You look like you got hit by a train!"

He winced as he stood and pulled on his trademark black sleeveless T-shirt, the same one he'd worn all those months ago the first time I saw him.

"Fell down the front steps of my condo. Tripped over a flower pot." He shook his head and chuckled mirthlessly. "Geraniums. Never liked them. That's what I get for trying to grow the stupid things."

Fell down the front steps. Tripped over a flower pot. Yeah, right. If that was the best bullshit story he could come up with, then his brains were scrambled, too.

Over the PA system, we could hear Bryan announce the start of the men's contest.

"Come on," Oven Mitts said, "let's go cheer for our guys.

Sounds like the poor bastards need it. Didn't you say the other team has a total burpees stud?"

He took a step and his knees buckled, nearly sending him to the floor.

"Tony, you need a doctor!" I said. "I'm taking you the ER!"

"No," he said, "the contest —"

"Fuck the contest!" I said. "Have you looked in a mirror? We might be calling a coroner, instead!"

He steadied himself and gently put both hands on my shoulders.

"Listen to me, Jack. We've got what, a half hour before they call us? Here's what I'm gonna do. I'm gonna go sit in the sauna, OK?"

"The *sauna?!*" I shouted. "Are you out of your mind?!"

"It'll loosen me up. Make me feel better. Then after you and I whip those EFC blowhards, I'll go see a doctor. Promise."

Whip those EFC blowhards?! Now I *knew* he'd banged his head. He'd be lucky if he didn't go into cardiac arrest any minute.

"Tony," I said, "forget the goddamn contest! What are you not getting here? YOU NEED MEDICAL ATTENTION, DUDE!"

He reached into his gym bag and pulled out a towel.

"Look, I'm not gonna argue with you," he said wearily. "I'm *doing* this contest, OK? Now go root for our boys. And don't come back here. Soon as I hear Bryan announce our match, I'll be out."

I watched in disbelief as he draped the towel around his neck and slowly shuffled off to the sauna. When I finally heard the wooden door creak open and slam shut, I went back to check on him. Peeking in the little glass window, I found him lying on the bench with his eyes closed.

The sight jolted me. *My God, was he dead already?!* In my mind's eye, I pictured the police interrogation that would surely follow:

Let me get this straight, Mr. Doherty. You came across an 80-year-old man with serious contusions and abrasions – and possibly a skull fracture – and didn't call 911? Instead, you left him ALONE? In a SAUNA? Sergeant, cuff this piece of shit and read him his rights.

Aw, c'mon, Lieutenant, lemme get a piece of him right here. Abandoning the poor codger like that...what kind of a sick, depraved monster does that to another human being? Just gimme five minutes with this scumbag . . .

But no, taking a closer look, I could see Oven Mitts' chest rising and falling gently. I said a silent prayer that he wouldn't die in what was, for all intents and purposes, a drab cedar closet with the temperature set at 175 degrees.

After that I went back to the contest and filled in the rest of the Big Five on my partner's frightful condition, including the ridiculous tale of how he got hurt and his even more ridiculous plan to still compete.

"He can't be serious!" Courtney said. "The guy could stroke out!"

"Oh, he's serious," I said. "Dead serious – if you'll pardon the expression."

"Then he's fucking delusional!" Harvey said. "He could barely *walk* when I saw him, never mind do burpees!"

Delusional was definitely the right word. There was no way Oven Mitts could pull this off, even given his god-like level of fitness. We would be forfeiting the final match, that much was clear. At the thought of this, I could feel the knot in my stomach loosening, the tightness in my shoulders dissipating.

At the same time, an acute sense of disappointment came over me. It felt as if we were letting down this tattered little gym that had become such a big part of my life, the place where I'd met some of the best friends I would ever have, the place where I finally began to address my deteriorating physical health and declining emotional well-being.

The truth was that despite my jitters, I'd been looking forward to this day for weeks. I was in the best shape I'd ever been – admittedly a low bar after years of fast food-gorging and beer-guzzling excess – and anxious to see what I could do against the other newbie on EFC.

There was also this: as much as I didn't completely understand it, I had developed a weird affinity for Oven Mitts. I *liked* being paired with him. Sure, from time to time, a silent loop played in my head: *Hey sport, are we forgetting something here? The man snuffed his wife! The mother of his kids! Are we gonna pretend that didn't happen?*

No, we were not. But the man had been good to me since we began training together, maybe better than good. He'd done an incredible amount of research on burpees and been generous with tips on the best way to do them. He'd also been gentle with criticism and magnanimous with praise.

I admired his competitive fire, too, along with his burning disdain for EFC and its membership rolls full of haughty big-money windbags who seemed to delight in mocking every other gym in the area.

My God, who *wouldn't* want to knock their dicks in the dirt?!

By this point, the men's contest was almost over. Predictably, the Ripped! team, composed of the hulking, muscle-bound trio of Rusty Quaranta, Matt Lito and Colin Terwilliger, was getting crushed.

With their baseball caps worn backward and hoodies, their camo pants and scruffy work boots, they resembled nothing so much as dockworkers just back from an early shift unloading refrigerators from a freighter at the Port of Baltimore.

It was hard to watch as they crashed to the mats like wounded elephants and moaned and strained to rise to their feet, their faces florid and hideously contorted from the effort.

The EFC team, on the other hand, was a sleek unit that appeared engineered from birth to excel at the most loathed exercise on the planet. Both of Lars' partners were trim, twitchy guys in their mid-20's who looked like they worked 14-hour days at a downtown brokerage, subsisting on Wheat Thins, Red Bull and NuVigil.

Not only were they cranking out burpees at an unnerving pace, but Lars himself was putting on another All-Galaxy performance. After he hit the 150 burpees mark, J. Kenneth Oberkfell began bellowing "NEW EFC RECORD! NEW EFC RECORD!" after every 10 new burpees the Norse wonder cranked out.

"Hell, the way he's pumping them out, it's probably a *world* record!" Mikey growled. I made a mental note to Google it.

"Funny, how *Mrs.* Lars is nowhere to be found," Courtney said with a knowing look. "Now why do you suppose that is?"

Not that Lars looked like he needed any more support. Perhaps out of sheer boredom, he took to taunting the Ripped! supporters as he approached his 200th burpee with a just few minutes left.

Each time he leaped to his feet, he waved bye-bye to them, wiggling his fingers for emphasis. When they booed, he grinned and windmilled his arms, eliciting even more Bronx cheers.

It was as if he'd morphed into some kind of pro wrestling

villain, one who'd smashed a folding chair over his opponent's head or kicked him in the groin and was now strutting about the ring while hearing it from the crowd.

When the final horn sounded, the EFC team danced around the room while their fans cheered and hugged each other, celebrating the lopsided 438-192 victory. The overall match was now tied at 1-1. Which is when Colin Terwilliger, no doubt embarrassed by the loss but mainly enraged by Lars' antics, jumped in his face.

Built like a giant sequoia with body art – and possibly evincing steroid-fueled psychosis, too – the 6-foot-8 Colin was a menacing sight.

"Motherfucker," he said heatedly, "that was some cold shit you did out there . . ."

"Cold…*shit*?" Lars repeated, seemingly baffled by the term.

"Disrespecting our fans, numb-nuts. Disrespecting me and my teammates. That what you rich jackoffs call sportsmanship?"

"Cold…*shit*," Lars mumbled again, still processing the phrase as if it were Mandarin Chinese.

But seeing the fury in Colin's eyes, Lars wisely issued an immediate apology, assuring that he'd meant no disrespect with the aforementioned, er, cold shit. This was accompanied by a sudden and loud burst of flatulence, the fear of getting pummeled apparently causing his cortisol levels to spike and his gut to stir violently.

Colin jumped back as a powerful stench wafted everywhere. Nevertheless, taking no chances on the possibility of bloodshed breaking out, J. Kenneth quickly ushered his prize robot from the room, with Lars' two fidgety partners also beating a hasty retreat.

When things finally calmed down, Jamison looked at his

watch and said: "OK, gotta roll." He gave me a bro hug and said: "Good luck with the contest – assuming your boy Oven Mitts isn't already zipped into a body bag back there."

"Whoa, what's this?" Harvey said. "Not sticking around for the final epic clash between the forces of good and evil?"

"Can't," Jamison said. "Duty calls. Baltimore's most trusted newsman has a rare Saturday assignment to get to."

"Let me guess," Harvey sneered. "Another big petting zoo expose?"

"No, it's that baby alpaca in Carroll County, isn't it?" Mikey said. "I *knew* he'd escape again. You can't trust those alpacas. They're tricky little bastards. Good to see our 'Most Trusted 24-Hour News Source' is all over it."

Jamison shot them dual middle fingers, waved to Courtney and left.

But who was kidding who here? There would be no "final epic clash" today. That dream was over.

As soon as a janitor or some other unsuspecting soul stumbled on Oven Mitts' lifeless body in the sauna, the locker room would be ringed with crime scene tape. And as soon as the first eyewitness told detectives "Come to think of it, the last person I saw him with was that Irish mook what's-his-name" they'd be issuing an arrest warrant for me and a SWAT team would be kicking in my front door.

Even as the announcement for the final match of the morning echoed over the sound system, I stood rooted in place, wracked with indecision about what to do. Which was when Bryan came up to me, a concerned look on his face.

"Where's your partner, Jack?" he asked. "Contest starts in two minutes."

This is insane! I thought. *It's totally not fair to keep Bryan in the dark! Not fair to the Ripped! fans who still think we have a shot to win this thing, either.*

"Bryan," I blurted finally, "I don't think our man Tony is —"

Suddenly, there was a burst of applause from the Ripped! supporters and Bryan said: "Oh, wait! Here he comes now."

Sauntering toward us and giving rah-rah fist pumps to the crowd was Oven Mitts.

36.

Unless it was his ghost.

I say this because the man approaching us now bore no resemblance to the poor battered wretch gimping around the locker room a half-hour ago. The transformation was breath-taking.

The swelling in his cheeks was mostly gone and his eyes were clear. He wore a long-sleeved T-shirt over his sweats that hid the injuries to his torso. The brown gunk from the gash on his forehead had been wiped away and the wound itself looked almost miraculously healed – no more than a thin scab remained.

Not only that, he was *smiling!*

This wasn't the wan smile of someone feigning good cheer during a health setback, either. No, this was the full ear-to-ear, 200-watt, I'm-the-biggest-swinging-dick-here smile that he'd flashed so many times before.

I stood there gawking at him. *How was this possible?! What in God's name had happened to him back there?*

It was as if he'd just returned from the famous healing shrine at Lourdes, not a cramped sauna reeking of Lysol and body odor. But when he clapped me on the shoulder and said "OK, let's go meet these EFC fuckwads," I thought: *Lourdes? With that mouth? Uh-uh.*

"Tony," I said, "you *really* shouldn't do this. After what you've been through, the strain could easily —"

He cut me off with a wave of his hand.

"Stop worrying, kid," he said. "What could possibly go wrong?"

"Oh, lemme see," I said. "How about internal bleeding? Ruptured kidneys? Stroke? Heart attack? And that's just me spit-balling here. Why don't we ask a certified medical professional?"

But he waved that off, too.

"You're watching too much 'Chicago Med,'" he said. "I'll be fine, Dr. Doherty."

I threw up my hands and followed him across the room.

Our opponents introduced themselves as Hal Reicher, the club member with the most seniority, and Mitchell Moranis, the newbie. Both sported the deep suntans that seemed de rigueur with the EFC crowd, the tans that screamed just-back-from-St.-Barts or played-18-holes-every-day-this-week.

We shook hands, after which Reicher felt compelled to add that he was vice-president of North American transactions at Citibank, overseeing assets of $50 billion.

"Is that right?" growled Oven Mitts. "Know what my bank does? They give you free Tootsie Roll Pops. Cherry's my favorite. But you can't go wrong with orange, right?"

I watched Reicher's grin slowly vanish, replaced by a quizzical look.

"You're only supposed to take one," Oven Mitts continued. "The lollipops, I mean. But I usually grab a whole handful. And nobody ever says anything."

Now the first signs of unease could be seen on Reicher's face. He looked at Moranis as if to ask: *What do you think? Certifiable whack-job? Or just a tad slow?*

Oven Mitts, on the other hand, was clearly seething.

Hal, Hal, Hal… major tactical mistake, I thought. *Flaunting your big job and wealth in front of a guy who spent a third of his life in the slammer? That's bulletin board material, my friend. That'll come back to haunt you if by some miracle Oven Mitts doesn't collapse out here.*

An uneasy silence descended on the four of us. We stood there sizing each other up. I put Reicher's age to be around 70. He had broad shoulders and a flat belly that signaled more than a nominal devotion to keeping fit in his golden years.

But he's no geezer freak like Oven Mitts, I kept telling myself. At least not like the Oven Mitts of yore, the one who didn't look as if he'd just been pushed off a cliff.

Moranis was the opponent who concerned me the most. He was maybe 10 years younger than me, trim and compact, the ideal body-type for burpees. In addition, he radiated an almost feral intensity, as if he'd sooner gnaw off a couple of his fingers than lose to the two unimpressive-looking mopes standing before him.

But there was no time to worry about whether Mitch was a ringer. The contest was about to start. As soon as the referees were in place, Oven Mitts and I went to our mats, bumped fists and wished each other luck.

"Remember, Jack, big smile," he whispered.

"Do me a favor," I whispered back. "Try not to die out here."

"That's the plan," Oven Mitts said.

I took one last look at Courtney, standing on the edge of the crowd. She blew me a kiss and pointed to three familiar-looking women in sleeve-less crop tops, yoga pants and pink Sketchers shimmying and sashaying off to one side.

The Oven-ettes were in the house!

I tried to alert Oven Mitts to their presence, figuring it might lift his spirits and enhance whatever strange mojo was having such a curative effect on his damaged body. But he was already in the zone: crouched in an athletic stance, weight evenly balanced, eyes locked on the clock.

Seconds later the horn sounded and the room exploded in noise.

At the risk of sounding immodest, I came out of the gate strong. *Very* strong. At least by my lowly standards. It turns out that doing burpees in front of a whipped-up crowd is completely different than silently struggling through them on your own in a musty corner of the gym.

Gone, for one thing, was the whole why-the-fuck-am-I-doing-this? doom loop that plays in your head when doing burpees solo. With a packed room cheering me on, no longer was I just some middle-aged dweeb with a dad bod reeling from a painful divorce, a man who spent his days pecking out desultory columns in a dying profession.

No, now I could almost convince myself I was some kind of hero! Oh, not a Marvel-type hero, not someone tasked with saving the earth from aliens bent on acquiring the Tesseract or anything. Let's not get carried away.

But I felt heroic nonetheless. Why else would all these people take time out of their busy weekend to shoehorn into a back room at an aging fitness facility to watch me and my partner? Why else would everyone be hooting and hollering and shouting our names to the heavens as we jumped around on some mats?

The surge of adrenaline coursing through my body would either propel me to burpees greatness or give me a goddamn heart attack. I prayed the first option would prevail.

Taking a quick glance at Hal Reicher and the wolfish Mitch Moranis, it was clear I was keeping pace with both of them. Neither was as formidable as I had envisioned. If Oven Mitts' spooky juju held and he could will himself to do even half the burpees he usually cranked out in our practice sessions, I felt confident we'd whip these two EFC frauds.

Except . . . something was terribly wrong with my partner.

From the outset, his movements were slow and stultified, like someone doing burpees underwater. *Maybe he's just warming up*, I thought. *Or toying with Hal and Mitch. Trying to get in their heads. Make 'em over-confident. Yeah, that's got to be it. He'll kick it into high gear any minute now ...*

Except...that didn't happen, either.

By the three-minute mark, he was moving even slower. We could hear him wheezing, and his arms wobbled visibly from the strain each time he dropped into the plank position. The gash on his forehead had opened, too. A trickle of blood ran down the side of his face and his mat was soon speckled with red drops.

Someone threw him a towel and he tried wiping the mess each time he climbed to his feet. But that only slowed him even more and he finally tossed the towel aside. His jaunty smile had disappeared too, replaced by a frozen rictus that was truly creepy to behold.

Quickly, the raucous chants of "TONY! TONY! TONY!" from the Ripped! supporters gave way to murmurs of concern. Which were nothing compared to the alarm bells clanging in my own head.

Oh, Jesus! I kept thinking. *He's gonna check out right here!*

Ten minutes feels like an eternity when doing competitive burpees. The mounting agony of the exercise makes it hard to concentrate. Now try doing burpees next to someone who's moaning and trembling and breathing as if on a ventilator – not to mention possibly hemorrhaging before your eyes – and all concentration goes out the window.

By the six-minute mark, Oven Mitts could barely lift himself off the mat and the trickle of blood had become a steady stream. I was still feeling OK, closing in on 70 burpees – a new personal record for the ex-fat boy! But when I saw him stagger to his feet, lose his balance and fall backward into the wall, I'd seen enough.

"Tony, stop!" I cried. "You'll kill yourself!"

I tried to wrap him in a bear hug, but he pushed me away. And when Bryan rushed over and implored him to quit, Oven Mitts shook his head.

"I'm . . *finishing*," he rasped, lurching back to his mat.

The next few minutes were a blur. Fuming over my partner's stubbornness – or was it some kind of sick desire to commit suicide in front of a hundred spectators? – I started banging out burpees faster than I ever had. It was a lunatic pace, really, completely unsustainable. Predictably, I was soon completely gassed.

The room had gone eerily quiet. Even the EFC supporters seemed transfixed by the passion play unfolding before them. Hal Reicher and Mitch Moranis, slowly and methodically, had pulled way ahead of us by this point. But all eyes were on Oven Mitts and his suffering.

After the final horn sounded, he lay on his back for several minutes, his chest heaving. When he finally climbed to his feet and looked at the scoreboard – EFC 159, Ripped! 119 – he shook his head dejectedly.

We congratulated Hal and Mitch, who had the good sense not to gloat before joining their crowd of jubilant supporters streaming for the exit. Out in the parking lot, we knew, the caravan of Jaguars and Lexus' and Mercedes was already forming for the victory celebration at the Prime Rib, the EFC happy place of ever-fawning maître d's, obsequious servers, $30 cocktails and $72 eight-ounce filets.

Just then, Oven Mitts' legs seemed to give out again. Before he could hit the floor, I took one of his arms and slung it over my shoulder. Harvey grabbed the other arm and he and Mikey helped me get him to a chair, where Courtney gently wiped the blood from his face with tissues.

"We're going to the emergency room," I said. "*Now!* Don't fight me on this!"

Oven Mitts grimaced as another wave of pain seemed to hit him.

"No," he said weakly. "Help me to my car. I'll go see my doctor. I *said* I'd do it when we were done here, didn't I? Well, we're done."

I couldn't believe what I was hearing.

"Tony, are you *insane!*" I said. "You can't *drive!* You'll pass out before you put the car in drive."

He managed a weak smile and patted my arm.

"I live 10 minutes from here, Jack. My doc's office is on the way. I'll be fine."

As usual, there was no arguing with him. The four of us helped him hobble out to his car. We lowered him into the driver's seat and he reached for a rumpled orange Orioles cap on the dashboard. As he fished in his pocket for the keys, tears welled in his eyes.

"I let you down, Jack," he said. "I let the whole gym down. Just thought I could . . ."

His voice trailed off, replaced by great wracking sobs.

"It was just a dumb burpees contest, Tony," I said. "One billion Chinese don't give a rat's ass and neither do I. Someday maybe you'll tell us the truth about what happened to you. But life will go on, partner."

After he drove off, Courtney said: "That almost sounded

wise and mature on your part."

"Oh, look at that," I said. "You're making me blush."

We rode back to her house in silence. I had never felt more exhausted in my life, physically and mentally drained. When we walked in the door, she pointed me to the bedroom.

"Sorry, hon," I said. "Way too tired for that now. You can make it up to me another time . . ."

She smacked me on the shoulder. "You idiot! I meant go take a nap!"

Oh. A *nap*.

Okay, that I could definitely do.

I didn't even have the strength to pull off my sneakers. The minute my head hit the pillow, I was out.

Ninety minute later, the ringing of my phone jolted me awake.

When I picked up, Harvey was shouting like a madman: "HOLY SHIT! HOLY SHIT! HOLY SHIT!"

37.

"Three Holy Shits!" I said, still groggy. "Must be something big."

"TURN ON THE TV!" he shouted. "CHANNEL 9!"

Then he hung up.

I stumbled into Courtney's living room, grabbed the remote and followed Harvey's instructions. Suddenly, there on the screen was Jamison, standing at a busy downtown intersection in a crisp Armani suit, holding a microphone and wearing the grave expression that signaled an event of some magnitude was unfolding.

Or at least one *not* involving a petting zoo.

"Again, this is a developing story," he intoned in his most sonorous voice. "What we know so far is that police are investigating an attempted armed robbery of a mother and her young daughter early this morning in the 300 block of Charles Street."

Ah, I thought, *no wonder it's called Charm City. What's more delightful than starting your day with someone sticking a gun in your face and snarling: "Give it up, motherfucker." Especially when you have your kid with you.*

"The woman," Jamison went on, "identified as 34-year-old Lucille Thompson, was opening her family's business, The Donut Dive, when she was accosted by two men at the store's front entrance. As one of the suspects held a gun to her head and tore a ring of keys from her hand, the other threatened to shoot her child and demanded money from the cash register."

"This, police say, is when the story took an amazing turn. A passer-by now being hailed as a hero heard the little girl's terrified screams and rushed toward the gunmen. He managed to disarm both with what one eyewitness described as 'some sort of martial arts technique, maybe kung-fu,' allowing Ms. Thompson and her daughter to slip into the store and lock the door, possibly saving their lives. At this point, the brave passer-by was apparently knocked unconscious by a blow to the head, then brutally beaten and kicked by the two suspects before they fled in a late-model Jeep Cherokee.

"To recap, all we know about the good Samaritan thus far is that he's an older man who wore workout gear and an orange Orioles cap. We also know he refused medical attention from paramedics at the scene and quickly disappeared into the crowd that had gathered outside the popular . . ."

Here Jamison's voice trailed off as he put his hand up to his earpiece and frowned. "OK, I've just been told a news conference about the incident is set to begin at police headquarters. So let's go there live now and have a listen . . .".

Seconds later, the stern-looking visage of Baltimore police commissioner Edmund Morris filled the screen. He stood in front of a bank of microphones flanked by the mayor, somber-looking city council members and the obligatory, over-caffeinated sign language interpreter.

"To follow up on our earlier briefing," the commissioner began, "we now know the name of the courageous citizen who put his life on the line this morning to prevent what could have been a horrific situation during the attempted hold-up of the Donut Dive in Midtown. He's been identified as Anthony Maldon, 80, of North Baltimore. I'll spell that for you now. It's M-A-L-D-O- . . ."

I heard a gasp behind me. Turning, I saw Courtney with a hand over her mouth, staring wide-eyed at the TV.

"We also learned," Commissioner Morris went on, "that Mr. Maldon checked himself into Greater Baltimore Medical Center this afternoon, where he was diagnosed with multiple internal and external injuries suffered during the encounter. He's listed in serious but stable condition and is scheduled to undergo surgery tomorrow morning. And now I'll try to answer any questions you might have . . ."

"Commissioner," a reporter asked, "did you say the man who foiled the robbery was *80 yeas old*?"

"That's correct," Morris said. He looked down at a sheet of paper in front of him. "We double-checked that. DOB is listed as February 10, 1933."

A murmur of incredulity rippled through the assembled media types. Courtney plopped down next to me on the couch, the two of us riveted by what we were seeing.

"With all due respect, Commissioner," another reporter began, "how the hell does a 80-year-old – a *senior* senior citizen, for God's sake! – fight off two armed thugs?"

Morris grinned and shook his head.

"Well, you'd have to ask Mr. Maldon about that," he said. "Whenever he gets out of the hospital. Judging by the severity of his wounds, that won't be for a few more days. The bad guys worked him over pretty good."

A moment later, the commissioner turned the briefing over to the mayor. The Honorable Bentley Aubrey III swaggered to the podium. Elected to office just one year earlier after a contentious campaign during which he vowed to "wipe out the criminal hordes plaguing our city," he was beaming.

"Notwithstanding the fact that a young mother and her

daughter could have lost their lives with another senseless act of violence and indiscriminate lawbreaking, this is a great day for the city," the mayor said.

Courtney and I looked at each other. *Huh? A great day for the city?*

"Now I'll tell you *why* it's a great day," the mayor continued. "Two words: citizen engagement. A lone citizen witnessed a barbaric act on the streets of Baltimore and said 'Enough is enough!' He took matters into his own hands and went after the two gunmen with no regard for his own personal safety. This is the message my administration has been preaching since Day One."

Whoa! I thought. *Isn't that kind of dangerous, Mr. Mayor? Urging people to confront vicious criminals armed to the teeth?* I made a mental note to rip the mayor in my next column and call out the lunacy he was advocating.

But right now he was on a roll, milking the moment for all it was worth.

"I am just so…so damn *proud* of Mr. Waldon," the mayor went on, appearing to grow emotional. The commissioner leaned over and whispered in his ear.

"*Maldon,*" the mayor corrected. "And if Mr. Maldon were here today, I would tell him: 'Sir, a grateful municipality thanks you from the bottom of its heart.' When he's all healed up, I fully intend to invite him to City Hall and bestow upon him the Key to the City."

The last Key to the City awarded by the mayor, I remembered, went to the Tony award-winning rapper and Baltimore native Lil' Crazee.

This quickly proved to be a tremendous source of embarrassment for the Aubrey administration after Lil' Crazee and three members of his entourage, following a night of non-stop partying, were arrested for possession of cocaine, public intoxication and urinating on the Rolls Royce Phantom of his hip-hop rival, Biggy Snooze.

"In addition," the mayor continued, "we're making plans to honor Mr. Maldon with a parade through our wonderful city. Members of my staff are already looking into available dates."

A *parade!*

I tried to picture Oven Mitts smiling serenely and waving from the top of a float as it inched down Pratt Street preceded by marching bands and Ravens cheerleaders and the Oriole Bird, with cheering throngs lined three deep on both side of the downtown thoroughfare.

Or would he opt to *walk* the parade route, shaking hands, kissing babies and posing for selfies with his joyful fans, their eyes aglow with hero-worship? Whether Oven Mitts would agree to be part of such an extravaganza was unknowable at this point. But this much was clear: for better or worse, the man's life would never again be the same.

"Finally," the mayor said, "with the blessing of the City Council, we're giving strong consideration to recommending Mr. Maldon for our civilian Medal of Valor. As will be recalled by my good friends in the media" – here he flashed the pained smile of a man with a urinary tract infection – "we have not awarded the Medal of Valor since Nestor Urias dove into the Inner Harbor a few years ago to rescue a drowning grandmother and her cat. . ."

"After which Nestor Urias probably died of typhoid," Courtney muttered. "Or E. coli. Or leptospirosis. Can you imagine jumping into that filthy sludge? Granny and her pussy-cat would've been goners if that was me who saw 'em go under."

As soon as the news conference ended, my phone started

blowing up with texts.

From Harvey, ever lyrical: "OMFG! You believe this shit?"

From Mikey: "Our boy Oven Mitts sure has balls. But maybe not brains."

From Jamison: "How did my suit look? Did the tie go with it? Too flashy?"

From Bryan at the gym: "Making plans for a 'Thanks Anthony Night' here. Still have half a keg of Shiner Bock left. Letting the Twitterverse know he's a Ripped! member. With all the pub he's getting, this might work out great for us! Even better than if you guys had actually won!"

From Jamison again: "What about my hair? Too wild? Ran out of styling gel . . ."

From Bryan again: "He's not gonna flatline in the hospital, is he? Talk about a total bummer for the party . . ."

That evening, the Big Five convened for dinner at the Naughty Leprechaun. Between pints of Guinness – Courtney kindly opting not to torture the barkeep by ordering a frou-frou cocktail – and heaping portions of fish and chips, we dissected the events of the day.

The consensus opinion: no one had ever seen anything like the ordeal Oven Mitts had put himself through that morning. And all because he didn't want to let down his gym buddies in a silly fitness contest??

How nuts was *that?* we wondered.

"He was straining so hard, it looked like his eyeballs might pop," Mikey said.

"And the bleeding!" Courtney added. "Like it would never end! What incredible fortitude that poor man displayed!"

"Well," Harvey said, "you know what they say about fortitude."

At this, the table grew silent, bracing for the worst.

"No," Mikey said finally. "What do they say?'

"Fortitude is the marshal of thought, the armor of the will, and the fort of reason," Harvey said.

We all stared at him.

"What?!" he said. "Francis Bacon. *Everyone* knows that quote."

As the rest of us dissolved in laughter, Mikey roared: "Once again, *nobody* knows that fucking quote! The question is: how does an annoying little twit like *you* know it"

Harvey took a gulp of his Guinness and sat back with his arms folded, a smug smile firmly in place.

"Well, I'm sorry I missed the drama at the gym," Jamison said. "But the story of Oven Mitts saving that mom and kid went all over the country. It was a helluva day to be in the news biz! If you don't mind me bragging a little, I'm super-proud of the station's coverage."

"Except that ugly suit of yours!" Mikey said.

"And the tie!" I said. "*Jesus!* Where'd you get that, Goodwill?"

"And your hair!" Courtney added. "Hey, Jaymo, here's a newsflash. They have these things called combs now. You should break down and get one."

Jamison's face turned crimson. But seconds later, he was laughing as hard as everyone else.

After dinner, we ordered a round of Bushmills. Climbing to his feet and holding his glass high, Harvey offered a toast: "To a speedy recovery for our brave friend Anthony Maldon! Better known to his admirers in this room as the great Oven Mitts!"

It was well after 10 by the time we wrapped up. As Courtney and I walked to the car, a full moon emerged from behind the clouds, the light shimmering off the water and bathing the harbor in a soft glow.

"Tired?" she asked.

I nodded. "Been a long, crazy day."

"Gee, that's too bad," she said, hooking her arm around mine. "I had something special planned back at my place."

"Do tell," I said.

"First I was gonna slip into this racy little number I got from Victoria's Secret. Then I was gonna smother you with deep, passionate kisses, including lots of tongue action, before I ripped off your clothes and threw you in bed for God knows what else. But, hey, if you're too tired . . ."

"Well, what do you know?" I said, smiling and drawing her close. "Guess who just got a second wind?!"

38.

"More coffee, Jackie?" Tom Halloran asked.

"I'm good, Tommy." Draining what was left in my cup, I added: "By the way, whatever this stuff is? *Way* better than the swill we usually have around here."

Halloran beamed.

"Sumatran Mandheling," he said. "One of world's finest blends. Thought you might enjoy a good cup of coffee to start your day."

Leaning across his desk, he pushed a tray laden with muffins and pastries toward me.

"Have one of those Florentine tarts," he said. "You look like you've lost weight. All that exercise, right? But you don't want to overdo it, Jackie."

I was actually having trouble deciding between the French chocolate éclair and the strawberry cream Danish, so I shoveled both on my plate. Halloran took a bite of his blueberry muffin and a rapturous look came over him. The only one not attacking this sumptuous spread was Mark Minske, who slouched against one wall with his arms crossed, trying to look disinterested.

Aside from the sound of rapacious chewing and the soft hum of the ceiling fan, the room was quiet.

Finally, Halloran cleared his throat.

"So," he began, "there's something we'd like to discuss with you . . ."

"*Erclor awrssome!*" I said.

"Beg pardon?"

"Sorry," I said. "Shouldn't talk with my mouth full. This éclair is awesome!"

"Glad you like it," Halloran said. "Anyway, we were wondering if you might consider —"

"In fact, *all* these are to die for!" I said. "Tommy, you *have* to tell me where you got them! What is that, a raspberry macaron? Pass that baby over here, willya?"

Halloran and Minske exchanged troubled looks. I knew just what they were thinking, too.

Here they'd had Debbie Nesbo summon their curmudgeonly metro columnist to an important Monday meeting – an elaborately-choreographed one, judging by the breezy opening banter, as well as the excellent coffee and breakfast fare served. Yet all the poor dumb bastard wanted to talk about were the stupid pastries.

You could almost hear Halloran telling himself: *Time to look into early retirement. I can't take much more of this crap . . .*

With a tight smile, he said: "The pastries are from Del Vecchio's over on —"

"Well, they're *fabulous!*" I said. "But now I'm stuffed. Might have to go home now and take a nap."

A hint of panic flickered in Halloran's eyes. I reached over and swatted him on the shoulder, leaving a palm print of powdered sugar on his dress shirt. "Tommy, I'm *kidding!* Who naps at 8 in the morning?! So what's on your mind, big guy?"

Looking vastly relieved, Halloran leaned back in his chair. He folded his hands together and looked down for a moment, weighing his words. It was the idiosyncrasy he favored when trying to project the image of a thoughtful executive editor, large and in charge.

"We're hoping you might consider doing a big takeout on your friend Anthony Maldon," he said. "You know, in light of the, er, *events* of this past weekend."

"Jack, the whole town's talking about this guy!" Minske said over my shoulder. He left his perch against the wall and plunked down on the chair next to me. "They want to know all about him! Who is he? Where'd he come from! How did he summon the incredible courage to do what he did – especially at his age!?"

"And we need *you* to tell us about him!" he continued. "You know him better than anyone! Give us his story! A story of hope! Of triumph! Of redemption!"

"YES!" Halloran said, pounding his desk excitedly. "Give us all that bullshit!"

"In other words," I said, "you guys want the same story I pitched to you weeks ago."

"Exactly!" Halloran said. "Except now there's a hook! The guy isn't just an ex-con who bumped off his wife, did time and wows people as a geriatric wonder at a local gym. Now he's a goddam civic hero! Hell, he's a *national* hero!"

"The networks can't get enough of him!" Minske agreed. "Lester Holt will have a reporter parachuting into his hospital room any minute now."

Halloran grabbed another muffin and took a savage bite. It caused a lone blueberry to fly in the air, bounce off his tie and land on his desk. Unbeknownst to him, the errant berry now lay squashed under his elbow, a dark blue stain spreading on his shirtsleeve.

"You probably saw we had Hector Ruiz do the second-day piece on what went down at the Donut Dive," Halloran continued. "Did an okay job, I guess. But that was just nuts-and-bolts stuff. Hell, a first-year J-school student could have written that."

Atta boy, Tommy, I thought. *Way to denigrate the efforts of a young, hard-working reporter. With that kind of support, I bet the kid's shooting his resume to the Post any day now.*

"The fact is, Jack," Minske said, "we need *you* to do the big-picture story on this guy. We need someone who can write the hell out of it. Plus someone Maldon trusts. Someone who has *access* to him."

Right now, the number of people with access to Oven Mitts was zero. I knew this because the Big Five had driven to Greater Baltimore Medical Center the day before to see him and were politely, but firmly, told he was still not allowed to have visitors.

A couple of unsmiling police officers wearing tactical vests and carrying automatic weapons were said to be stationed outside his room to enforce this edict, as well as to ensure that the two thugs Oven Mitts battled at the Donut Dive – still on the loose – didn't return to finish him off.

The doctors were being close-mouthed about Oven Mitts' injuries, although hospital administrators had promised a press briefing on his condition soon. So we had left a nice goody basket for him at the front desk filled with wine, cheese, crackers and dark chocolate.

I had slipped my business card in there, too, with a request to call my cell when he felt up to it. If anyone was going to tell the story of Oven Mitts writ large, it was going to be me. Not that I was about to share that desire with Halloran or Minske. Better to let them squirm a while.

"So how about it, buddy?" Halloran said. "Can we count on you for this one?"

I didn't answer right away. Instead, I helped myself to another cup of coffee. I took my time adding a generous amount of milk and two packets of sugar. Now the only sound in the room was the tinkling of spoon against ceramic as I stirred the brew.

"Know what I was just thinking?" I said finally. "Funny how things just pop in your head, isn't it? Anyway, I was thinking about how long it's been since my last raise."

The two editors exchanged more anxious glances.

"A raise has such symbolic importance, don't you think?" I went on. "It lets an employee know he's valued. That management appreciates the effort he puts in day after day. That his talent and drive and dedication are –."

Halloran couldn't take any more.

"HOW MUCH?!" he blurted. Then, forcing a tight smile: "How much did you have in mind?"

"Oh, I don't know. I'd say $50K sounds fair."

Halloran's face turned pale. He looked like a man about to have a seizure.

"JESUS CHRIST, JACKIE!" he thundered. "THIS ISN'T SILICON VALLEY! THE PAPER'S BLEEDING MONEY! YOU KNOW WE CAN'T AFFORD THAT!"

"Fine," I said, climbing to my feet. "Well, thanks for the grub. I'm sure Hector Ruiz will do a fine job on the big Maldon profile."

I started to leave and Halloran grabbed my arm.

"Whoa, whoa, wait a second!" he cried. "Goddammit, will you sit down?! All right . . . lemme think, lemme think . . .I'll have to talk to the publisher, of course. But maybe we can find a way to . . . *Christ*, Jackie, that's a lot of money!"

A thin bead of perspiration appeared at the top of his forehead. He wiped it with a napkin, smearing a glob of the styling gel he'd begun using on his thinning hair.

Watching him fidgeting and ruminating aloud, I knew a raise was no sure thing. The word around the newsroom was that the new publisher – to use an old expression – threw around nickels like they were manhole covers.

It was also true that the *Herald,* like every other paper in the country, was losing print subscribers at an alarming rate. But digital subscriptions were said to be booming. Maybe, with some creative accounting, Tommy could find a way to tap that rising digital stream to keep his devoted, hard-working columnist happy.

"Another thing," I said. "*If* I do this story, I'm doing it my own way. I don't want some idiot editor on the verge of a nervous breakdown hovering over my shoulder, asking every five minutes if it's done. Or telling me *how* to write it."

"Hell, write it any way you want!" Halloran said. "I could even see it as a personal essay! 'Donut Dive Hero With Sordid Past Bares All to *Herald* Pal!'"

Minske chimed in: "Or how 'bout 'My Wife-Killer Buddy: Man of the Hour Prevents Deadly Sweet Shop Assault?!'"

I made a silent vow to disembowel both of them with a rusty screwdriver if either of those headlines ran with my story.

Before the two could suggest something even *more* dumb, I said: "By the way, I'll be needing some time off."

"Sure, sure, no problem," Halloran said. "Just get the Maldon piece done first, okay?"

Minske fixed me with his reptilian grin, meant to seem friendly and empathetic, but which somehow only made him appear even *more* cold-blooded.

"Going anywhere special, Jack?" he asked.

"Maybe. Might be getting married."

This was a bit of a white lie. Courtney and I were getting along wonderfully. I had no doubt I was falling for her big-time – if I wasn't totally smitten already. But neither of us had brought

276

up the m-word in our conversations.

Deep inside, we were both still hurting from our previous marriages, scarred by the lies and the cheating that had blind-sided both of us, wary of jumping too soon into another relationship that could blow up in our faces all over again.

But who knew what might happen a few months from now?

If I let my mind wander, I could picture the two of us going off to someplace warm, maybe in the Caribbean. And maybe, as we stood on a dazzling white beach one evening, the moon shimmering off the turquoise-blue water and a soft island breeze blowing, I might get down on one knee, pull a ring from my pocket and . . .

But that was getting ahead of things. All I wanted now was another French éclair.

God, they were awesome!

Acknowledgements

Many thanks to "first readers" Mike Davis, Vince Jones, life-long buddy Steve Korn, Tom Pannone, David Robinson, brother-in-law extraordinaire Bill Rose, Janet Schurman, Lori Sears and Gerry Shields.

Thanks to everyone at Apprentice House Press for giving this book life. And a special thanks to the AH publisher and great friend, the unflappable Kevin Atticks. When he said he loved the book, my spirits soared.

About the Author

Kevin Cowherd is the New York Times best-selling author of *Hothead* and five other baseball novels for young readers written with Hall of Famer Cal Ripken, Jr. and published by Disney-Hyperion Books

Cowherd has also written six books of non-fiction. His 2019 book *When the Crowd Didn't Roar: How Baseball's Strangest Game Ever Gave a Broken City Hope* was featured as one of the five best new sports books in the *Times' Summer Reading* issue that year.

He was an award-winning sports columnist and features writer for *The Baltimore Sun* for 32 years, and has also written for *Men's Health, Parenting* and *Baseball Digest* magazines.

He lives with his wife, Nancy, in Cockeysville, Maryland.

Learn more about his work at his website: kevin.cowherd.com.

Apprentice House Press
Loyola University Maryland

Apprentice House Press is the country's only campus-based, student-staffed book publishing company. Directed by professors and industry professionals, it is a nonprofit activity of the Communication Department at Loyola University Maryland.

Using state-of-the-art technology and an experiential learning model of education, Apprentice House publishes books in untraditional ways. This dual responsibility as publishers and educators creates an unprecedented collaborative environment among faculty and students, while teaching tomorrow's editors, designers, and marketers.

Eclectic and provocative, Apprentice House titles intend to entertain as well as spark dialogue on a variety of topics. Financial contributions to sustain the press's work are welcomed. Contributions are tax deductible to the fullest extent allowed by the IRS.

To learn more about Apprentice House books or to obtain submission guidelines, please visit www.apprenticehouse.com.

Apprentice House Press
Communication Department
Loyola University Maryland
4501 N. Charles Street
Baltimore, MD 21210
Ph: 410-617-5265
info@apprenticehouse.com • www.apprenticehouse.com

Printed in the USA
CPSIA information can be obtained
at www.ICGtesting.com
LVHW050923240224
772719LV00012B/939